"You ha[ve] You've al[ways had too many] rules.

Her amused expression disappeared. "Without rules you have chaos."

"Too many rules and you never get to live," Eli told her. "You should try a pet. Add a little chaos to your life. I bet you'd be surprised at what you've missed. Animals put the unconditional in love."

A shadow flitted across her face and was gone. "Unlike humans."

He stared at her until she met his eyes. "Some humans love that way, too."

As expected, she looked away. "I'd better get to bed. It's been a long day."

"And tomorrow will be longer. In Pine River, Wisconsin, people go to bed early and get up the same."

"Nothing ever changes around here, does it?" she noted, and stared down at her feet.

Eli put his finger beneath her chin and raised her gaze to his once more. He winked and lied through his teeth. "And nothing ever will...."

Dear Reader,

Those of us who have pets know about unconditional love. I was never much of a dog person—until a Labrador named Jake entered my life, then left it far too soon. Not a soul got near my sons if Jake was around. Oh, he was polite about it—putting his body in front of the children and nudging them away from strangers until I called him off. For that he earned my everlasting respect.

Our new dog, Elwood, hasn't got the knack of earning my respect yet. Of course, he's a puppy. As my husband says, "The lights are on, but no one's home."

When I was playing with ideas for a Superromance, the concept of unconditional love kept whirling in my head. It was a short trip from unconditional to everlasting. My favorite types of books have always been those where the hero loves the heroine all his life but she never knows it—until the book, of course.

Eli Drycinski loves three things—animals, Pine River and Gwen Bartelt. Unfortunately, Gwen has three rules by which she lives—no kids, no pets, no everlasting love. What's a small-town veterinarian to do?

Eli's solution? Use the single month Gwen is at home following the injury of her father to show her that the three things she wants least are actually the three things she wants most.

I hope you enjoy Gwen's discovery of Eli's love and all the magic Pine River has to offer. Jake and Elwood are there, too. I couldn't resist.

Please visit me at my Web site: http://www.eclectics.com/lorihandeland/

Lori Handeland

Doctor, Doctor
Lori Handeland

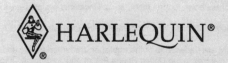

HARLEQUIN®

TORONTO • NEW YORK • LONDON
AMSTERDAM • PARIS • SYDNEY • HAMBURG
STOCKHOLM • ATHENS • TOKYO • MILAN • MADRID
PRAGUE • WARSAW • BUDAPEST • AUCKLAND

ISBN 0-373-70969-2

DOCTOR, DOCTOR

For my sister-in-law, Joan Handeland.
You know why.
And my brother-in-law, Mark.
For being smart enough to marry Joan.

PROLOGUE

IN THE FIRST six years of his life, Elijah Drycinski moved a hundred times. Well, maybe not a hundred, but it seemed that many. People called him an army brat. He understood the *army* part—his daddy was ''the Colonel.'' But *brat* was kind of mean. His mama said so.

He tried to be a good boy, but sometimes bein' good was hard. Especially when you were lonely, and no one wanted to be your friend but the animals.

Eli liked animals a whole lot. They didn't care that he was new in town. They didn't care that he didn't know any of the kid games everyone else played, on account of he never stayed in one place long enough to learn 'em, and his mama and the Colonel were sort of old and didn't play much.

Eli's parents loved him; they just weren't quite sure what to make of him. Eli never brought kids home to play; he always brought animals home to live—which made his mama kind of nuts. But animal friends were better than no friends.

Which was what Eli had one bright summer morning, two days after the Colonel had left the army for good and moved them to Pine River, Wisconsin—forever, he promised. No friends but Mr. Squirrel.

"So what do you do here in Pine River?" Eli asked of the gray squirrel in the tree.

Eli knew squirrels didn't talk to people, but what could it hurt for him to talk to a squirrel? He'd discovered that the more an animal heard his voice, the better the animal behaved around him.

"Are you talking to that squirrel?"

Eli clamped his mouth shut, turned around and shook his head at the little girl who eyed him from the next yard. He'd been caught by other kids talkin' to animals, and while *Dr. Dolittle* might be a nice movie, when kids shouted the name at you that wasn't very nice at all.

"Sure were."

She marched into his yard as if she owned it. She was definitely a girl, 'cause her yellow hair was in pigtails, but she wore pants and a T-shirt, and she was as dirty as any little boy. He liked her right away.

"Squirrels can't talk," he sneered, and kicked the dirt with his sneaker.

The girl came over and kicked the dirt right back at him. "Can, too. Only, they talk squirrel, not people. But I figure if people can learn to talk Spanish and French they can learn to talk squirrel."

Eli stared at her in amazement. He'd often thought that himself. But no matter how hard he tried, he never could understand squirrel or dog or cat or any language but people.

"So can ya, huh? Can ya talk squirrel?"

"Nah," he said. "I was just foolin' around."

"Oh, I do that sometimes, too."

Eli glanced at her to see if she was teasin'. But she wasn't, or not so's he could tell. She was smilin' at him as though she liked him, or at least he thought that was what her smile meant. Eli wanted a friend. He'd never had one that wasn't an animal. But he was afraid—afraid that if he tried to be her friend she'd laugh, then run away, and he'd be alone again with the animals.

The Colonel always said only cowards didn't take chances. Eli's dad wasn't thrilled with his gentle, animal-loving son, so he often said things like that to make Eli toughen up. But Eli couldn't help it that whenever someone threw a ball his way the ball hit him in the face.

Since Eli had never been a coward, he took a chance—and it was the smartest thing he ever did. "You want to play with me?" he asked.

"Sure."

As easy as that, they became friends. Gwen Bartelt accepted Eli for who he was—a quiet, shy boy, who was smarter than most and related better to animals than people. She never made Eli feel embarrassed or weird; in fact, she made him feel special.

Not until high school, when hormones raged and love became real, did Eli understand all that he felt for her. Because he knew Gwen better than anyone else, he also knew that he had to let her go if he ever expected her to come back.

So he never told her of his love, and when she left,

he smiled, waved and pretended he was happy, even as his heart cried.

Then he waited for Gwen to come back of her own free will—but she didn't.

CHAPTER ONE

Steven Bartelt requests the honor of your presence at the marriage of his daughter, Guinevere, to Lance Heinrich, M.D., on Saturday, the seventeenth of June—

SCRITCH!

Eli ripped the invitation in half. Childish, true, but tough. Gwen was his. She'd been his since...since...

Since the very first day he'd seen her. He'd always believed they belonged together. He figured eventually she'd see it, too.

He hadn't wanted to push; he knew Gwen well enough to understand that speaking of love would be a mistake. Gwen had watched her father turn into a cranky old man at the age of twenty-nine because of love, and she wanted nothing to do with the emotion. Too bad, because Eli loved her with all his heart, and he always would.

Propping his hip along the front porch railing, Eli stared down the quiet side street where he lived. Pine River was always quiet. Maybe that was why she'd left.

An odd thud from the backyard started his dogs

yapping inside. Eli might not have a passel of friends, but he had a gaggle of pets. Not much had changed over the years. Every stray in the vicinity still found its way to Eli's house.

His gaze wandered next door. Why hadn't Doc told him about Gwen's engagement? Sure, Gwen's dad was the same workaholic small-town doctor he'd always been and rarely took time for any talk beyond "Hey, Eli, how about them Packers?" But you'd think the man would have mentioned his daughter's wedding.

Unless, of course, Doc hadn't known, either. Gwen could easily have printed the invitations on her own. She and her father had never been close, despite the fact that her mother had died when Gwen was two and Doc had raised her. If you called paying the bills and hiring Eli's mom to take care of her raising a child.

Eli sighed. Who was he to judge? The townsfolk said Doc had never been the same after his wife died, and that was understandable. Doc had always blamed himself for his inability to save the woman he'd adored.

Eli glanced at the heavy sheet of paper crunched in his hand. Guinevere and Lance... Geez, were they serious? Gwen had probably gotten a few chuckles over the names, but Eli wondered if old Lance got the joke. If he didn't, he wasn't the man for Gwen.

No one was the man for Gwen but Eli. So what was he going to do about it?

"Doctor! Doctor!" The strident voice came from

the backyard. The panic in that voice brought Eli to his feet.

Nancy Davidson, face as white as a fresh sheet of typing paper, stood between the two houses. Nurse Nancy, as everyone called her, was Doc Bartelt's right hand. She was unflappable—or had been up until now.

"It's Doc," she shouted. "Come quick."

Eli jumped down the steps and sprinted across the lawn and into the backyard. Doc lay on the ground, his leg bent at an impossible angle, his face whiter than Nancy's. The ladder leaning crookedly against the side of the house gave a clue to what the odd thump of a few moments earlier had been.

Nancy fell to her knees and checked Doc in perfect nurse fashion. The routine seemed to soothe her, and her hands stopped trembling.

"What happened?" Eli asked.

"I told him not to climb up there and clean the gutters. All the rain's made the ground soft. You're just begging for trouble to go up on a ladder in springtime. But do you think he'd listen?" She snorted.

"Contrary to what you might believe, Miss Smart Aleck, you are *not* my mother," Doc snapped, though pain drew his mouth tight. The man might resemble Alan Alda with his long, lean build, but in quiet voice and manner, he wasn't even close.

"Well, if he's this feisty it can't be that bad," Eli observed.

"Quit talking like I'm not here or too senile to understand. It's broken."

"I could figure that out for myself," Eli said.

"Get me a Tylenol No. 3, Nance. And you, boy, set the leg."

"Me?"

"They call you doctor, don't they?"

"My patients mostly call me moo and oink."

"Ha-ha. Fix it."

Eli glanced at Nancy, who rolled her eyes, confirming Eli's suspicion. Doc didn't want to go to the hospital. He'd try anything to stay in Pine River.

"I can't set your leg, Doc. I'm a vet."

"Well, at least look at it. Make all that education your parents paid for worth something more than horse healin'."

"If you were a horse, I'd be your doctor."

"If I were a horse, you'd shoot me."

"Don't think it hasn't crossed my mind," Nancy muttered.

Eli hid a smile. The two of them were always sparring. Doc was a crusty old coot, though he had to be in his midfifties at most. Still, he cultivated the cranky, small-town-doctor persona.

Nancy, a friend of Gwen's from school, had grown up knowing Doc. She thought that gave her a right to tell him what to do. Doc didn't.

Nancy tried to rip Doc's pants leg so she could see better. She didn't have much luck so she scowled at Eli from her position next to the prone man. "Do you think you might *do* something? From what I can tell this is an open, compound fracture."

Which meant the bone protruded from the skin. Eli hated when that happened. "Yuck."

Nancy rolled her eyes. "Wuss. Get down here."

When Nancy said "Jump!" the correct response was "How high, ma'am?" So Eli went down on his knees. "Did you call for an ambulance?"

She gave him a withering glare. Nurse Nancy knew emergency procedures. "You know how long that will take."

Pine River was thirty miles from the nearest hospital—small-town life at its most dangerous.

Eli found his pocketknife and slit Doc's pants farther. "Excellent work, Doc. You're going to need a pin in this."

"Goody," Doc spat from between clenched teeth. "Nance, the Tylenol and an antibiotic, hmm?"

Eli did what he could, but basically he was a horse doctor. Doc needed a human one. When the ambulance came, Eli gratefully turned his patient over to the experts.

"I'm going to be in the hospital a few days, then out of commission awhile." The paramedic loaded Doc onto a gurney.

"Should have thought of that before you did a Peter Pan off the ladder," Nancy said.

Doc turned to the paramedic. "Could you make her go away?"

The young man gave Nancy a wary look. "I don't think so, sir."

"That's what I figured. Nancy, cancel my appointments. Get a temporary replacement."

"You know how that will go."

Doc sighed, and for just a minute, Eli felt sorry for him. Pain in the behind that he was, the man was devoted to his patients and the town. Pine River was not the number-one choice for new doctors. Doc had needed a partner for years; there just weren't any to be had. The money stank, the hours were worse and the prospects for advancement mighty slim.

"Try anyway." The paramedic started to take Doc away. "Wait!" Doc held out a hand to Eli. Surprised, Eli took it. "Call Gwen. Tell her..."

Eli waited, expecting declarations of love for the man's only child. "Yeah, Doc, what should I say?"

"Tell her to get her butt home."

Doc disappeared into the ambulance, the doors slammed shut and the vehicle rumbled off. Eli stood there dumbfounded.

Nancy appeared at his side. "Some bedside manner, huh?"

"Pain makes you say crazy things."

"Maybe. Then how would you explain his everyday manner?"

"Old age?"

"The man is fifty-six years old. My mother, who may I say is as happy and spry as a lark, has calluses older than him."

"Only fifty-six, huh?" That must be right. As long as most folks could remember, Doc Bartelt had been the doctor in Pine River—for nearly thirty years anyway.

"So are you going to tell Gwen to get her butt home, or should I?" Nancy asked.

"You."

"Coward."

"That would be me."

Nancy grinned. "All right. I'll call her before I call the patients." She stared in the direction of the long-gone ambulance and an odd sort of wistfulness came over her face. "I'd sure like to go with him, though."

"He'd want you to call the patients. You know how he is."

She snapped back from wherever she'd been and became once again Nurse Nancy, Doc's right-hand woman, though she didn't look too happy about it at the moment. "Patients first. Always and forever."

Eli stuck his hands in his pockets. His fingers touched the torn wedding announcement, and he caught the glimmer of an idea.

Until he heard Gwen pronounced another man's wife there was always hope. Eli had one month before the wedding, and he meant to make the most of it. He would do what he must to force Gwen to see the truth. He'd just discovered a truth of his own.

He should never have let her go.

THE PHONE RANG, shrill in the depths of the day. Gwen Bartelt did not flinch or gasp; she barely woke up. With practiced ease she found the phone on her nightstand, punched the button, her eyes still closed, and brought the receiver to her ear. "What?"

"Gwen?"

Her first name spoken in a familiar voice made Gwen's eyes snap open. She could see nothing but the faint green glow of the phone from the corner of her eye. The heavy curtains on her windows blocked out every snatch of light. She had spent a fortune on those curtains. In her profession a good day's sleep was priceless.

Gwen sat up, rubbing at thick and grainy eyelids. How long had she been asleep? Not long enough.

"Nancy?"

"I'm sorry. I woke you up, didn't I?"

Shaking her head, Gwen tapped the light on her nightstand and squinted at the clock—10:30 a.m. Lovely, she'd been asleep for half an hour. No wonder she couldn't seem to get her mind around… something.

Her sleep-fogged brain cleared with the speed thunderstorms raced out over Lake Michigan. Phone calls that did not begin with "Dr. Bartelt, we have trouble in the ER" meant one thing. Bad news.

"Is something the matter with Doc?"

"Damn right. He's too stubborn for his own good. I told that old goat not to climb that ladder, but did he listen? No-o."

"Nancy!" Gwen bit out, tired, impatient and scared. "Focus! What happened?"

"He's in Mercy Hospital, having his broken leg put back together with a pin." Silence descended over the line, then a question tumbled free. "Can you come home?"

Gwen stared into the semidarkness and thought of

home. She didn't want to go. Then Nancy said the one thing that could make her go where she had not been for a very long time. "He asked for you, Gwen."

"Really?" The needy note in her voice embarrassed her. She'd have thought her father would chew nails before he'd ask for anything, especially for the prodigal daughter to return home.

"No, I lied." An exasperated growl that was so "Nancy" Gwen almost smiled traveled across phone line. "Yes, really. Will you?"

Gwen needed nothing less than to take time off one month before her wedding and honeymoon. Her fiancé, who also happened to be her boss, would be put out. He would pout. She couldn't resist.

"I'll be there this afternoon," she said.

THE FIRST SIGHT of Pine River always made Gwen want to cry. Perfect little town, so pretty and sweet, with pines along the river, just as the name promised.

She drove past the large, colorful sign at the city limits that announced: Pine River. Come For A Visit You'll Stay For A Lifetime. Midwest propaganda at its finest.

"It should say, Just A Visit Seems Like A Lifetime," Gwen muttered.

Though she'd lived in Pine River the first eighteen years of her life, she'd always wanted out. She couldn't remember the mother who had died when she was two, but everyone else in town did. They said

Gwen looked like her, talked like her, walked like her. No wonder Doc could barely stand the sight of her.

Well, she'd left the place behind and been nothing but happy ever since—except for missing Eli. She'd seen him sporadically after graduation, when she'd driven off to Milwaukee and he'd gone to Madison, but not at all in the past five years. Oh, they'd written and they'd phoned, but she missed having her very best friend in her life. Unfortunately, Eli loved Pine River and he wasn't ever going to leave.

Gwen winced as the bright May sunshine hit her sore eyes. She was running on adrenaline and caffeine. There'd been no sleep for her after Nancy's phone call.

Pulling to a stop in front of the rambling three-story house where she'd been born, Gwen stared out the windshield for a long moment. The place had always been too large for just her father and her, but it had been in the Bartelt family since Wisconsin was admitted to the Union over one hundred and fifty years before. Back in the days of large families, this house had been full of love, laughter, children. Now it looked pretty unloved, sad and empty—which, Gwen acknowledged, was most likely a reflection of her mood than anything else.

If she were a patient, she'd tell herself her recent depression was common enough on the threshold of changing your life forever. Wasn't that what wedding jitters were all about? But to be honest, the cloud that seemed to follow her everywhere, like Pigpen's little ball of dust, had appeared long before the ring on her finger.

Nancy emerged onto the porch, waved, then hopped down the steps and approached the car. As always, the woman didn't have a spot on her white nurse's outfit. Gwen couldn't believe Nancy hadn't told Doc where to get off with his insistence that this nurse wear a traditional white uniform, just as all his other nurses had. At least the triangular nurse's cap wasn't perched atop Nancy's head. That would have been a bit much. Instead, her long, slightly curly, chestnut hair was secured in a thick braid down her back.

Gwen got out of the car and they hugged. Nancy was taller and bigger boned than Gwen, but her bright-blue eyes and freckles made her appear smaller and younger than she was. An attractive, amusing, intelligent woman, why on earth was she devoting her life to Doc?

"I thought you'd be here long before now." Nancy rubbed Gwen's shoulder a moment in a silent show of sympathy before releasing her. "What happened?"

Gwen sighed. To drive from Milwaukee to Pine River took three hours with luck, much longer than that if you were Gwen Bartelt and bad luck was your middle name.

"Traffic," she said shortly, unwilling to go into all the other things she had needed to attend to before leaving her condominium on the east side of Milwaukee: call Lance, get a week off, listen as he begged her to stay—not for love but because it would mess up the schedule—ask her neighbor to pick up the mail and water the plants...

"Ah, traffic." Nancy nodded. In Pine River the word *traffic* in conjunction with Chicago, Minneapolis or Milwaukee always brought on long faces and frowns. Though most Pine River folks didn't venture into traffic, they'd heard all about it.

Gwen and Nancy walked toward the house, and as was her way, Nancy answered questions Gwen hadn't even asked yet. "Doc's fine. Resting while comfortably drugged. He's going to be in the hospital a few days with light traction before he can get a cast and come home. I doubt he'll be able to work for a month."

"He'll be able to hobble me down the aisle, won't he?"

Nancy stopped and faced Gwen. "If I were you, I wouldn't even go there, girl."

"Huh?"

"Your father is hot as a hornet about your getting married to a guy he's never heard of. He got the invitation, bitched all morning, then stomped out to do the eaves and fell on his butt."

Guilt washed over Gwen. She should have told him in person. There still would have been a scene, but maybe Doc wouldn't be in the hospital. She pushed the guilt aside. With a head harder than the average brick, Doc would have gone up on that ladder sooner or later, regardless of what had been in the mail that morning.

"He's never met Lance," Gwen pointed out, "because he refuses to leave this town or his patients."

"He's been to Milwaukee a few times."

"For a conference or a consult. Yippee."

"At least he went, Gwen."

Gwen blushed. True enough. She'd been so busy with work, and so darned glad to get out of Pine River, she hadn't come back at all. Until now.

"You could have at least brought up the fact that you were dating seriously before springing a wedding on him."

Gwen shrugged. She could have. But she just knew her father would loathe Lance. Doc was an old-school physician who abhorred the namby-pamby elite. Lance was the elite of the elite. Even his name would send her father off on a bender of sarcasm. So why was she marrying the man?

She'd been lonely most of her life; only Eli had helped. But sooner or later Eli would marry and have as many kids as he had dogs—that had always been his dream.

Gwen winced. Then he would be lost to her forever. She'd begun to pull away from him several years ago so that when the man who was her best friend found a new one her heart would not shatter.

Lately the loneliness had begun to prey on her. She got on well with Lance, and they shared a vision for the future—brilliant careers augmented by perfect partners. She had no illusions that Lance loved her, just as he had no illusions that she loved him, which was the way they both wanted it.

No kids, no pets, no everlasting love—three very good rules—because if everlasting love knocked on Gwen's door she was going to throw the bolt and hide under her bed.

She'd seen what that kind of love did to a person, and she wanted no part of it. What she wanted was a sane, mutually satisfying relationship. If Lance died or things didn't work out, she'd be sad, but she'd survive. Unlike her father. He might breathe and walk and work, but he wasn't really living, and he hadn't been for almost thirty years.

"Earth to Gwen." Nancy waved her hand in front of Gwen's eyes. "Where did you go?"

"Memory lane. Sorry. This place has that effect on me."

Nancy's eyes darkened, but she didn't commiserate. One of Gwen's favorite things about Nancy was that she knew sometimes sympathy only made matters worse. "Let's go inside and put away your suitcase. Then we can drive to Mercy. I canceled your dad's patients for today and tomorrow, though God knows what we'll do for the next month."

"You drove to Mercy and back, then made all those calls? Damn, you're good."

Nancy's lips curved as she shook her head. "You know how Doc is. Patients first. I stayed here and Eli went over to Mercy. He just got back."

Gwen's gaze went to the house next door—a house where most of her happy memories of Pine River resided—just as two black rockets of fur shot from the backyard and headed straight for them.

Nancy saw them coming. "Sit!" she snapped.

The two identical black labs skidded to a halt, their rear ends sliding along the ground and hitting their front feet. Gwen's gaze went to their mouths and stuck there. Something furry hung out.

"What do they have in their mouths?" Gwen asked, though she really didn't want to know.

"Oh, no! Drop it!"

Obediently, the labs opened their jaws, and two scraggly, wet bits of fluff landed at their feet.

"Please don't tell me they've brought us dead things."

"No. They wouldn't hurt a flea. They're just possessed." Nancy took a step toward the dogs and the balls of fluff, which had begun to tumble about and mew. At her approach, the dogs started to wiggle their rumps and wag their tails. "Stay." They stilled. "Where did you get these?" Nancy demanded, as if the two would tell her.

Their mouths opened in doggy grins, tongues lolling, and Nancy gave an exasperated sigh. "These two bring home every cat in town. They don't hurt them. They just want to carry them around and get them all slimy. They're the scourge of the neighborhood."

Gwen's lips twitched. She couldn't help it. The dogs' initial glee had turned to expressions of abject embarrassment as Nancy talked about them. Obviously, they'd been down this road before.

"Elijah Drycinski," Nancy shouted. "Get out here!"

The screen door opened and Eli stepped out. Gwen's mouth fell open. What had happened to him?

Maybe she hadn't seen him in five years, but she would remember if Eli looked like a *GQ* model. He'd always been just Eli, the guy next door and her very best friend. Shy and sweet, but smart, gentle with animals, uncomfortable with people—except for her.

He'd never been *that* tall or *that* muscular. He'd worn glasses and kept his hair so short he didn't need to comb it. Who was this man over six feet tall, with biceps bulging out of a black T-shirt that stretched over an equally well-endowed chest? The rugged, manly face, upon which perched no hint of glasses, appeared a bit familiar, and the black hair that had always been too short to curl now wound below his ears and flashed blue highlights in the sun.

"What the…?" Gwen murmured.

Nancy chuckled. "I always said he'd be a late bloomer, but you wouldn't listen."

"Bloom? He looks more like he detonated."

"Gwen?" Eli shaded his eyes against the late-afternoon sun.

Though his voice had changed years ago from a boy's to a man's, it now held a hint of hoarseness, a worldliness unlike the Eli she knew, which sent an odd skitter down Gwen's spine. Goose bumps raised on her legs. Only a reaction to a cool spring wind, she assured herself. She'd worn shorts to travel, and in May Wisconsin, shorts were almost always a mistake.

As Eli approached, a smile of welcome spreading

across his face, unfamiliar lines created by sun and wind and cold deepened about his black eyes, altering his countenance in new and intriguing ways.

She was staring and she needed to stop. Gwen stepped forward, arms spread wide for a welcome home hug. "Hey, Eli."

Instead of hugging her back and letting her go, Eli pulled Gwen close to his remarkable new body, then brushed her lips with his.

And the world did a funny sort of shimmy.

CHAPTER TWO

ELI'S MOM ALWAYS SAID, "Begin how you mean to continue." And since Eli meant to continue with Gwen straight down the aisle, the first order of business was for her to stop seeing him as the amiable boy next door and start seeing him as a man she could love.

He only gave her the merest brush of lips, a chaste, welcoming kiss no matter where you lived, but she jumped as if he'd stung her, and when he raised his head she stared at him as if he'd sprouted a beanstalk from his ear.

Though he wanted to tug her close and hold her tight, tell her everything he felt and beg her to stay with him forever, he wasn't as dumb as he looked. That would be the quickest way to see the back end of Gwen's car disappearing down the highway. He had to play this right or lose everything.

So he smiled as if he hadn't a care in the world, ignoring her puzzled frown—and Nancy's knowing smirk. "Glad you're home."

Even though her scent enticed him, seduced him, made him want to do crazy things in the middle of the day, he stepped back. Gwen always did smell like temptation in the rain, and the sight of her made him think of cool vanilla ice in the midst of a desert summer.

Though he could tell by her face he appeared different to her—he'd grown a few inches in several directions since she'd seen him last—she looked exactly the same to him. Dark-blond hair, brown eyes, a complexion that would tan light gold with only minimal time in the sun. The present porcelain shade of her skin revealed her work habits even more than the fatigue in her eyes.

In her simple summer shorts and top the shade of sand and the setting sun, she made him think of deserted beaches and tropical nights. Long legs; slim build; elegant, capable hands.

Eli swallowed, and so as not to be tempted any further toward liberties he dared not take, he turned to Nancy. "You bellowed?"

"Your animals were out cruising again."

Eli winced. "How many this time?"

"Only two because I made them sit and stay. Can't you break them of that? I thought you were a dog doctor."

"I thought so, too, but they don't seem impressed." Eli turned to his dogs, who looked suitably abashed. They were afraid of Nancy, along with the rest of Pine River, though they tried with all their doggy hearts to make her love them. They couldn't understand why she didn't succumb. Everyone else did.

"Jake! Elwood!" Ears perked at the sound of their names. "No cats."

"Wait a minute," Gwen interrupted, laughter in her voice. "Their names are Jake and Elwood?"

Eli had been explaining those names for a year now. No one ever seemed to get his joke. He had no doubt Gwen would.

"Yeah, so?"

"And that would be because…?"

Eli shared Gwen's smile. God, he had missed her. "They bring home every cat in town. No matter what I do, they won't stop because they're—"

"On a mission from God," she finished.

They laughed, and it was as if the years apart had never been.

"What are you guys talking about?" Nancy demanded.

"The Blues Brothers," Gwen said, as if that explained everything, which for the two of them, it did.

"Eli always says that when people ask him about the names, but I don't get it."

"It's a movie."

"That much I know."

"Jake and Elwood, the Blues brothers, are on a mission from God. They demolish Chicago."

"Aha," Nancy said. "I see where this is going."

"Eli and I must have watched that movie a dozen times in high school. We had hysterics every time."

"You always were two peas in a pod."

That was what Eli was counting on. He just had to remind Gwen of everything they had shared and nudge her bit by bit toward the realization that the rest of their lives should be shared, as well.

"Have you watched it lately?" he asked.

"Not since I left Pine River."

"We'll have to remedy that while you're here."

Her smile froze. For a moment she looked caught in a trap. Then she straightened, and it was as if the Gwen he'd always known was gone, replaced by this long, cool woman in tan shorts. "I don't plan on being here very long."

Nancy and Eli exchanged a glance. They'd see about that. "I'll drive you to the hospital," Eli offered.

"I know where it is."

"Really? I thought you'd forgotten this section of the state altogether."

"Don't start, Eli."

"Hey, you know your dad will."

"I'm used to Doc. I stopped listening to him years ago."

"Maybe that's your problem."

"Who said I had a problem?"

"If everything is fine, then why are you stick thin and ghost pale, with purple circles under your eyes and tension lines around your mouth?"

"Whoa!" Nancy held up her hand. "Them there's fightin' words. I'll just put Jake and Elwood in the house. When you two finish round one, you'll find me in Eli's truck." Nancy stalked off, snapping her fingers at the labs, who, after lingering gazes of adoration for the kittens tumbling on the lawn, followed with their tails between their legs.

Eli turned to Gwen. The hurt in Gwen's eyes had Eli wishing he'd kept his mouth shut, but seeing her all worn-out made his chest hurt. He knew Gwen. She was Superdoctor. To admit exhaustion would be failure—and failure she would not allow. She tried so hard to be unlike Doc she didn't see how very like him she was.

Before Eli could say anything else, a pickup truck stopped in front of his house. Pete Jones, a farmer from the outskirts of town, leaned over and shouted through the passenger window, "Hey, Eli, you want to bring my kittens over here?"

Gwen snorted. "Everyone knows where to come when they're missing a cat, don't they?"

"They used to blame coyotes. Now they blame Jake and Elwood."

"And they're usually right."

"They're always right," Eli muttered, picking up the still-damp balls of fluff and taking them to Pete.

"I see Gwen's home." Pete waved and Gwen waved back. "She's lookin' good."

Pete and Gwen had dated. Lucky for Pete, he was safely and happily married, with five kids and eighty dairy cows; therefore Eli did not have to kill him.

Eli leaned into the open window. "Doc broke his leg this morning."

"I heard."

Shaking his head, Eli absently petted the kittens. The Pine River grapevine was amazing, as always.

"Who's going to be our sawbones until Doc is back in commission?" Eli shrugged. "You think Gwen will stick around?"

Eli could only hope Doc found the right words to get Gwen to stay. Even though he wouldn't wish a compound fracture on his worst enemy, Eli had to admit Doc's accident had been fortuitous. He didn't know what he'd have done about Gwen otherwise. Gone to Milwaukee, pounded on her door and dragged her away with him?

Eli sighed. Caveman he wasn't, but if that was what it took, that was what he'd do. He'd waited long enough for Gwen to come to her senses on her own.

WHEN GWEN AND ELI reached his Ford SUV, Nancy handed Gwen a pillow and pointed at the back seat. "Time for you to take a catnap."

"Why? So Jake or Elwood can bring me home in a doggy bag?"

"Snot," Nancy muttered, and got into the front seat with Eli.

Gwen climbed into the back, and her gaze met Eli's in the rearview mirror. He raised his eyebrows in an expression that plainly said: *Why argue with Nancy? You'll only get a headache.*

Gwen returned his wry smile and lay down. She couldn't stay mad at Eli for more than a minute. He'd only been telling the truth. She *was* exhausted—in body, mind and soul. Of course she'd never admit that, but truth was truth.

Shutting her eyes, Gwen enjoyed the warmth of the

sun and the fresh spring breeze through the half-open windows. Shadows of the trees danced across her closed eyelids, making her remember summer afternoons with Eli, lying lazily beneath the oak tree in his backyard, sharing their dreams, drinking Kool-Aid.

Nothing had ever been that peaceful or easy again. Eli had that effect on her. With him she could be who she was. Because he was her friend and not her lover, she knew that no matter what she did, he would always be there for her—at least for as long as he could be.

"How're your mom and dad?" Her voice sounded sleepy and Gwen let her eyes stay closed.

Though Eli's parents had originally retired to Pine River, the long winters had worn thin and they'd moved to Tucson several years ago. Katie Drycinski had been the only mother Gwen ever knew, and she'd been a good one. Gwen was ashamed to admit she had not seen Mrs. D. since the last time she'd seen Eli.

"They love Arizona," Eli answered. The peace Gwen had hoped to find listening to the familiar cadence of his voice did not overtake her. Instead, she experienced again that odd shiver as his new husky tone slid across her skin like warm water.

"Do they love Arizona even when it's 110 degrees in the shade?"

"They come home and harass me then."

"Do you fly west in March when winter in Wisconsin isn't so fun anymore?"

"Wish I could, especially when I'm in a cow barn, stripped to the waist, up to my shoulders in cow and it's forty below."

"Mmm, nice image."

Actually, the image of Eli stripped to the waist wasn't all bad. She'd like to see that, minus the cow. Gwen rubbed her eyes. She must be tired if she was fantasizing about Eli half-naked.

What had gotten into her? She'd never thought of Eli like this. He had been her friend and nothing more, because a friend was what she needed. Lovers were a dime a dozen. Friends were forever.

"Why don't you let Nancy watch the Blues Brothers and you can head for the desert?"

"Speak for yourself, honey. I'm not watching the twin terrors."

"They're very well behaved," Eli protested.

"Until they smell cat."

"I'm working on it. It's embarrassing for the local vet to have dogs who covet feline flunkies."

Gwen giggled. Eli always could make her laugh. "So why *don't* you spend March in sunny Arizona?"

"I can't leave my patients, Gwen. There is no one else."

Gwen's laughter died. "You sound just like Doc."

"Thank you. He's an admirable man."

Gwen went silent, her mind drifting on a sleepy haze. Doc was an icon in Pine River. Like his father before him, he'd been present at the births of half the town, the illnesses of all and the deaths of many.

Gwen would admire him, too, if she could get over a lifetime of neglect.

Oh, she'd never wanted for anything—except love—and you could live without love. She was proof of that. But he'd never needed her, never needed anyone but his dead wife. So Gwen had grown up feeling that if she disappeared from the face of the earth, no one would notice. Except for Eli, of course.

The truck slowed, turned, stopped. ''There she is. Mercy Hospital.''

Gwen sat up. The place had expanded since she'd been here last, as a volunteer aide during high school. The ER at Mercy was a far cry from City Hospital in Milwaukee. People died at Mercy; it was inevitable. But they rarely died in quite the same fashion as people died in Gwen's ER.

Of late, the job she'd always dreamed of was more a nightmare than a wish come true. Working in the emergency room of a big-city hospital had always seemed like the way to help the most people, but the longer Gwen worked there the less she felt as if she helped anyone at all.

Eli opened her door and held out his hand. *Such chivalry,* she thought. *Does he think I'm near collapse?*

Trying to reassure him, Gwen gave a great big happy smile before aligning her palm to his. A curious tingle went up her arm, and she pulled herself free, unnerved at the odd response. Her smile dissolved.

"What's the matter?" He continued to hold out his hand.

"Nothing." Gwen got out of the vehicle on her own. She had to get a grip. Quickly. Before Eli noticed the strange effect he was having on her and asked more direct questions. She would have no idea what to tell him.

They followed Nancy across the parking lot, then Eli took the lead to Doc's room. Once there, they paused outside.

"You go in first," Eli said.

"Can't we all go in together?"

"He was kind of loopy when I was here before. We'd better go one at a time."

Gwen frowned. She'd never seen her father loopy. She wasn't sure if she wanted to.

Eli nodded toward the door. Nancy gave her a little shove.

Gwen would have liked to run all the way home to Milwaukee, but she'd come this far...

So she stepped into her father's hospital room. In that big white bed, with his leg in traction, he appeared both smaller and older than she remembered. Gwen fought a rush of sympathy. Her father had never needed or wanted anyone's sympathy. He'd always held his pain close to his heart, where it festered. She swallowed the bitterness she had hoped to conquer. Here, faced with both the man and the memories, it returned.

His eyes snapped open, pinning her at the foot of his bed. For a moment Gwen imagined she saw love and tenderness there, but she must have been mistaken, because his words held neither.

"Didn't think you'd come."

"Couldn't believe you asked." She winced at the sarcasm in her voice. She and her father had been picking at each other for years. Her mother would have been horrified—or at least Gwen thought she would have been. She'd never known her mother at all.

Doc sat up, grimaced, then waved Gwen off when she would have helped him. "I did a dumb thing," he began.

Gwen very nearly gaped. For Doc to admit himself at fault was nothing short of miraculous. She sat down heavily in the chair next to his bed but kept silent, curious what else he might admit.

"I'm going to need help."

Now she did gape. The words *need, help,* and *I* in a sentence from Doc occurred about once in every never.

"What kind of help?"

"Doctor help."

"Should I buzz someone?" Gwen half stood, reaching for the call button attached to his bed. "Do you need more pain medication?"

"Not yet. But they'll be in here soon enough to dope me, and by then I'll want them to. So let me talk and don't interrupt."

That sounded more like the Doc she knew. *I'll talk and you listen.*

"I'm going to be out of commission for at least a

month. Could be six to eight weeks in a cast—well, you know that as well as I do. But the beginning is going to be tough, and I know I'm not going to be able to do my job the way I should.'' His lips tightened again, this time with annoyance over the truth rather than pain. ''I need someone to take over for me until I can manage again. I want that someone to be you.''

''We've had this conversation before—''

''I'm not asking you to be my partner. I'm not asking you to stay here forever. I'm asking you to give your father one month of your life. Without a doctor around here, people die. Even *with* a doctor, they die.''

A shadow passed over his face, and Gwen knew he remembered her mother, his wife. A car crash on a lonely country road and she'd died in his arms, despite everything the great Doc Bartelt had done to save her. That was why Gwen had run as fast as she could from any suggestion of practicing in Pine River. She did not want to watch someone she knew or loved die in her arms; so she'd gone where she knew no one—and she hadn't loved at all.

''You have vacation time coming, don't you? Comp days? Something?''

Though they rarely spoke, and saw each other even less, her father understood her well—or at least knew her work habits. Probably because Doc took off even less time than she did—in the vicinity of little to none.

''I've got some time,'' she answered grudgingly.

"So take it."

"I saved it for an emergency."

He flicked a finger at his broken leg. "Looks like an emergency to me."

"Can't you get a temporary doctor?"

He snorted. "Sure. Tons of decent physicians are knocking on my door to inquire whether they can help me take care of the people in my town for a few weeks' stint."

"There has to be someone."

"There isn't. I need a competent physician, right now. You're elected."

"Well, *un*elect me. I'm getting married in a month."

"So get married in a month, but in the meantime help out your father."

"I'm an ER physician, not family practice."

"Think you'll be bored in little old Pine River?"

Gwen shrugged. She *did* thrive on the fast pace of the ER. People who worked in one had to or they'd never manage. But there was also a high burnout rate, and of late she'd begun to understand why. Still, she was very, very good at her job—one of the best. Yet she had no doubt that in Pine River, no matter how good she was, she'd always be less than Doc.

"Do you remember what your mother said when she first saw you?"

Gwen narrowed her eyes. "Low blow, Doc."

He shrugged. "Desperate times, desperate measures. So what did she say?"

"'This one will save the world,'" Gwen recited.

She'd heard the story of her birth countless times, and her mother's words had sent her into emergency medicine. What better way to save the world? Unfortunately, in Milwaukee she rarely felt she was doing more than sticking her finger in a disintegrating dike. No matter how hard she worked, the disasters kept on arriving.

Silence descended—heavy, charged, waiting. Gwen braced herself. The bombshell was coming.

"I need you to save my world, Gwen."

She looked at her father and she yearned to say yes. He'd never needed her before, and she'd talked herself out of needing him—of needing anyone.

The voice of temptation whispered that even though he needed her now for his patients, at least he needed her, and maybe if he admitted needing her, he might admit loving her. She'd been waiting a long time for her father to say those words. He probably wouldn't—or maybe, like her, he couldn't.

She *wanted* to say yes, but she was all grown-up now, with places to go, people to see, patients of her own, for crying out loud. So instead of giving in to temptation's voice, Gwen stood and walked to the door. Without looking at her father again, she whispered, "I can't," and slipped from the room.

CHAPTER THREE

ELI DROVE HOME from Mercy Hospital amid silence so taut the air vibrated. Nancy had gone in for a brief, strategic visit with Doc after Gwen came out, and had obviously gotten the lowdown. Eli knew what Doc had asked of Gwen because he'd suggested it, but from the "Don't talk to me" expression in Gwen's eyes and the tightness of Nancy's lips, Gwen had been less than thrilled with the prospect.

Eli had figured on that. He hoped that given time to think, Gwen would see she was needed in Pine River the most. She *was* a doctor; therefore need should count for something.

"Who's that?" Nancy spoke for the first time as Eli pulled into his driveway and shut off the engine.

Gwen, who had been pretending to be asleep all the way home, sat up. "Where?"

Nancy jumped out of the truck without answering and sprinted across the lawn. A pickup sat crooked in the driveway, and a man pounded frantically on the front door. "Doc! Doc!" he shouted.

"Ken Barrabs, what are you bellering about?" Nancy demanded.

Gwen got out of the truck. Eli followed.

Ken turned and relief spread over his face. "We called and no one answered. We paged Doc, too."

Nancy cursed. "The beeper's probably going off in his pants somewhere in the garbage at Mercy."

The blank look on Ken's face revealed he hadn't heard the latest gossip on the vine; his next question confirmed that. "Where's Doc?"

"In the hospital with a broken leg."

Ken went white and grabbed the porch rail. "It's Sadie. She went into labor and the baby's comin' real fast."

"Let's go." Nancy took his arm.

"But what about Doc?"

"I know how to deliver a baby, Ken."

"But...but this isn't like the other times. Somethin's not right."

"Did you call Mercy to send an ambulance?"

"Of course. But I don't think they'll get here in time. There's an awful lot of blood. Her mom said I needed to get Doc over there come hell or high water."

"Well, Doc isn't coming. You've got me."

"And me." Gwen stepped forward.

"You?" Nancy sounded skeptical.

"I've been delivering babies in the ER for quite a while now, and there's always something wrong if they walk in my door. Does Doc have a traveling bag or something?"

Nancy stared at Gwen for a long moment, then gave a short nod. "Get in the truck and I'll grab the bag from the hall."

Gwen started toward Ken's vehicle. Eli just stood there until she turned around. "Aren't you coming?"

"Why?"

"Ken's going to need someone to hold his hand. They always do."

Eli nodded. He didn't know Ken well, but he'd delivered a calf or two over Barrabas's way. He supposed his hand was better than no hand at all.

Eli jumped into the back of the truck as Nancy arrived with a huge briefcase that looked to weigh about twenty pounds. She chucked the case into Eli's lap. He grunted. Maybe thirty pounds. Nancy followed the case, and before she could settle in, off they went.

From the small back seat of the pickup, Eli studied Gwen. After talking to her father, she had emerged from the room paler than when she'd gone in, the dark circles that concerned him turned to purple bruises beneath her exhausted eyes. Now her entire demeanor had changed. No slouching, no sighing. Dr. Bartelt was in control.

"How long has she been in labor?" Gwen asked.

"An hour."

"Water break?"

"Yep."

"How far apart are the pains?"

"Three minutes when I left."

"Three?" She tilted her head with a frown. "How many children has she had before this?"

"Three. Their grampa took them back to his place."

Gwen waved that off. "Did the others come fast?"

He shrugged. "Seemed like she took her sweet time."

Gwen rolled her eyes. "Let's put it this way. Did you get to the hospital?"

"Barely."

"Damn. You'd better put this truck into gear, Ken."

The Barrabas farm lay only five miles down the road. With Ken driving, they got there in record time. As they piled out of the vehicle, an earsplitting shriek rent the air. Everyone froze but Gwen. She yanked the bag from Eli's hands and ran for the back door.

Gwen reached the house while everyone else still stood by the truck. Adrenaline pumped through her veins. She jumped up the porch steps and burst through the door. Hoisting the heavy doctor's bag higher in her arms, she sprinted up the stairs as another shriek kicked her heart into overdrive.

Gwen stepped inside a room filled with sound and movement. There was a lot of blood, all right.

In the movies deliveries looked easy and sweet, with happy mothers in fresh nightgowns and clean, pink babies wrapped in bunting. But childbirth was never very pretty, not clean and not neat. Bringing babies into the world was hard, sweaty, bloody work—not for the faint of heart on either side. Though at least you had something to show for your trouble when you were through. If everything went well. Gwen planned to see that everything went well.

Sadie appeared wrung-out. Her mother didn't look

much better. They both glanced hopefully at Gwen as she came in. Their faces fell.

"Who are you?" Sadie's voice had gone hoarse.

"Dr. Bartelt."

"No, you aren't."

Gwen sighed. *See?* her mind taunted. "I'm Gwen, Doc's daughter."

"Where's Doc?" the mother demanded.

"Gone. I'm filling in." She winced at that admission. She was only filling in for the night, she assured herself.

"We want Doc."

"Well, you got me."

Another pain took Sadie, and Gwen brushed the mother aside. Most women in end-stage labor didn't care what you did, who you were or anything else, as long as you got the baby out.

Gwen lifted the sheet, checked the patient and cursed beneath her breath. Nancy appeared at her side. "Frank breach," she stated, something Gwen already knew.

"What's that mean?" the mother asked.

"Rear end first."

"That isn't right!" Sadie wailed.

"No shit," Nancy muttered, and Gwen gave her a silencing frown.

"I want to push."

"Not yet." Gwen opened the bag and rummaged about. "Pant. Don't push." She turned to Nancy. "Too late for a C-section, even if we could do one here."

"Baby all right?" Nancy asked.

"Without a monitor, I can't be sure, but his little butt looks healthy enough at the moment."

"Healthy enough to wait?"

Gwen eyed Sadie. "I don't think so. Even if we get paramedics in time, they won't know dink about birthin' babies like this. Let's get him out of there."

"Do you know how?"

"Yes."

"Have you ever delivered a breach?"

"Yes."

"And everyone was fine?"

"Except for me. I had heart failure. Now, get me the soap, gloves and an episiotomy scissors. Have the anesthetic and sutures ready."

"Yes, Doctor." Gwen glanced sideways to see if Nancy was being sarcastic, but she had already gone off to do what Gwen had asked. Nancy was a professional first—a pain in the behind second.

"Where's Daddy?" Gwen asked the room at large.

"He fainted the last two times," the mother answered with a sneer in her voice if not on her face. "That's why I'm here."

"Fine." Since she didn't need a fainter on top of everything else, Gwen left Daddy to Eli and got to work. "Sadie? On the next contraction, I want you to push. Mom? Get on the bed and hold her shoulders up." She glanced at Nancy. "Here we go."

In short order a baby was born. His first cry sent goose bumps over Gwen's flesh. The tears in Sadie's eyes made Gwen choke up, too, but she swallowed the unaccustomed emotion and went about her business. Only when the mother was stitched up, cleaned up and resting on the stretcher, showing a healthy baby to his father, did Gwen relax.

Everyone else followed the mother and child out of the room and down to the waiting ambulance. Gwen sat on a chair and put her head in her hands. Adrenaline was great until you hit the shakes that followed.

"I've never seen anything so beautiful."

Gwen didn't look up. Even with the changes in him, she'd know Eli's voice anywhere. "They were something, weren't they?"

"I meant you."

Gwen dropped her hands, confused at his tone. Eli leaned in the doorway, staring at her. He'd been different since she came home. That kiss for one thing. Oh, sure, he'd just pecked her lips, but she'd felt the touch all the way to her toes.

She needed to get a grip. In a month she would marry the perfect man for her. Lance knew what he wanted; Gwen wanted the same things. Now was not the time to feel strange stirrings of hunger for her best friend.

Gwen flushed—from the direction of her thoughts and the expression in Eli's eyes. He stared at her as if he'd never seen her before, as if he wanted to cross the room, sweep her into his arms and kiss her, really kiss her, this time.

The frightening thing was—she wanted him to.

So she made a joke to dispel the odd tension. "I

always look my best after emergencies. The sweat of pure panic gives me a healthy glow.''

"You didn't panic. Far from it. If you hadn't been here, Gwen, this would have been a disaster.''

"The paramedics got here.''

"But would they have been in time? Would they have known what to do?''

"Probably not,'' she answered.

"You can see how much you're needed here. Why can't you admit that and stay?''

"I'm needed in Milwaukee, too.''

"Are you really? How many doctors do they have at that hospital? Here, we only have you between us and catastrophe.''

"You're exaggerating.''

"If you save one life—and I think you just saved two—wouldn't it be worth a month of your time?''

She began to clean the instruments, roll up the ruined sheets, pack away what had not been used. Eli was right. But she still didn't want to stay. "You know how much this place gets to me,'' she murmured.

"I know. But I don't think you ever gave Pine River a fair shake. Stay, Gwen. Let me show you the town through my eyes.''

She scowled at him. "Fair shake? I'm *from* here. You can't change my mind about Pine River. There are too many bad memories.''

"What about your memories of me?'' His voice was quiet, a comfort she'd never noticed before. "Are those bad?''

"You know they aren't. They're the only good ones."

"We could make more good ones." Gwen sighed, but before she could refuse, he spoke again. "I never thought you were selfish or a coward."

"Maybe I'm both. I can't help it if this place makes me want to cry. Wherever I go, whatever I do, I'm reminded of a woman I can't even remember."

"You need to get past that if you're ever going to move forward with your life."

"The way Doc has?" She couldn't stop the sarcasm in her voice, even if she'd wanted to.

"You need to make peace with your past, with this town, with your mother and especially with Doc. This is your chance."

"You make it sound like a gift from above."

"It could be, Gwen, if you let it."

NANCY CREPT INTO Doc's room after visiting hours. No one would say anything even if they caught her. But she didn't want to chat with the nurses about work or boyfriends or anything else.

Not that she had any boyfriends to chat about, but that was beside the point. She wasn't a saint or a virgin, but that was only because she'd made herself date boys in an effort to get over the man who'd taken her heart—even though he'd never know about it. And just as she'd suspected, none of the boys ever measured up to him, so she'd stopped beating her head against that particular wall.

Doc slept, which was as it should be. With an injury like his, they'd keep him on pain medication for a few days, and that would make him dopey. He'd sleep and sleep healed better than anything.

Nancy took the chair next to Doc's bed and just watched him sleep. Thirty-two years old and she was working her life away. Why not? Did she want to get married just to be married, have children just so she'd have them? *No.* She wanted to marry the man she loved. She wanted his children, or none at all. Unfortunately, the man who held her heart was a man whose heart was already taken by another.

She continued to watch Doc sleep as her mind drifted. Once upon a time she and Gwen had been friends. Not best friends, of course. Eli always held that place in Gwen's heart. Now Nancy was starting to wonder if Gwen held a bit more serious place in Eli's heart.

Wouldn't it be wonderful if Gwen came home to stay? Doc would like that, even though he'd have his wisdom teeth pulled before he'd admit it. Old coot.

Her attention returned to the man in the bed. He slept soundly, peacefully, looking his age or younger for the first time in a long time. Fifty-six wasn't so old, not that anyone could tell *him* that.

Temptation was a familiar enemy. Nancy had resisted it for years. But today had been too long and too hard for her to resist temptation any longer.

Before she even realized what she was doing, Nancy reached out and touched Doc's face. She had never once touched him like this. Her hand trembled and she yanked it back. But when he didn't awaken, she touched him again, brushing his fading blond hair from his forehead, then skimming his lips with the tip of one finger. Her eyes burned, and before she could do something really stupid, Nancy fled.

How could she ever compete with a dead woman?

GWEN WAS TOO WIRED to sleep, a common occurrence after an adrenaline rush followed by the shakes. Often when she worked and there was a trauma—there was always a trauma—her body would scream exhaustion, but her mind would not shut down and let her sleep. So she would come home and play solitaire for as long as it took to relax.

From what she'd garnered by talking to other physicians, the horrible hours of residency—days without rest, sleeping at the drop of a hat or not at all, a doze here, a nap there—ruined sleep patterns for a long time, if not forever.

Her father had often walked the halls in the middle of the night. Back then Gwen had thought he missed her mother—and he no doubt had. She hadn't figured out until residency that he'd probably had sleep disturbances, too.

She wandered the dark house. The place was familiar, but so many things were new. That chair, those books; several fish swam in a bowl atop the bookcase. Her father had never kept pets before. Though fish weren't exactly petlike, still they were alive and in the house. Amazing.

On the desk next to the bookcase a new picture

frame stood in an old position. Gwen moved closer. The picture within the new frame was the same.

"Mother," she whispered, and nearly pressed her nose to the glass.

Looking at Elizabeth Bartelt was like looking in a mirror. Betsy her husband always called her, if he spoke of her at all. How could Gwen resemble so closely a woman she'd never known? Genes were an amazing thing.

Twin shadows drifted across the light of the moon that poured through the floor-length front window. When she looked outside, nothing was there. Or at least not anymore.

She returned her attention to the picture, then a thud split the silence of the room. Did someone need medical assistance?

Gwen crossed to the door. "Who's there?"

Her answer was a slight whine, a sound of pain, then scratching against the wood. Gwen turned on the porch light and flung open the door.

Jake and Elwood shot into the house like balls from a cannon. They didn't bark because their mouths were full. Instead, they headed straight for the kitchen at the back of the house.

"Hey, get in here!" Gwen ran after them.

They hit the kitchen floor and skidded across, nails scritching, feet scratching. Jake—or was it Elwood?—slammed into Elwood—or was it Jake?—and they both collapsed in a heap at the back door.

"Stop that!" she admonished. Big mistake, be-

cause they must have thought she said, "Drop that!"
So they did.

Twin bits of fur flew from their mouths, cater-
wauling loud enough to rattle the eardrums. The animals shot toward Gwen, and for a minute she thought
they were rats, of the drowned variety, since they
were gray-brown, rat-size and sopping wet. She
shrieked and jumped on the kitchen table, only to
have her poor, beleaguered brain register that they
had been cats, not rats. This was, after all, Jake and
Elwood that had come to call.

The cats tore off toward the living room. The dogs
followed, but much more slowly since they couldn't
seem to get traction on the tile floor. Gwen climbed
down from the table and grabbed the first weapon she
saw—a pie spat—then chased after them.

Too late. The cats sat on the bookcase, dipping
their paws into the fish bowl, nudging at the glass
with their heads. The dogs leaped in three-foot-high
leaps, trying to get to the cats.

"Sit!" Gwen shouted, but she hadn't the presence
of Nancy and the dogs kept on jumping. Slowly,
slowly, as if in a bad movie, the fish bowl slid toward
the edge of the case. Gwen ran, catching the thing
just before it fell. Fish water sloshed down the front
of her nightgown.

And that was when Eli walked in and started laughing. She threw the pie spat at him. The utensil slapped
harmlessly into the door above his head, which made
him laugh harder. Since she wanted to throw something else, badly, she swept the cats to the floor—

where they promptly took off into the night, braying hellhounds at their heels—and set the fish bowl back on the bookcase.

"I fail to see anything funny about this."

He kept laughing. "That's because you aren't looking at you."

She crossed the room, not stopping until they were toe-to-toe. The night air brushed her wet gown and she shivered. Her nipples hardened, pushing against the damp material. Eli stopped laughing and a new expression came over his face. His gaze dropped and when he stepped closer, his breath caressed her neck.

"Wh-what are you doing?" Whose voice was that coming out of her mouth? She sounded sleek and sexy, like a 1-900 operator. Maybe; she'd never heard one. She certainly sounded nothing like Dr. Bartelt— ER physician extraordinaire.

"You're cold."

He gathered her into his arms, but it was nothing like the other times he'd held her, few that they had been. He was big and strong, in charge now, so different from the Eli she'd grown up with—the boy who'd come to town alone and remained alone, friends only with the animals, until they'd discovered each other. Back then it had been the two of them. Oh, she'd had other friends, Nancy for one, but no one had ever been what Eli was—and no one ever would.

"I'm n-not c-cold." She shivered again.

"Liar," he whispered.

As the familiar scent of Eli washed over her she

felt as if she were discovering him all over again—or maybe discovering the man he had become while she was away. At least the essence of him still remained—the Eli she trusted.

His lips brushed the top of her head, gentle and sure, before he tilted her face up to his. "Should I kiss you, Guinevere?"

He used her real name and brought to mind their childhood when they'd played Knights of the Round Table. Despite her name, Gwen had always been Arthur. And Eli? He'd been Galahad, the virgin knight, which made her wonder...

She was wondering far too much lately. Insane things like how would he taste if she ran her tongue along that pulse at the side of his neck? What would happen if she leaned forward and pressed her lips against his?

Kiss Eli? Such a thing had never entered her mind—until this morning, and strangely she felt as if she fantasized about the forbidden.

She waited too long to answer his question; perhaps because while her body shivered and shuddered, her mind shouted, *No, don't kiss me and change everything!* Even as her secret, fantasizing, treacherous heart called, *Yes, kiss me. Kiss me now.*

She swayed toward him; her head tilted back, an answer without words that shouted just the same.

He smiled, a dangerous heated smile in the midst of the night. When he smiled like that he didn't look like her best friend at all; he looked like a secret lover.

His kiss was not hello, or goodbye, or anything she

could put a name to beyond more. More than she'd ever had, more than she'd ever wanted, more than she'd ever dreamed.

He took her lips gently at first—nibbling, tasting, tempting. His fingers in her hair, he tilted her head so he could delve more deeply within her seeking mouth. She lost all thought of right or wrong, who he was, who she was. The only thing she knew was that she wanted to keep kissing him—forever and a day.

The first touch of his tongue along the seam of her lips made her start, but instead of pulling away she pressed closer and opened to him. Someone gasped. He or she? What did it matter? He was doing amazing things with that mouth—things that made her shiver with cold and shudder with heat.

Her fingers spread through his hair, holding him to her, needing him still. She matched the rhythm of his tongue with her own, learned the contours of a man she'd known forever but had never really known until today.

How long did he kiss her, standing in the doorway, lights in the house silhouetting them for the entire town to see? Gwen only cared about the kiss until a car honked a block down; it was nothing to them, but Eli kicked the door shut, and the slam brought her back to herself.

She tore her mouth free. His lips appeared swollen and wet. Hers must be the same. His eyes half-closed, he observed her warily, as if afraid she'd bolt and run all the way back to Milwaukee. Not a bad idea.

Her cheeks heated, and her eyes went wide with

shock. What had she done? Kissed her best friend as though she wanted to yank him down on the floor and have hot, heavy sex in the hallway.

Gwen groaned and tried to pull away, but Eli held on tight. "You're not running, Gwen. Not this time. Pine River needs you. Your father needs you. This is your chance to make things right all around. Will you stay? Please?"

Since he wouldn't let go, she hid her face along his chest. His shirt smelled like Eli, citrus soap and heated man in the cool of a spring night. She burrowed against him; his arms held her just right. No matter what had happened, the implications of which she wasn't up to handling right now, Eli was her friend and she'd trusted him all her life.

So she gave the only answer she could. "Yes, I'll stay. For a month."

And as soon as the words were out of her mouth, Gwen wanted to take them right back.

CHAPTER FOUR

ELI HELD GWEN because she let him. He had no illusions she'd stay in his arms, fall into his bed, confess everlasting devotion. This was Gwen, and he knew her better than she knew herself. She needed to be held; he was her best friend. It was as simple as that.

She would forget about the kiss, pretend it had never happened. If he didn't mention it, she never would.

Perhaps that was for the best. He knew better than to tell her the truth—that he'd been dreaming of kissing her like that for too many years to count. He wasn't a virgin or a fool. He'd kissed other women. But none of them had been Gwen, and no kiss had ever been like that one. Magic happened rarely, but it happened. And the quickest way to kill the magic was to talk about it.

So he would let Gwen pretend the kiss had never occurred. Heck, he'd better pretend that himself or he'd be mooning about and wind up bitten by a patient for his trouble. Eli had a plan, and it did not involve Gwen running away before he could convince her that she loved him.

The plan was seduction—her mind, her body and her heart. First the mind. He would make her see that this town could be the home she'd never let it become, and her father's practice could be the job she'd never let herself want. Eli was betting Gwen's exhaustion came not only from too much work but too little joy in it.

Too soon she disentangled herself from his arms, and after filling his lungs with the familiar, yet new, scent of her hair, Eli let her go. As expected, she ignored the kiss completely. "Don't you have to go after the Blues Brothers?"

Eli shrugged and leaned against the door. "They'll come home eventually."

"With their mouths full of cats?"

"Probably."

"Are they brain damaged or something?"

"They're puppies. Same thing."

"Puppies? They're huge."

"Their bodies are willing, but their minds just aren't able." She stared at him blankly. "Labs don't grow a brain of any worth until they're about two."

"And people actually spend money for those dogs?"

"A lot of money."

"Don't they drive you crazy?"

"Not me."

She tapped herself on the forehead. "How could I forget? You're every animal's best friend."

"No, I'm your best friend." Her slight smile at his words encouraged Eli that he was on the right track.

He would be her friend first, because a friend was what Gwen needed the most. She always had. And when your best friend became your lover, that was the best friendship and love affair of all—or so Eli believed.

"I like labs," he continued. "They're happy-happy. For them life is beautiful. Always. More people could use that in their lives, don't you think?"

"Too happy-happy for me."

"That's why dogs need to be matched with their owners, just like a medicine has to be matched with a disease."

"Interesting metaphor." Her voice was dry.

"But true. Hyper people should not have hyper dogs."

"Should anyone?"

"Depends on what you're after. Dalmatians, for example, are very energetic and sensitive. Probably not the best choice for a busy household full of small children. But they do well in search and rescue. They're relentless." He paused, realizing he had climbed onto one of his particular soapboxes, the matching of pet to master. "I could go on and on."

"I'm sure you could. Your devotion to the ever furry is one of the things I love about you."

Eli tried not to get his hopes up too much. Gwen tossed around the word *love* with the carelessness of one who did not understand its worth. He planned to rectify that.

"You ever try one of those invisible fences?"

Eli snorted at that particular memory. "They ran right through it."

"No way."

"Uh-huh. There was a cat on the other side so they took off after it. The fence shocked them, but since they were on full speed ahead, they were past the line before the pain registered. From then on the thing was useless. To Jake and Elwood a shock is worth a cat any day."

"So, two years of that—" she waved her hand at the door "—for ten years of bliss?"

"Pretty much."

"And you wonder why I have a no-pets rule?"

"You have too many rules, Gwen. You always have."

Her amused expression disappeared. "Without rules you have chaos."

"Too many rules and you never get to live. You should try a pet. Add a little chaos to your life. I bet you'd be surprised at what you've missed. Animals put the unconditional in love."

A shadow flitted over her face and was gone. "Unlike humans."

Eli stared at Gwen until she met his eyes. "Some humans love that way, too."

As expected she looked away. "I'd better get to bed. It's been a long day."

"And tomorrow will be longer. In Pine River people go to bed early and get up the same."

"Nothing ever changes here, does it?"

Eli put his finger beneath her chin and raised her

gaze to his once more. He winked and lied through is teeth. "And nothing ever will."

ELI LEFT without kissing her again. In a way Gwen was disappointed. Where had that man learned to kiss?

She was grateful he hadn't brought up the topic. She couldn't understand why her best friend was suddenly kissing her passionately. She could understand even less why she was liking it—with equal passion. She didn't want to talk about what had happened and discover things that were better left undiscovered. Since Eli hadn't said anything, or kissed her again, she'd pretend the embrace had never been.

Easier said than done.

After shutting off all the downstairs lights, Gwen climbed to her second-floor bedroom. The place looked untouched, as if she'd never left. The third floor housed her father's bedroom and private office. He would not be using either one for a while.

Gwen found it oddly comforting that Doc had not turned her bedroom into a guest room or a library or a storage room. Which was silly. She should be annoyed that he'd left the place waiting—as if she would come back and live there someday.

That was something she never planned to do. Even now she wondered if she'd sleep. A tiny pulse of panic beat at the back of her head and her throat had gone tight. Maybe she should have asked Eli to hang around. She could talk to him about anything—or at least she always used to.

Certainly she could have talked to him about a fear she knew was irrational but could not get rid of anyway. She definitely couldn't tell her father she was afraid *his* worst nightmare would become *hers*.

Tomorrow she would practice medicine in Pine River. Gwen swallowed and her throat crackled with the effort. Not practice, exactly—she'd be filling in. The reassurance fell flat. She would see patients and they would see her. Someone could die. Someone she loved.

"You're being foolish," she murmured, throwing off her still-damp nightgown and scrounging for a T-shirt to sleep in.

Doc was in traction, so he was relatively safe from disaster. Everyone else she cared about had been doing just fine without her. Why would any of them suddenly jump in front of a bus just because she was back in town?

"Now you're being morbid, which is quite a stretch for an ER doctor. Besides, there aren't any buses in Pine River."

Gwen giggled at the wayward whim of her thoughts. When spoken out loud they sounded every bit as ridiculous as they were.

As she climbed into bed, her gaze wandered over the room. Certain items turned her giggles into a grin.

Eli was right—she'd only remembered the bad things about Pine River. But looking at her teen years spread about like a collage, she remembered some of the good times, too.

Her pompoms were shoved between the curtain rod

and the wall. Blue-and-gold plastic curlicues drizzled over her rose-dotted draperies. Just seeing them made her remember football games beneath the lights, the crisp fall air cool on her cheeks, her body warm from the dance. Then afterward, soft drinks at the McDonald's on the interstate, laughing and joking with her girlfriends, driving home with the boyfriend of the month.

And every night before she went to bed, there was Eli. Always Eli.

Gwen's gaze went to her window, and she climbed out of bed to kneel next to the sill. She twitched the curtain and gazed across the short space between her window and Eli's.

Light illuminated his bedroom. Books covered every surface. His bed was unmade. He still slept there, even though his parents were gone and he could move into the master bedroom if he chose. The place made Gwen dizzy with déjà vu.

Then Eli stepped into her vision. His back to the window, he pulled off his shirt, the slow slide of cotton across the supple expanse, combined with the flex of work-defined muscles, was nothing like her memories. Her déjà vu evaporated on a sharp intake of breath, which sounded loud and alien in the nighttime stillness of her room.

In days gone by she would have called to him. Then they would have talked across the short distance until one of their parents made them stop. Or, if it was warm enough, they would have met in the backyard—sometimes hers, sometimes his—lain in the grass, watched the stars and talked about every secret of their hearts.

Now Gwen jumped out of sight and let the curtain fall back into place. She did not want Eli to come to the window and reveal that his front was even more attractive than his back. She didn't think she could talk to him and not stare at the brand-new body she found far too appealing.

Gwen had never been attracted to good looks. They faded fast, like cut flowers in a vase. Not that she didn't drool over Antonio Banderas like any woman with eyes, but that was different. She'd never get to see Antonio walking about half-naked next door—more's the pity.

Eli had said nothing ever changed here. Which was one of the reasons Gwen had left.

But Eli was wrong. Everything was different. And she had no idea what to do, how to feel—an uncommon occurrence for a woman who had always done all that she could and felt nothing that she did not wish to feel.

Exhausted, Gwen fell into bed and dreamed of Eli in ways she'd never dreamed of him before. She awoke with the dawn amazingly refreshed, and lay in her bed staring at the ceiling, thinking of him.

Would she be able to look Eli in the face and not remember what she had seen last night, what she had dreamed until this morning? She was a doctor. She knew you could not control what you dreamed, and often a dream did not mean what you thought. Just because she'd dreamed of Eli naked did not mean she lusted after him.

A sound of derision escaped her mouth. She could kid herself all she wanted, but she'd always been partial to the truth. Eli's new body aroused her, while his familiarity comforted her. She was drawn to him in different ways, yet deep down she felt the same way, too.

With a shake of her head and a long, long sigh, Gwen got out of bed. She was sure Nancy would show up by eight or nine, despite the fact that there were no appointments and no Doc. Gwen needed to call Lance and explain. He would be upset. His perfect schedule would be thrown into a furor. Lance disliked furor, which made Gwen wonder how he had ever ended up as head of an ER.

But before she made that call, Gwen could use some time alone with her thoughts and an up-close-and-personal meeting with some coffee, then she would face her brand-new world.

A short while later, once she'd showered and dressed, she emerged onto the back porch. The steam from her thermal coffee mug wafted over her face as she sipped, the heat a beguiling contrast to the chill dew on the grass and the cool early-morning air that brushed her damp hair.

She set her cup on the porch rail and searched the pocket of her jeans for a hair band. After scooping the shoulder-length strands together, she secured them in a high ponytail to keep the wet from her neck. A movement in the next yard caught her attention and

Gwen stepped to the end of the porch in time to see Eli, fully dressed in black jeans and a blue work shirt, disappear into a storage shed set at the back of his property.

The shed was new and huge. The lots in Pine River had been divided and built upon in the 1840s, which made them large indeed, nearly five acres apiece. Despite the size of the land allotment, the Bartelt home and the Drycinski home stood close together. The structure on the Drycinski property had been built after the original house burned down.

Eli's place dated from 1950 and had been built at the lot line as an in-law residence. Generations of Bartelts had lived on both lots, until Doc's parents had died just before Gwen was born. Later Doc sold the place to Colonel Drycinski.

Gwen's maternal grandparents had left town shortly after her mother's funeral—unable to bear Pine River following the loss of their only child. Gwen had seen them sporadically until they died about five years ago. She was certain her resemblance to her mother had kept them at a distance, too.

She frowned. Doc had lost his parents and his wife in the space of a few years, then been deserted by his in-laws. If such a thing had happened to one of her patients, she'd recommend grief therapy. Since there had been no such thing when Doc's losses had occurred, she could see why he had gone a little bonkers in the grief department.

Understandable, even forgivable if you considered what he'd had to endure. Gwen shook her head. Why was she thinking all kinds of new things about the same old people?

A thump and a muffled curse from the open storage shed had Gwen taking a last swig of her coffee before leaving the cup on the porch and crossing her yard to enter Eli's. What did he have in there anyway? The place was far too big for a lawn mower—or ten.

Outside, she hesitated. This was Eli's land, Eli's shed. Heaven knows what he was doing inside. Sacrificing chickens? Not Eli. His soft heart would never allow him to hurt a living thing, even if he hadn't been committed to saving all creatures great and small.

Gwen stepped inside and blinked. *A menagerie.* She should have known.

Every hurt animal within a twenty-mile radius ended up on Eli's doorstep. Not because of any Dr. Dolittle-like ability to talk to them or for them to talk to one another about him, but because people all over the state knew Eli was a pushover for anything with four legs or more.

"Sh," Eli whispered, bending in front of a cage that housed a very nervous-looking hawk. "You can go back to the wild blue yonder this weekend. I promise."

The hawk ruffled its feathers and poked out its neck as if to say, *I'll believe that when I see it.*

Gwen watched Eli work. He was so at home here— something she could never be. He was so at ease with himself—something he'd never been before. What had he said about his dogs? They thought life was beautiful—and by deduction, Eli must think that, too. For a moment Gwen wondered what it might be like to see the world in such a way.

Eli chuckled at his hawk, and the warm, joyous sound trilled down Gwen's spine, making her shiver. She rubbed her neck, vowing not to come outside again with wet hair until it was at least seventy degrees in the shade. She ignored the little voice that said wet hair had nothing to do with the way she felt. That little voice had been far too yappy of late.

Eli continued to feed and water and talk to his guests, so engrossed in his task he did not notice her standing in the open doorway, even though most of the animals looked in her direction curiously.

There were cages of various sizes, some empty, but not too many. From her position she saw a sad-faced opossum, a twitchy rabbit, even a shy-eyed fawn in what appeared to be a jumbo dog cage. A soft mew drew her glance to the right. Green eyes stared at her amid a gray puff of fur. She hoped Jake and Elwood hadn't actually hurt one of their cat toys.

A splash brought Gwen's attention back to Eli, who leaned over a huge horse trough in the corner. "And how are you today, Mr. Frog? Is your leg well enough that I can put you back in the river?"

Gwen smiled at the memory of the first time she'd seen Eli. He'd been talking to a squirrel that day. Perhaps things had not changed so much after all.

Splish-slash. "I think you're fine. But watch out for those boats next time. They don't care if you're the biggest bullfrog in town. They'll run over you anyway.''

''Were you talking to that frog?'' she asked.

Eli started, turned about and his hair fell into his eyes. He shook his head.

Gwen stepped inside. ''Sure were.''

Shoving the hair out of his face, Eli left a track of water across his brow. He reminded her so much now of the boy he had been; her throat tightened with nostalgia. She crossed the room, reached up and traced the water away with her thumb.

His gaze captured hers and she froze, her hand hovering in the air between them as the scent of Eli washed over her and the memories exploded against her will—their first kiss, his bare chest beyond the window, her dreams of him all night long. Woman's dreams in the bed of her childhood about a man who was no longer a boy.

Dropping her hand, she spun away. ''So tell me what you have here.'' Her voice sounded shrill, breathy and demanding. She swallowed and tried for a lighter tone. ''Pine River Humane Society in your own backyard?''

He came to stand at her side, and she glanced at him from beneath lowered lashes. He looked at the cage in front of them and not at her. Eli had always been more interested in animals than people, and Gwen understood that. She'd always understood everything about Eli. Until now. Or maybe it was herself she no longer understood.

''If there's a humane society, I guess this is it.''

He opened the cage and pulled out the chicken. The way he held the animal comfortably in the crook of his arm, murmuring nonsense and checking her wing, made Gwen want to cuddle up to his side just as the bird did. Gwen spared a moment to be embarrassed that she'd ever joked, even in her mind, about him sacrificing one.

"When did you build this shed?"

"Hmm?" He turned his attention from the chicken to her, as if coming to the surface from beneath deep water. His long, tanned, capable fingers still moved over the bird's feathers—soothing, stroking. Gwen couldn't take her eyes off them. "About two years ago. The house started to smell like a barn."

She raised her gaze to his. "You kept them in the house?"

"I couldn't very well throw them outside, could I?"

Gwen laughed. "Only you would look at it that way. You don't *have* to help every animal dropped on your doorstep."

"Yes," he said, "I do."

In that quiet statement lay the essence of Eli. He could no more turn away an injured or abandoned animal than Doc could turn away a patient. The two men were alike in a lot of ways, and that made Gwen very nervous.

"The city doesn't mind if you run an animal shelter?"

"I'm zoned for a veterinary clinic. Most of the animals are patched up and reintroduced into the wild in very little time at all.''

"Most?''

He shrugged. "Some don't make it. Some come back, regardless, like pets.''

"And then what?''

"I find a place for them in a domestic environment—home, zoo, wildlife refuge.''

This was something Eli had always dreamed of doing. As a child he had brought home a lot of strays. He got to keep a few, but more often than not the Colonel took them away when Eli wasn't looking.

Gwen's eyes burned when she thought of all the times Eli had cried on her shoulder after his father had gotten rid of a cat or a dog or a rabbit he'd bandaged and loved. The Colonel had been doing what he thought was right. In the end, Eli's gentle, animal-loving soul had persevered. Gwen wondered if Eli and his father got along any better now than they had then.

"What did the Colonel say about your shed?'' Eli snorted, which said it all. "Not impressed, huh?''

"Very little impresses the Colonel.''

The resignation in his voice touched her. Eli had often tried to be what his father wanted—a he-man son the Colonel could brag about. Her gaze flitted over the bump in his nose from the high fly ball he hadn't caught, then lowered to the crooked pinky finger on his right hand, which had come from his only week in tackle football.

What must it be like to know your father considered you a failure, even though you'd achieved everything you'd ever dreamed of? Doc considered her a traitor, not a failure, but was there much of a distinction? Yet Eli never seemed angry at the Colonel, only disappointed in himself. Which made Gwen angry at the Colonel.

Eli deposited the chicken in the cage and latched the door. "I had to stop worrying about what the Colonel thought of me. I'm not an ax murderer or a bank robber. I don't even cheat at solitaire. There's nothing wrong with me. I'm just me."

"Damn right."

He smiled. "You always were first in line to defend me against every dragon—real and imagined."

She sniffed. "Someone had to."

"You don't have to anymore. Maybe *you* should stop worrying about what Doc thinks of you."

"I don't care what Doc thinks!"

"No?"

"No!"

"If that was true, you wouldn't be trying so hard to prove you're right and he's wrong. You wouldn't be so mad at him. Once you decide that who you are is okay with you, that little knot in your gut—" he flicked his long fingers upward in a gesture reminiscent of a magician "—just disappears."

"What little knot?"

Eli reached out to brush a fingertip across her belly, just beneath her breasts. "That one."

The muscles in her stomach jumped at his touch.

Her gut roiled on only coffee, and the knot she'd denied having tightened to a slick, cold ache.

She backed away, afraid he'd touch her again, or make her admit things she hadn't admitted even to herself. "I-I have to go and call Lance. Tell him I'm staying a month."

"Bet he'll love that."

"Bet not," she muttered, continuing to back away, trapped in Eli's calm, dark gaze.

"You want to watch out, Gwen."

"I know how to handle Lance."

"I'm sure you do. I was talking about the Blues Brothers. You're going to trip over them."

Gwen stopped backing up and glanced behind her. The twin labs sat at attention directly in front of the kitten's cage, mouths open, tongues lolling and drooling. She frowned at Eli. "They didn't hurt that one, did they?"

"Of course not." He looked offended. "Someone left it on my doorstep. I've been searching for the perfect mommy for her. Want a shot?"

"Me?"

Eli's face went still at the horror in her voice. "I didn't ask you to drown her, Gwen. I asked you to take care of her."

"No pets, Eli. I mean it."

"I assume from your horror-stricken face at the word *mommy,* no kids, either."

"No kids," she agreed.

"What other rules do you have?"

"No everlasting love."

The words fell between them like a brick through a glass roof. "Pretty lonely life you're planning."

"But it's my life," she snapped. "So let me live it."

"Knock yourself out." He turned his back on her.

She blinked, shocked at his dismissal. Glancing at the dogs, she found them gazing at her with sad, disappointed eyes. Even the kitten's plaintive mew sounded like a reproach. Gwen tightened her lips and stomped out of the shed so she didn't have to listen to any more.

CHAPTER FIVE

"STAY," Eli ordered as the dogs began to follow Gwen. The quickest way to make her loathe animals would be to give her too many doses of the Blues.

Seducing Gwen was going to be harder than Eli had thought. He believed she loved him. She thought only as a friend. But the way she'd kissed him last night, the way her eyes had followed him this morning, Eli believed she could come to love him the way that he loved her. Truly, madly, deeply, forever.

So how was he going to convince her that the three things she feared the most were really the most beautiful things on this earth?

"Meow!" Cleo yowled, swiping her paw across the sniffing, snuffing, searching nose of Elwood.

He yelped, sneezed and rubbed his snout against Jake. "Told you so," Eli murmured. "Love her to death and she'll hate you for it. Cats just aren't impressed with undying devotion. Ignore them and they'll come running to you. Pretend you're busy with more important things. Like learning the meaning of the word *no*."

The two hung their heads. "Hey, I didn't mean no now. I meant in general." They slunk off anyway, casting expressions of pathetic, undying devotion his way.

Eli turned back to Cleo. "See what I mean? Do I look like that whenever Gwen comes into a room?"

The kitten tilted her head as if to say, *You don't really want me to answer that, do you?*

Eli sighed. Perhaps he needed to take his own advice—to a point. He wasn't going to ignore Gwen completely. He had to lure her back to him with promises of the perfect friendship they'd shared. If she needed him again as she'd always needed him before, he could make her see all that she'd missed by leaving Pine River, all that she'd missed by leaving him.

Her silly rules were killing her from the inside out and might be a big problem for him in the end. She'd looked at Cleo as if the kitten were evil incarnate. If Gwen couldn't be swayed by that sweet little face, how could she possibly be swayed by Eli's everlasting love?

COWARDLY AS IT WAS, Gwen left a message with Lance's receptionist, saying that things were much worse in Pine River than she'd thought—like that was a surprise—and she'd be staying until June. At least by the time she had to talk to him about this he'd have gotten half of his fuming over with. Lance was not one to keep disappointments bottled up inside where he kept all his emotions.

He was the first man she'd dated who'd praised her cool reserve, who liked her just the way she was.

According to Lance, she was pretty, efficient, brilliant. What more could a man ask for?

What more indeed, Gwen had thought to herself, remembering all that had gone before.

In the past, her relationships floundered quickly when she was unable to move past the first stage. Her work was her life. She could conjure up little in the way of warmth or affection. Perhaps because she had no idea how. The only person she'd ever felt strongly about had been Eli—and for Gwen those feelings belonged to Eli and no one else.

So when Lance had asked her to marry him, saying she was just the kind of woman he needed, she'd agreed, because she'd come to believe that he was just the kind of man she needed, too.

The front door opened. Footsteps moved toward the office and clinic. A few moments later Nancy took a seat at the table.

"Been to the hospital yet?"

Gwen shook her head. "Figured I'd go see him tonight."

Nancy frowned. "I meant for rounds."

"Rounds?"

"You know, where the doctor goes and checks on his patients who are in the hospital."

"I know what rounds are, Nancy. Why should I have to do them?"

"Because it's your job. You're supposed to check on Sadie and the baby."

"I'm not a pediatrician or an OB-GYN."

"You are now. Along with podiatrist, geriatrician,

dermatologist, psychologist—you name it, you're it. So get your rear in gear.''

Gwen had saved two lives yesterday, but already she felt inadequate. "I guess I got out of the habit of following up. Once I stabilize people in the ER, I ship them out and that's that."

"Well, you aren't in the ER—you're in PR."

"Public relations?"

Nancy raised an eyebrow. "Pine River."

The doorbell rang several times in succession and then the door banged open. "Help!" a man shouted. "We've got trouble out here."

Nancy hurried from the kitchen, Gwen at her heels. When Nancy stopped at the entryway to the clinic, Gwen bumped into her back. "ER, PR—what's the difference?" Nancy muttered.

Gwen peeked over Nancy's taller, broader shoulder. "Not much, from the looks of things."

Urging Nancy aside, she stepped briskly into the examining room to attend the farmer with his hand wrapped in a bloody towel. As Gwen washed her hands and got to work, her feelings of inadequacy faded.

Hours later she was still at it. Once the word got around that she'd stitched up the gash in Floyd's thumb, put there by a close encounter with a manure spreader, given him antibiotics and a lecture on farm machine safety, the horde had descended.

Strep rash on a five-year-old girl, plantar wart on an eight-hundred-year-old man, burned wrist for the home ec teacher, goat-bit butt for the 4-H leader. Just another day in paradise.

Gwen was setting the last stitch into the scalp of Johnny Kirkendal, whom she'd privately dubbed "Johnny Be Bad," and was considering the dispensation of tranquilizers for one and all, when she noticed Nancy wasn't running around like Eli's dogs.

She'd been answering phones, scheduling appointments and helping Gwen in the exam room as if today were no different from any other day. Gwen frowned. She didn't recall her father's practice being like this, but then, she'd been a teenager—translate selfish and oblivious to anyone but herself. If Doc had been this busy, day in and day out, no wonder he'd had Mrs. Drycinski take care of her.

Putting aside such disturbing thoughts to finish Johnny's head, she bandaged the wound and prescribed a painkiller. "No more Spiderman imitations for you, young man," she admonished as she pulled off her gloves.

"But he—he—he always walks down the side of buildings." Johnny's breath hitched as he fought to stop crying long enough to explain the truth. "And he—he—he sticks like glu-u-u-e."

"Well, *you* didn't, and if you don't want to have ten stitches next time instead of five, you'll stick to scaling the ground and not the barn."

Johnny nodded, but Gwen knew a repeat offender when she saw one. He'd be back. Maybe not tonight, maybe not tomorrow, but soon. With a sympathetic glance at his stoic-faced parents, Gwen showed them to the door.

The waiting room was deserted. "Thank God," she breathed, and collapsed into the nearest chair.

"You can get right back up, Doc. You still need to check on the Barrabas baby and Sadie."

"Nancy," Gwen moaned. "Slave driver."

"That's my name—don't wear it out," Nancy sang as she cleaned up the exam room.

"Is it always this busy?"

"Mmm?" After yanking the soiled paper drop cloth off the examining table, Nancy crumpled it into a ball. "Pretty much. Doc's the only game in town— and for miles around. You might get some midnight callers, too."

A shadow memory flitted through Gwen's mind of a knock, muffled voices, smothered cries, her father's deep, soothing voice in the night before she drifted back to sleep. People had come whenever they needed him and Doc had always been there. For them.

Gwen hauled herself upright and pitched in with the cleanup. "Thanks for all the help. I would have panicked without you."

Nancy raised an eyebrow. "I've never seen you panic, Gwen. I doubt I ever will. You're too much like your dad for that."

Gwen winced. "What makes you say so?"

"Some people are beyond panic, and most of them are doctors. You have to be of a certain temperament to do what you do every day. With Doc, I've only seen him get calmer over the years."

"Doc? Calm? The man's a volcano. He erupts over the slightest thing."

"Not under duress he doesn't. There isn't a calmer, saner voice amid chaos than your father."

Once again the dream memory of a quiet, gentle voice against the echo of tears drifted through Gwen's mind. Why hadn't she remembered that before?

"I think the more Doc sees of life and death," Nancy continued, "the less there is for him to get upset about. He's faced pretty much every disaster to be had around here, and he's come through fine."

Fine was a matter of opinion. Doc had been there at the death of his wife, but Gwen doubted he'd ever faced it.

"What I'd like to know is what's your excuse?" Gwen cast a narrow look at Nancy, which she ignored. "Have you seen twice as much in that big-city place, or do you shut everyone out so nothing touches you at all?"

"Who made you my analyst?"

"Me." Nancy grinned, unrepentant. "Never mind. Let's finish up and we can go to the hospital together. Can you drive? I'm meeting a date there."

"Date!" The word shot out of Gwen's mouth like an olive pit.

"Yes, date. I do have them." For some reason she didn't appear happy about it.

"Great," Gwen said, a bit too heartily. "A doctor?"

Nancy wrinkled her nose. "I don't think so."

"What's the matter with doctors?"

"Nothing if you're sick. Everything if you want some attention."

"Most women would kill to date a doctor—money, prestige, class."

"If you divide the money by the hours, doctors who deserve the title make less than I do. Then there're the pagers going off at any given moment, interrupted dinners, lives, dreams. I'll pass, thank you very much. Now I have to change."

She walked off in a huff and Gwen had to wonder what she'd said to get Nancy so worked up when a day full of blood and assorted other bodily fluids hadn't turned a hair on the woman's head.

"Hmm," Gwen murmured. "I think there's a special doctor somewhere in Nurse Nancy's past. I wonder who it is."

AFTER COMING OUT of the house and slapping a pager into Gwen's hand with a short "Here. You're on call until I say you aren't," Nancy had gone silent. She seemed to have her mind on something, or someone, else, and after a few lame attempts at conversation Gwen gave up and drove.

Nancy looked good. She'd freed her hair and the heavy, waving mass spilled over her shoulders, sparking rays of amber and russet in the fading sunlight. Her dress, a peach knit, clung to her curves and showed off a figure never before revealed in her usual nurse's whites or off-day jeans.

At the elevator, they parted company. "I'm going to check on Doc," Nancy said. "See when he'll be released. I have half an hour before I'm supposed to meet Brett.''

"Brett, huh?'' Nancy scowled at Gwen's teasing tone. "He works here?''

"He's a physical therapist, Dr. Nosy.''

"And you've been dating him how long?''

"It'll be ten minutes, ten minutes after he shows up.''

"Oooh, first date. And that dress? You must really like him.''

Nancy shrugged and got off the elevator. As the doors closed, Gwen caught an expression on Nancy's face that wiped the smile right off her own. Nancy looked as if she'd just lost her best friend.

Gwen took a step forward, hand out to stop the door from closing, but she was too late and the doors whooshed shut. She doubted Nancy would tell her anything anyway. The woman had never been very forthcoming about her love life, which was somewhat odd considering their friendship.

The elevator opened on the maternity floor. Gwen checked in at the nurses' station. A pediatrician had examined the baby to make sure there were no immediate problems from the difficult delivery. So far, so good, though Gwen would recommend visits to the orthopedist for the first year. A breech birth could cause hip and leg displacement not visible to the naked eye—even a doctor's.

Chart in hand, Gwen traveled to Sadie's room. The door stood open and Gwen stepped inside. The setting sun washed over the bed, illuminating mother and child in shades of pink and gold. Gwen stilled and watched Sadie feed her child.

Sadie reminded Gwen of the sculpture of the Madonna behind the altar at St. Bart's. The utter love and undying devotion on her face was so plain Gwen's eyes burned with the intensity of the beauty.

The baby, bundled in the blue hospital blanket, with a matching cap upon his tiny head, made a lot of noise for one so small. Sucking sounds warred with sighs of contentment, and a shriveled little fist shot from the blanket and waved about as if he were cheering himself on.

Gwen had never viewed anything this exquisite, nothing this peaceful or right. She'd delivered babies countless times, but she'd never had the privilege of seeing them after they left her ER. The feeling of success that flowed over her now gave a joyous closure to the case of Sadie Barrabas and child.

Sadie looked up and smiled when she caught sight of Gwen hovering just inside the doorway. "Doctor! I was hoping you'd come."

She reached down and made a fast move with her fingers near the baby's mouth. A pop, like the cork on champagne, though not quite so loud, emerged from the bundle. "Come look."

Gwen moved to Sadie's side and bent to peer at the face. He resembled a very old man in a blue baby hat. Gwen smiled. "Cute."

"Here." Sadie shoved the bundle at Gwen. Shocked, Gwen took it and stood, hands outstretched while the bundle twisted and turned. "I think he wants to burp."

Gwen blinked at Sadie. "You want me to—"

"Please."

Gwen frowned and stared at the baby. "Uh." She turned him to the right, then the left. "Which way?"

Sadie laughed. "You look like you've never held a baby before."

Gwen tried to remember when she'd held a baby that wasn't slippery and in need of a good washing. She always handed them off to the nurse so she could attend to the mother. Gwen couldn't recall ever holding one who was sweet-smelling and clothed.

"Just put him up to your shoulder and pat him. He's too little to have a preference yet."

Gwen shrugged and did what she was told, laying the baby along her body, chin over her shoulder, before she tapped him.

"Harder, Doctor. He won't break. You'll be here till Judgment Day if you tickle him like that. You'd think you'd never done this before."

Sadie watched her so closely Gwen figured she was catching on. She tried to appear confident, as if she burped day-old babies every day, but when he actually burped she got so excited she blew her cover. "I did it!"

"You sure did." Sadie tapped her lip with her finger. "What kind of doctor are you exactly?"

"Trauma."

"Hmm. Well, I guess I'm lucky you were around. Thank you, Dr. Bartelt."

Gwen smiled as a warm, cuddly feeling spread over her from the inside out. Few people came back and thanked her in the ER. Most of them never saw her face; they were in too much trouble. And that was fine. The pace of her profession did not leave time for thank-yous or baby burping, and she'd never noticed or cared. Maybe because she'd never experienced the flip side.

"What's his name?" she asked.

"Michael Bartelt Barrabas."

Gwen blinked. "After me?"

"Who else?"

Gwen's eyes stung again and she hugged the baby tighter. He emitted an admirable belch and something wet hit first her shoulder, then the floor. He began hiccuping and Sadie held out what appeared to be a cloth diaper.

"Consider yourself baptized."

Gwen lowered Michael, who gazed at her with unfocused eyes amid a face full of slightly digested milk. Her shoulder looked the same.

"Sorry," Sadie said, but she didn't appear sorry at all; she looked like she might laugh at any given moment.

Michael gurgled; bubbles frothed his bowed lips and his mouth went slack as he fell asleep. Gwen wiped his face and he never even twitched.

She examined him, then his mother. By the time she left she was as confused as she'd ever been. Here was life instead of death, joy rather than heartache.

And she craved more of it.

What had happened to the woman unrattled by death, unfazed by heartache, unmoved by tears? Had Gwen left her in Milwaukee? And if so, did she ever want that woman to come back?

DOC WAS CRANKY. And not the usual "I'm busy, don't bother me" cranky. He was out and out "bored to death, shoot me in the foot for some excitement" cranky.

Not that he hadn't had visitors and gifts and phone calls. He had. But had his daughter shown up? Had his erstwhile nurse brought him anything to read? Had they answered the bloody phone at his own house when he'd called to check in?

The answer to every one of those questions was— "Hell, no!"

He hadn't heard a word from anyone since Nancy had called last night to tell him about the Barrabas incident. He'd wanted to hear the details from Gwen, but apparently he'd have to pull them from her like gum from the bottom of his shoe. If she ever showed up. Doc growled and jabbed the channel change button on the remote.

Thank God he did not have time during the day to waste on television. And what a waste it was. Soap operas? How could people watch those things? Year after year yet. Just listening to the actors talk for two minutes made him want to shake them for two hours. How could they recite dialogue like that and not laugh their asses off?

And game shows? What a load of morons. Did they

advertise for stupid people to appear on those things? Or just folks who had no lives and a lot of bounce?

Then there were the talk shows. People weren't actually telling the truth on those things, were they? He was a doctor, had been for thirty years, and some of the stuff they talked about on those shows made his stomach turn and his eyes cross. They *had* to be making all that up.

Doc clicked, flipped and clicked some more. "Where's a Clint Eastwood movie when you need one? Or John Wayne? Those guys kept quiet but said a lot."

The door to his room opened. He knew it was Nancy immediately. He didn't know how he knew, he just did. Nancy had become so much a part of his life he had no idea how he'd managed before she came along.

"Well, it's about damned time," he began, then stopped in midtirade when he caught sight of her. "Nancy?"

"Who else?" The staccato clip of her high heels only drew his gaze to her legs. Damn fine legs. Doc choked, then pulled his eyes, and his mind, back to her face.

"You okay?" She poured him a glass of water, which gave him time to recover and to get a very good look at her dress and all that was in it.

Nancy handed him the water. Dazed, Doc took it, sipping as she fussed with his pillow and covers. Her scent washed over him—familiar, yet intriguing. She smelled like Nancy—soap and evergreen shampoo—

and she smelled like a stranger—some French perfume she never wore to work.

"There." She sighed, satisfied, and perched on the chair at his bedside, acting as if she wanted to jump up and race out at the slightest opportunity.

"Got somewhere to be?"

"No, I dress like this every day to come visit cranky old coots in their hospital beds."

"Might help 'em."

She blinked. "Excuse me?"

"You in that dress could cure just about anything."

A frown creased her face. "Is that a compliment?"

"Of course. Haven't you ever heard one before?"

"Not from you."

It was his turn to frown. Was that true? No, he was certain he complimented her on her work. She was a top-notch nurse, even though she was a pain in the behind. One put up with attitude for genius.

"I expected to see you before now. And where's Gwen?"

"With Sadie."

"Just now?" he roared. "What's she been doing all day?"

"Calm down. This is the first minute's peace we've had since Floyd nearly lost a thumb this morning."

"Manure spreader?" Nancy just raised her eyebrow at the rhetorical nature of the question, and Doc snorted. "Go on."

Nancy did. When she got to Johnny Kirkendal, Doc groaned. "Again? Was there any room left in his file to write anything?"

"Barely. That kid is an accident waiting to happen."

"That kid is an accident happening on a weekly basis." Doc chuckled. "Some of them are like that. They grow out of it."

"We can only hope he grows out before he goes under."

"Little morose, are we?"

Nancy shrugged. She seemed sad, and that was not like Nancy. "You wanna talk about it?"

Her eyes snapped up to his, surprise evident. She wore makeup tonight, which made her lashes appear incredibly long, her eyes shone bluer and her freckles had disappeared a bit too much for Doc's liking. Those freckles were a part of the Nancy he knew so well. Or the Nancy he thought he knew. She was really very pretty.

Something flickered in her eyes that made him interested, curious, and he stared harder, squinting at her face until her cheeks darkened, and she looked away.

"Talk about what?" Her voice sounded hoarse.

"You got a cold?"

She cleared her throat. "No. I'm fine. When can you come home?"

"Tomorrow."

She nodded and a lock of hair fell over her shoulder, then drifted across the curve of her breast. Doc's stomach did a funny dance, and his curiosity shifted lower. His indrawn breath echoed loudly in the quiet room. He hadn't felt *that* in…aeons.

Nancy jumped to her feet. "Are you in pain?"

Leaning over the bed, she placed her palm on his forehead. A memory came to him of the same touch in the midst of his agony, a loving brush of fingers through his hair, across his lips while he tossed against a drugged sleep, then a trill of male awareness that had followed him down into the depths of the night.

He shoved her away. "Quit fussin'."

Her hand dropped slowly to her side. Doc waited for her to tell him to shut up and get over it; she'd fuss if she wanted to. Then they could start arguing and he could stop feeling strange. But when she remained silent and didn't touch him again, Doc looked up, confused, to catch the sheen of tears in her eyes.

"Nance?"

She turned away, but he caught her hand and held on even when she cursed and tugged. After a moment she stilled, but before he could question her again, the door opened and a young man stuck his head in.

"Excuse me. Ready to go, Nancy?"

"Sure, Brett." She tugged on her hand, and this time Doc let her go. "See you tomorrow, Doc."

The young man eyed Nancy as if she were the house special at the Crystal Café. He all but licked his lips, and Doc's fingers curled into fists. He glared at the injured leg that prevented him from standing up and towering over Nancy's date. He might be older and thinner than that kid, but he was taller—Doc was almost always taller. Never before in his life had he wanted to use his height to intimidate as much as he wanted to now.

He had a sudden urge to order the two of them home by eleven, and that urge made his stomach shimmy again. He must have eaten something that didn't agree with him. Which wouldn't be surprising in a hospital.

As they were walking out of the room, the young man asked, "How come you had to check on him? Isn't he just your boss?"

Nancy's voice sounded sadder than ever before. "Yeah, I guess that's what he is."

The door whooshed shut. Doc had never felt so old in his life.

CHAPTER SIX

GWEN'S VISIT WITH Doc did not go well. She'd thought he would want to know about his patients and the delivery of the night before, so she told him, but he didn't seem to be listening.

She'd expected snarls and sarcasm. What she got was far from it. Doc sat in his bed like a lump for so long she actually looked at his chart to see if they'd overmedicated him. She wouldn't put it past anyone to slip Doc the hospital equivalent of a mickey just to shut him up. The worst patients were those who knew too much.

But he'd taken nothing stronger than ibuprofen, and in truth he should be taking more than that. "Don't you want some Demerol?" she asked.

"No." He continued to stare at the television, flipping channels mindlessly, until she wanted to take the control from his hand and stomp on it. A common female reaction to a man with the television remote in his hand, Gwen was certain, but very unlike her.

"Leg hurt?"

"Hell, yes."

"Then why don't you take a pill?"

"Why don't you take a walk?"

"That's better. For a minute there I thought they might have done a personality transplant while they were fixing your leg."

"Ha-ha. Go home."

Gwen did. Since she wasn't used to seeing patients after the fact, she had no idea if his behavior was typical postsurgery depression or not. She'd ask Nancy in the morning.

By the time she reached Pine River, Gwen was hungry and tired. Not a pleasant combination by any means. She wanted to snarl and stomp. Lucky she lived alone.

As she pulled into her driveway she glanced at Eli's house. A shadow flitted beyond the living room window and she smiled. Though she wanted to be alone right now more than she'd wanted to be alone for a long time, the thought that Eli was only a few feet away comforted her. Hadn't it always?

Gwen walked through the house, relishing the silence after the day's commotion. Being an only child, sometimes she craved solitude. Lance never understood how she could just be by herself for an entire day and love the space. He had come from a family of four, and you'd think he'd crave solitude after never having any. Instead, he couldn't seem to amuse himself very well at all.

Her stomach growled a reminder. "All right, all right." Gwen stuck her head in the refrigerator. "Cheese, sausage, crackers and a wine cooler. I think today warrants a bubble bath smorgasbord."

Another thing Lance didn't understand—her penchant for eating, drinking and reading in the tub. Warm water, fragrant bubbles, books and snacks—what wasn't to like?

Gwen took her haul and headed upstairs. Forty-five minutes later she came back down refreshed, renewed. As she went to put her plate and bottle in the kitchen, the blinking light on the answering machine atop the counter called her name.

Guilt flooded Gwen. What if someone needed her? She wasn't used to being on call. ER physicians worked long shifts—sometimes as long as twenty-four hours—but once they were off they were off.

Her heart had already begun to beat a painful rhythm of panic, when she remembered the phone in the kitchen was the personal line. She'd been wearing a pager since Nancy had shoved one in her face, so if there'd been a medical emergency, she'd have known about it.

She took a deep breath and punched the play button. Lance's voice flowed out. "Guinevere, please tell me the message I received wasn't true. You cannot leave me in the lurch for an entire month. My schedule is a disaster. I need you. Come home." *Click.*

A snort of laughter erupted from Gwen. He didn't need *her* per se; he needed her hands in the ER. Once such a need had made her feel complete.

Today? Not so much.

The dogs started barking outside, and Gwen meandered to the large window at the front of the house. Moonlight shone on newly mown grass like silver atop an emerald. Eli and the Blues Brothers cavorted beneath the stars.

A smile curved Gwen's lips as she watched them tumble on the ground. They rolled about like the puppies they were. Eli pinned first one dog and then the other. When he stood, they sat, quivering in expectation until Eli pulled something from his pocket and tossed it as hard as he could. The two were gone in a flash of black legs, racing after the most fascinating thing in their world—a tennis ball.

As if he sensed her watching, Eli looked toward the house, then up at her window, staring for a few moments before turning away. Had he been hoping she stood there, as she had all those years ago, waiting to tell him about her day, hear about his, then dream together of all the days to come?

The dogs returned from their search-and-rescue mission and followed Eli into his backyard. A yearning to join them filled Gwen and she moved toward the kitchen door.

She should really call Lance and tell him her message was true; she had no intention of coming back before the aforementioned month was up. Need was relative—and her relative needed her. Gwen had no doubt her fiancé would attempt to convince her that *he* needed her desperately and City Hospital needed her even more than that.

Gwen knew better.

She stepped onto the porch. The night was warm; summer approached. Her cotton lounge pants and matching peach top fluttered in the breeze that rustled trees heavy with buds. Tulips and daffodils sprouted next to the house. His back to her, Eli stared up at the night.

Long and lean, his shadow spread out from his feet in her direction, as if pointing a path straight to him. His hair sparkled silver beneath the light of the moon, curling over his collar, inviting her touch.

In the house, the phone began to ring, a distant demand. Gwen knew who it was.

Feet bare, she ran across the grass, feeling more alive than she had in a long, long time.

ELI SENSED GWEN even before he heard the door shut on a quiet click. He did not turn. He wanted her to come to him without being asked. Seduction required patience and skill. A lure, a promise, a trace—nothing solid, nowhere exact.

The distant ring of a phone reached him and Eli stifled a curse. If she went back in to answer it, tonight would be lost. He had time but not eternity— to make her love him anyway. Once she did, eternity was theirs.

Eli held his breath, sent up a prayer, and seconds later the grass rustled at her approach.

"How's Doc?" he asked.

She stopped a few feet away. "Mad at the world."

The sight of her hit him in the gut with the force of a wayward soccer ball. She smelled like peaches; her hair was damp; her cotton trousers and shirt covered her from ankle to neck—nothing alluring about them at all. She could not know that the simple, innocent slope of her collarbone enticed him more than the shrouded weight of her breasts or the curve of her thigh pressing against the cloth as she moved closer.

Eli swallowed and kept his eyes on her face. "Mad at the world? Same as usual, then?"

"Pretty much. He's coming home tomorrow."

"Yippee."

"Funny, that's what I thought."

They shared a smile before Eli held out his hand. "Want to sit awhile?"

She stared at his hand as if she couldn't quite decide what he wanted. Patience his gift, Eli waited, and when she stepped forward and aligned her palm to his, he smothered his relieved exhale. She trusted him more than she trusted anyone. She knew him in her heart as he knew her in his. He only had to teach her the magic they could make together, and in the end everything would be all right. He held on to that thought.

"I want to show you something." He led her behind the menagerie shed, toward a grove of trees that separated his yard from the rest of his property.

"What—?"

"Just wait." He wanted her to view the prize beneath the light of a night moon; no words would soil the power of its enchantment.

Stepping through the trees into a clearing he had shaped for a night such as this, Eli drew Gwen after him.

"Oh, Eli," she whispered, and squeezed his hand. Fashioned of knotty pine, the gazebo gleamed.

Windows now empty to the spring breeze, when the dog days of summer arrived, along with the bugs, screens would fill that emptiness. As the chill of fall spread, glass could be exchanged for the screens.

Inside, atop the matched plank floor, benches upholstered in evergreen spanned each wall of the pentagon. The roof was made of Plexiglas, so they could lie on their backs and watch the drift of the stars and the sky no matter if it rained or it poured.

Eli had known the gazebo was for Gwen the moment he'd seen it on display at the state fair last August. He'd had the parts stored in the shed until the last snow melted and only finished attaching the roof a week ago. He'd bought the building on hope and built it for the dream. Looking at the gazebo now made Eli wonder what he'd have done if fate had not brought Gwen home. How long until he'd hated the sight of the place? How long until it reminded him of his foolishness in ever hoping or dreaming at all?

Together they moved to the door. Before he could reach for the handle, Gwen released him and skipped inside. Standing in the middle, she leaned back, staring at the stars. Palms out, she turned a single, slow revolution.

Eli remained outside looking in, fascinated with the sight of her. Since she'd come back she'd seemed more like Doc on a bad day and less like the girl he'd fallen in love with. He'd feared that girl gone forever, smothered by pain, the life in her choked by too much heartache.

"It's perfect, Eli." She pulled her gaze away from

the stars, and he saw the Gwen he adored waiting behind the cool of her eyes. "Aren't you coming in?"

His superstition dissolved, and he brushed aside the remnants along with the cobwebs above the door.

Inside, with her so near, he went dizzy with a hunger too familiar, yet somehow new. He sat on the nearest bench to keep from pulling her close and burying his mouth against the fragrant skin where her neck met her shoulder.

She looked at him strangely but did not comment on his sudden silence. Taking a seat on the other side of the gazebo, she leaned her arms along the open window and her head out into the night. "Where did the bad dogs go?"

His heart stuttered. For a moment, his mind full of her, he couldn't remember where they were. Then his breath escaped on a sigh. "Inside. This time of a night, if they scent a deer they're off. I'm not in the mood to track them down."

"I think you mean cat."

"That's a given. But a deer would take them far and wide."

She sat up. "They can't actually catch a deer, can they?"

Eli snorted. "No. But don't tell them that. They like to pretend."

She giggled—there was no other word for it—and Eli remembered all the other times he'd made her laugh. Gwen had been a sober child, a serious young woman, but with Eli she had often laughed.

"You haven't changed," she said. "You still talk

to your animals like they're people and give them personalities.''

"They have personalities.'' He shrugged. "And I've always enjoyed talking to those who don't talk back.''

"Don't we all?''

A companionable silence settled over them. Separate yet connected, they shared the night. Once upon a time they'd talked for hours about every little thing; they'd spent silent hours, too, that had been every bit as remarkable as the time filled with words.

Eli could tell by the way she sighed and shifted that Gwen had something to say. He kept quiet, knowing she would tell him when she wished or not at all, as the situation warranted. He only hoped she wasn't trying to tell him how much she loved Lance Heinrich. That he did not want to know.

"I held the Barrabas baby today.''

His eyebrows shot up, but all he did was murmur, "Mmm.''

"He threw up on me.''

Her voice contained a note of wonder not often associated with being barfed on by a baby. Eli waited.

"I liked it.''

"The throwing up?''

She laughed. "No, the holding.''

"Mmm,'' he agreed.

"I rarely get to see what happens after I've done my job. Never bothered me, either. I was already on to the next trauma, the next day, the next shift. I save lives. I know that.''

"So what's the problem?"

"I might know it intellectually, but emotionally maybe not. It felt wonderful to see with my own eyes and touch with my own hands something good that came about because of me."

"I bet Sadie feels even better."

She frowned, cut him a glance, then ignored the implication, as usual. "I was thinking all the way home...."

She trailed off and stared into space, obviously thinking again. "You were thinking?" he urged.

"When I get back to Milwaukee I'm going to follow up more. I'm sure if I *see* that I'm helping people, that nagging feeling of..."

She stopped and her lips compressed into a tight line as if to keep the next words from escaping.

"What nagging feeling?"

"Never mind. Where did you get this gazebo?"

Eli stood and crossed the tiny space between them to sit next to her on the bench. "Don't change the subject, Gwen. This is me you're talking to."

Her shoulders raised and then lowered on a long, sad sigh. "I feel like a failure and I don't know why."

"Failure? You? Superwoman?"

She allowed a small smile. "Me. I...I haven't been happy for a while."

Eli should whoop and shout. Gwen had just admitted what he'd been hoping for. If she wasn't happy in Milwaukee, if she'd agreed to marry Lance for something other than love, Eli had a better chance to make her see how wonderful life could be in Pine

River with him. But the sadness in her voice called to the heart that loved her, and regardless of what it might mean to him, he couldn't be happy if she was not.

"Maybe you just need a break. Maybe being here will be good for you."

"You call this a break? I worked harder today than I have in a long time."

"And do you feel sad?"

She went still, then tilted her head to peer into his face. "No. I'm tired, but it's good tired. As if I've been jogging or digging in the garden."

"And what do you feel like after a day at City Hospital?"

A crease appeared between her eyebrows. "As if I've been running in circles and getting nowhere. Saving life after life, but the dead just keep piling up. It's a losing battle. I can't win no matter how hard I try, no matter how long I stay there."

She leaned her head on his shoulder. The scent of her hair, of her, tickled his nose and sent a shaft of lust much lower. And though the windows were open and the ceiling like glass, the gazebo seemed too small for both of them and stifling with a sudden heat.

Eli rubbed his cheek along the top of her head like a contented cat, while his body hummed with an awareness that was both sexual and peaceful.

"You're such a good friend, Eli," she breathed.

His desire and his peace dissolved on the night.

ELI'S SHOULDER stiffened beneath Gwen's cheek. She raised her head. His profile appeared chiseled from wood.

"Hey, what's wrong?"

"Nothing. I should go in."

"Me, too."

By the time she got to her feet, Eli was across the floor, as if he wanted to get away from her.

He opened the door and stepped back to let her through. As she passed close to him, Gwen hesitated, then looked into his face. She saw nothing in his eyes to make her stomach shift and roll, no reason for the pull that began low and deep.

Without warning the memory of his kiss the night before whirled over her, and her breath caught with a strange emotion—something akin to what she felt when a particularly harrowing trauma wheeled into her ER—excitement, adrenaline, a near-sexual rush. What on earth was the matter with her?

She licked her lips and tasted him. His gaze heated, dipped to her mouth, then back up again. He did not look like the boy she remembered, or the man she thought she knew.

Since she'd returned to Pine River, nothing had been as she remembered. Not even him.

"Why did you kiss me last night, Eli?"

He gave a small start, as if her question was not what he'd been expecting. She had not planned to ask, either, but now that she had, she really wanted to know the answer.

Instead, Eli asked questions of his own. "Why do you think, Gwen? Why did you kiss me back?"

She pondered those mysteries. She'd kissed him back because…because… She couldn't remember thinking at the time. All she'd been able to do was feel, and perhaps that wasn't so bad. Perhaps she thought too damned much.

Was it so terrible that she'd kissed Eli? The man could kiss her like she'd never been kissed before. All too soon she would never be kissed like that again.

Gwen frowned. Never to be kissed again so that her heart thundered and her blood slowed. Never to be kissed so that her busy little brain turned to mush. Never to feel as if nothing else mattered but the man and the moment, every problem minor as long as his arms held her tight.

Those kinds of thoughts led to disaster and heartache. If you felt that strongly for another human being you were asking to die a living death when you lost him or her. She had spent a lifetime watching just such a death.

And she'd vowed never to let such a thing happen to her.

Gwen stepped through the door without answering his questions. And Eli, being Eli, did not press; he let her go.

Despite her well-earned exhaustion Gwen slept fitfully; odd dreams she could not quite remember chased her throughout the night. When her doorbell blared, she groaned and rolled out of bed feeling as if she hadn't slept at all.

Trudging downstairs expecting to find an emergency all over her porch, she blinked, owl-eyed, when Nancy shoved inside. "Forgot my key. Why's the door locked, anyway? You sick? It's after nine."

Gwen scrubbed at her eyes, squinted into the sun and slammed the door. Shuffling toward the kitchen, she ran into Nancy ahead of her.

"Coffee," she croaked. "Move it or lose it."

Nancy laughed. "You're just like your father before coffee."

Gwen scowled. "You're one of those cheery morning people, aren't you?"

"Someone has to be."

"No, they don't. Get out."

"I brought doughnuts."

"Put them down, then get out."

Nancy ignored her, proceeding into the kitchen. Since she put the doughnuts down and started to make coffee, Gwen didn't have to hurt her. Even when Nancy started to hum while measuring coffee grounds and water, Gwen only *thought* of murder. She was too tired to act on the notion.

"Do you dare behave like this in front of Doc?"

"Every day."

"He must love you with all his cold, cold heart." The glass carafe rattled alarmingly. "Careful. I need that coffeepot and all that goes in it."

"You need to watch your mouth, Gwen."

"Huh?"

"You father is a good man. A gifted doctor. People adore him around here."

"They should. He lives for the people."

"You have a bad attitude, young lady."

"Who made you my mother?"

Nancy winced and her face whitened as if in pain. Gwen got up and went to her. "Hey, what did I say?"

Nancy shrugged off Gwen's comforting hand. "Never mind."

"No, really, tell me what's the matter. Was your date a jerk?"

Nancy's laugh ended on a watery half sob. "No more than any other."

"Why's that?"

"I'm just not interested."

"So get one that interests you. There have to be a ton of guys who would love to spend time with you."

"Not in Pine River. I guess you've been gone awhile, but you can't have forgotten what it's like."

"I haven't forgotten, but explain anyway."

"The men my age are all married."

"Find a younger model."

"They're all married, too. I'm not a spring chicken, Gwen."

"Neither am I, but who's counting?"

"My damned biological clock. Can't you hear it ticking?" She poured water into the automatic coffeemaker. "Sometimes the thing wakes me up at night. Doesn't yours?"

"Hell, no!"

But even as she said it the memory of a warm, compact body against her breast, the scent of powder and milk, caused a funny little tug near her heart.

"It will." Nancy nodded sagely. "Soon."

Gwen shook off the odd feeling. "I doubt that. You want a baby." She lifted one shoulder. "Have one."

"In Pine River? I don't think so."

"You don't *have* to stay here, Nancy."

Her smile was sad. "Yes, I do."

"Then pick a guy, any guy."

"None of them can be the man I want."

"You're that choosy?"

"No. I just know who I want."

"Go get him, tiger."

"Easy for you to say. You've never wanted anyone like that."

Gwen looked at Nancy's haunted face, which reminded her a lot of someone else's, and hardened her resolve. "And I never will."

Nancy sighed, pushed the start button on the coffeemaker and moved to the back window, where she stared out at the bright spring morning. "Must be surgery day at Eli's."

Gwen joined her in time to see a sweet, young, blond thing bounce up Eli's front steps and disappear inside. "Who's that?" she barked. Nancy tilted her head and raised an eyebrow at Gwen. "I mean..." Gwen cleared her throat and asked nonchalantly, "Who's that?"

"Eli's assistant. Candi."

"You've got to be kidding."

"No, she's his assistant, all right."

"She looks like she's twelve."

"You didn't see her from the front. She's definitely not twelve."

Gwen grunted. "What kind of name is Candi?"

"Cutesy for Candace. And she's twenty-two. Over the age of consent."

"Consent? For what?"

"Whatever. Coffee's ready." Nancy left Gwen alone at the window.

She stared at Eli's house, but Candi never came back out. Nancy handed her a mug of coffee. Gwen nodded her thanks and sat at the table. "What kind of assistant?"

Nancy took her time selecting a cherry-filled, sugarcoated dose of fried dough. "Veterinary assistant, what else?"

"Maid?"

"Ha. Did she look like a maid?"

"Cook?"

"Oh, I'm sure she can cook, but not the way you're thinking."

"Nancy, you're being deliberately obtuse."

"What do you want to know?"

"Is that child after Eli?"

"Yep."

Gwen sagged back in her seat and shoved a cruller in her mouth to keep from snarling. Nancy's smile didn't improve her mood. Gwen swallowed. "What's so funny?"

"That bothers you?"

"Eli deserves better."

"You've never met her."

True enough, but logic did not seem to be high on Gwen's list this morning. "Does he date her?"

Nancy's smile faded. "Eli doesn't date anyone."

"No one?"

"Here, there. Once or twice. No one lately. I'm sure he has the same problem as I do. And since he rarely leaves Pine River, I'd say he doesn't do much dating at all." Nancy shrugged. "The old-timers wonder if he's gay."

Gwen snorted her opinion of that before she had a chance to realize how such an opinion would sound. When she glanced across the table, all she saw was the tail end of Nancy's smirk.

"Just because a man has standards doesn't make him gay."

"Trust you to defend him."

"What does that mean?"

"You always defended him, Gwen. From everyone, even the Colonel."

"Someone had to."

"Did you ever consider why that someone had to be you?"

"Because I know Eli. And he's…he's…he's special."

"I agree. But if he's so special, then why are you marrying another man and Eli's alone?"

"He's my best friend, not my lover."

"Why not?"

"Lovers come and go. Friends are forever."

"But what happens when your best friend becomes your lover?"

"Ew!"

"Stop that! Think about it. Wouldn't such a love be the best love of all?"

"It could be my worst nightmare."

"Could be. Or maybe it could be a secret dream come true."

"I have no secret dreams."

"Maybe you should, Gwen." Nancy touched her shoulder with a gentleness reflected in her eyes. "Maybe you should."

CHAPTER SEVEN

"I HEARD Gwen Bartelt is back in town."

Eli grunted as he positioned a German shepherd named Spike on the operating table. Spike liked the ladies a bit too much, so he'd been brought in for an attitude adjustment. Poor Spike.

"Have you seen her yet?"

Eli glanced at Candi, who was setting out the instruments. She had her back to him, so he couldn't see her face. But her voice sounded funny. He should know. Candi talked a lot.

Eli preferred working alone, but he needed help one day a week when he did small-animal surgery. Candi was good with animals. She also worked at the Crystal Café, so her hours were flexible. He'd learned to ignore her chatter, and after a while she usually wound down.

"Have you?"

At Candi's unusual persistence, Eli frowned. "Seen Gwen? Of course. She's my neighbor."

"And what else?"

Eli, busy with Spike, wasn't really listening. "I don't understand."

"She's not the woman for you."

He glanced up. "Why would you say that?"

"She's not going to stay. She's always hated Pine River."

"You don't even know her."

"Everyone knows Doc and they talk about Gwen. How she's from here, but she never fit in. How you weren't born here, yet you love the place as much as old man Garret, whose great-granddaddy stole his farm from the Ojibwe. Small towns don't usually take to folk the way Pine River's taken to you, Eli. You might be eccentric—all those strays and fixing up animals that should really be road kill, then sending them back into the wild—but since you're a dog doctor..." She shrugged. "People understand."

Annoyance flashed through Eli, and he returned his attention to Spike—someone he could understand. "I didn't realize my life and Gwen's were the main topics of conversation among the counter squatters at the Crystal."

"They talk about everyone. The old guys have nothing else to do."

"Why would you listen?"

"Anything to do with you interests me." Eli frowned and looked up to find Candi right on the other side of the table. "I love you, Eli. I have since I saw you get off the bus when you came home from college to stay."

She leaned across the table and kissed him. He was so shocked, he let her. Until her tongue touched his lips and he jumped back as if bitten.

"You're kidding, right?"

"Of course not. I saw you that day and you were like a different person. When you left you were skinny...big hands and feet, huge glasses. Geek with a capital *G*. Then you come home a doctor." She lifted one shoulder. "A dog doctor, but still a doctor. And you've filled out, grown up. Your glasses are gone."

"You like how I *look?*"

"What's not to like? You're gorgeous. We'd be so good together. And our children would be beautiful. You're a little stiff with people, but that's where I come in. I can talk to anyone. Think of how our life could be, Eli."

He did and he wanted to run and hide. He still wasn't used to the way women reacted to him since he'd grown into his hands and feet, gotten contacts and begun to lift animals that weighed more than he did. That kind of habit did wondrous things for the pectorals.

In his mind Eli was still the odd, clumsy child everyone smiled about behind their hands. Not that people here hadn't accepted him—they had. But as Candi said, it was with a smirk and a wink. He was different, always had been. The fact that Pine River liked him anyway was one of the things that made him love the place so much.

Lately though when he glanced in the mirror he didn't recognize himself. To have someone say they loved him because of how he looked... It would be funny, if it wasn't so sad.

"That's not love. I'm not sure what it is."

Hurt passed over Candi's face. "I'm not a child. I know how I feel. I'd be the perfect wife for you. I was born here, and I don't mind staying. I could help you in your work. We could have so much. If you'd quit thinking of her and look at me."

Eli looked. Candi might have the body of an adult, but he still saw a child. Besides, she wasn't Gwen and she never could be.

"I'm sorry, but I don't feel that way about you. I never pretended—"

"No, you never did." She gave a dramatic sigh that had him thinking of soap opera actresses and teenage girls. "You've been nothing but a professional. And I found that so exciting. The more you ignored me, the more I wanted you. I thought if I hung around, if I was everything you needed, I could make you love me."

He blinked. *Make* him love her? That was impossible. But wasn't that what he'd been thinking about Gwen? If he was everything she needed, if he was patient and true, eventually she'd love him. Was he as delusional as his assistant? Was there as little chance of Gwen loving him as there was of him loving Candi?

No. He wouldn't believe that. Gwen had responded when he'd kissed her. He had seen in her eyes that she cared for him deeply. He believed she already loved him, way down where love lived. He was fighting her fear of love itself, not fighting her love of someone else. He wasn't forcing her to feel what could not be forced. He was leading her toward something that had been destined for a very long time.

He truly loved Gwen—the girl he'd grown up with, the woman she hid beneath the cool mask. He didn't love her for a pretty face or a great ass. Not even for a calm capability in the face of disaster, or a mind that understood science several levels above his own. None of those things, or perhaps all of them. He just loved her and he'd never stop.

"It doesn't matter, does it?" Candi asked. "I can talk and talk, I can love you forever, but you love her."

He could tell by Candi's face that she couldn't believe he'd pick Gwen over her. Most men would say he was an idiot. Candi was a hottie. But then, Eli wasn't most men.

She wanted to fulfill his every dream. But she couldn't, because his dream was Gwen. Even so, when tears filled her big blue eyes and she ran from the room, Eli secured Spike and went after her. He wasn't heartless. He might not believe she knew what love was, but Candi believed love was him.

Eli caught up to her on the porch. "Wait, Candi." She stopped at the top of the steps and he could hear her crying. He wasn't sure what to say. "Um—are you coming back to work?"

"I don't—" *hitch, hitch* "—think so."

Eli sighed. She'd been a very good assistant; whether because she wanted to impress him or because she truly liked animals, it didn't matter. He'd miss her.

"You're wasted at the Crystal. You might want to think about becoming a vet yourself."

She laughed, though he could still hear the tears. "I'm not a brainiac like Gwen. I barely got out of school. I wanted to *marry* a doctor, not *be* one."

"You're selling yourself short."

She turned and approached him. Eli resisted the urge to back up when she came far too close. "Can I ask you one thing?" He could only nod. "Why her?"

Candi appeared so honestly lost, so deeply hurt. Though he knew that the shallowness of her devotion would ensure a quick recovery, Eli couldn't help but smile gently and cup her cheek. "You said you fell in love with me when you saw how I'd changed?"

She nodded, rubbing her cheek against his palm, sighing like a teenager. "Gwen thought I was special when I was nothing more than a geek with a capital *G*."

Confusion filled her eyes. She had no idea what he was getting at, and it didn't matter. Eli leaned down and brushed a kiss over her perfect forehead. "Good-bye, Candi. Good luck."

He returned to the operating room and stared down at the anesthetized dog. "Ah, Spike, love stinks, doesn't it?"

A soft snore was his only answer.

GWEN HADN'T meant to spy. She *wasn't* spying. She was in her own yard. On her own porch, thank you.

It wasn't her fault if Eli wanted to smooch in broad daylight.

Watching him cup that girl's cheek, stare into her eyes, whisper sweet nothings, then kiss her gently on the brow, as if they had all the time in the world for kissing other places later, made the coffee and fried dough in Gwen's stomach do a little dance.

She stomped inside and slammed the door before she had to see any more. Nancy had said the child was chasing Eli. She had neglected to mention that Eli wasn't running away very fast.

Not that it was any of Gwen's business. Eli owed her nothing. Just because he'd kissed her once as no one had ever kissed her didn't mean anything. Not to her; or to him, obviously. They were adults. Things like that happened. You didn't dwell on them.

So why did the sight of Eli kissing Candi make Gwen want to sit down and cry? Right after she beat her fists against the wall for a few hours.

The phone shrilled. From the clinic, where she restocked supplies, Nancy yelled a distant query.

"Got it!" Gwen shouted, and picked up the receiver.

"Guinevere?" She closed her eyes. *Lance.* Just the man she didn't want to talk to. "Where have you been? I've phoned several times."

"I've been at the hospital. On duty. Working. I'm sorry I was unable to return your call."

A pause. "You say that as if I were a patient, Guinevere. I'm your fiancé. And as such I think I have a right to be consulted before you make a decision like this."

"What decision? There was no decision involved."

Liar! Liar, liar. Wasn't that how an old song went? Gwen hated that song.

"You *decided* to take a month's leave to work in Nowhere, Wisconsin."

She might have called Pine River that herself on occasion, but that was like calling your brother stupid. *You* could, but no one else had better try.

"The town is named Pine River, and I didn't realize I needed your permission to help my father."

"Now, Guinevere, you're jumping to conclusions. I never said anything about permission—even though I am, technically, your boss. It's just that I need you here."

Once, not so very long ago, Lance's need of her had been like a drug. She couldn't get enough of it. She was a need junkie. Maybe that was why Pine River called to her now as it never had before.

"My father needs me more."

"But, baby." Gwen gritted her teeth. When Lance called her baby she wanted to slug him, but he kept right on doing it. "I'm going to be your husband. I really need you in the ER."

Those two sentences did not go together. The fact that Lance thought they did only proved how little their personal relationship meant—a truth that had never bothered her before.

"But, *honey,*" she said with a syrup-laden twist

that was lost on him, "what kind of wife would I make if I left my father flat on his back in traction?"

"Mine?"

Exactly, Gwen thought, and she didn't like that image. If she hadn't planned to stay in Pine River before, she certainly would now. Lance ought to remember that theirs was a partnership, not a dictatorship. Though the relationship might not be based on love, it could at least be based on respect.

"I'll be back for the wedding," she said. "If you miss me before that, you know where to find me."

Gwen hung up while Lance still sputtered.

"If he doesn't show up here in the next few weeks," Nancy said from the kitchen doorway, "I'd dump his ass."

Gwen burst out laughing. She'd been doing that a lot lately, and it felt good. "Nancy, you are a prize."

"That's what I keep telling your father. But he won't believe me."

"Men."

"Yeah, men."

Shaking their heads, the two mulled over the mysteries of the opposite sex. Then Nancy threw her arm around Gwen's shoulders and pulled her close. "So, who gets to pick up Doc? You or me?"

"Flip you for it."

"Loser has to pick him up?"

"Certainly not the winner."

They collapsed against each other giggling like kids.

Gwen decided it also felt good to have a pal.

NANCY WASN'T laughing when she lost. For the first time she could recall, she did not want to see Doc, and she couldn't figure out why.

Was it because last night she'd caught a glint of something different in his eyes? Admiration? Appreciation? A flare of heat?

All these years she'd loved him from afar, and she'd known he would never love her back. Psychologists would say she'd chosen an unavailable man on purpose. No threat there. But that theory applied to women who had been abused, physically or emotionally. Nancy had lived a pristine childhood. She had no reason to avoid men.

So why Doc? She'd asked herself that often enough in the still of the night. He was cranky. He was stubborn. He was old. He was taken.

He was also smart, gentle, devoted and handsome. Why should age matter if love was involved? A good argument, were she not the only one in love.

Last night she could swear he'd seen *her* and not Nurse Nancy. She hadn't known what to do, what to say, so she'd fled.

Her date had been a disaster because she had been thinking of Doc's eyes, of his hand grasping hers, of his voice whispering, ''Nance?'' as she'd always yearned for him to whisper it. And when Brett had kissed her good-night, she hadn't been thinking of him.

She'd been thinking insidious thoughts, such as: *What if I don't settle for just being his nurse? What if being near him isn't enough? What if I take a chance? And give him one, too?*

Thoughts like those were dangerous because thoughts like those led to action. And once you *did* something there was no going back to the way things had been.

Nancy pulled up to the hospital entrance to find Doc already discharged and awaiting her in his wheelchair. One look and she knew she'd imagined the soft heat in his eyes the night before. She'd imagined the heat because she'd wanted to see it so very much.

Which was pathetic and had to stop. So when Brett walked out and helped her load the wheelchair, then smiled the smile that had made her say yes to a date in the first place, she said yes again when he asked her to dinner the next night.

Chances were for the young and foolish, and Nancy had never been either one.

GWEN SAT at the reception desk, wondering what she was supposed to do during off times like these. They never happened at City Hospital. Then the front door opened and a woman nearly as old as God walked in.

She had to be that old because Sandra Guiley had been ancient when Gwen was a child. Still, the woman didn't use a walker or even a cane. She moved straight and sure, at home with her body and herself. Her face was lined, though not heavily, and her black hair, which hung to her waist in a ponytail, held only a few streaks of gray—the same streaks that had been there when Miss Guiley had taught seventh grade. Even her eyes were the same; sharp and gray, they never missed a thing, and they stared at Gwen as if they had seen the world so they were not impressed with her.

"Where's Steven?" she demanded.

Gwen blinked. She hadn't heard Doc called Steven in...oh, about forever.

"He's—"

"And where's that nurse? I like that girl. No nonsense. No giggling foolishness like I get from that twit who helps next door whenever I take Fifi to have her nails trimmed. What are you doing here, Guinevere?"

"I'm—"

"Never mind. In here. My chest hurts."

Gwen got to her feet in a hurry. Chest pains were nothing to fool with, especially in a woman like this. Still, despite said pain, the woman beat Gwen to the clinic, and climbed onto the exam table while Gwen hunted for her stethoscope.

"When did the pain start, Miss Guiley?"

"Ms. Never been married. Never plan to be."

Gwen's lips twitched, but she managed to keep her doctor face in place. She wondered when Miss had gone Ms. and what Pine River had thought about that.

"Fine, Ms. Guiley, when did the pains start?"

"Start? They never end. I come every Thursday at four and Doc checks me over. Where is that man?"

"I guess you haven't heard—"

"Heard what, girlie? Get to the point."

Gwen took a deep breath. She'd have gotten to the point a long time ago if Ms. Guiley had stopped interrupting her. "Doc broke his leg. He's on his way home now, but I'll be filling in for him while he's laid up."

Ms. Guiley grabbed the stethoscope from Gwen's hand and spoke into the receiver. "About damned time."

Gwen jumped and yanked the thing out of her ears. "Pardon me?"

"Doc's needed help since 1982."

Gwen sighed and unwrapped the blood pressure cuff. "I'm not staying, Ms. Guiley. I'm just filling in."

"Hmph. In my day, children helped their parents. Took care of them when they were sick, took over for them when they became too old to work."

"You want to tell Doc he's too old to work?"

Ms. Guiley cackled. "No, sir! I'm not a fool. Still, your mama would have loved to see you working together."

Gwen, in the midst of pumping the cuff around Ms. Guiley's scrawny arm, froze. "You knew my mother?"

"Of course. Class of…" She scrunched her face into an expression of intense concentration. "Nineteen—nineteen something or other. Do you think you could release that doohickey? My arm's gonna explode."

"Oh!" Gwen released the pressure cuff. "Sorry."

Ms. Guiley shrugged. "Am I gonna die?"

"Not today. Your pressure's lower than mine. Your

heart beats like a bull. But just for fun, I'm going to schedule you for an EKG at Mercy.''

"Had one last month.''

"And?"

"I've got the heart of a seventy-year-old.''

Gwen didn't think that was particularly good, but Ms. Guiley seemed proud. She'd have to hunt up her chart and find out just how old this woman's heart was.

"So what does Doc do for you every Thursday at four?"

"Same's you. Except we have a shot and a beer afterward.''

Gwen gaped. "Excuse me?"

"You heard right. It's the only way he gets me back here once a week." Ms. Guiley winked. "I'll meet you in the kitchen, girlie.''

She jumped off the exam table and set off at an able clip. Gwen dove for the chart file and yanked Guiley out of the *G*s. In Doc's precise handwriting she read: "Sandra Guiley. Age unknown. Chest pains since time began. Check her over once a week. EKG once a month. Promise her a shot and a beer to keep her coming back. If she isn't dead yet, that won't kill her.''

Gwen frowned. She didn't approve, but she'd talk with Doc about his methods later. After making a note on the chart, she joined Ms. Guiley, who had already helped herself.

"Sit down and visit a spell, Guinevere.''

Gwen sat, shaking her head when Ms. Guiley offered the whiskey in her direction. Gwen wasn't much of a drinker. She'd discovered that alcohol disturbed her sleep, and she had sleep disturbances enough.

Ms. Guiley stared at her over the rim of her shot glass. "You look just like Betsy. It's uncanny."

Gwen forced herself to remain seated. It wasn't as if she hadn't heard this before, just not in several years. In Milwaukee she was Dr. Bartelt—Gwen to her friends, Guinelot to Lancelot. She was never Betsy's daughter, and she liked it that way.

"I remember once when your mama was little..." Ms. Guiley paused to sip the amber liquid, savoring the flavor as if it were spun from gold.

Gwen sat, tense and miserable. Stories about her mother always made her sad. She'd never known the woman, though everyone else had, and whenever they looked at Gwen they all remembered Betsy.

"She was a sweet child, though one for trouble was Betsy."

"Trouble?" Gwen's interest perked up. No one had ever spoken about her mother in anything but saintly attributes. Maybe that was part of the reason the stories were so hard to listen to. No one could be that perfect.

"For certain," Ms. Guiley said, taking a healthy gulp of her beer. "Not mean, like. Mischievous. But she was so cute and earnest everyone forgave the little things she did."

"Like what?"

Ms. Guiley lifted an eyebrow. Gwen was surprised

herself. She'd never voluntarily asked to hear a memory of her mother.

"I taught third grade back then. She put a garter snake in my desk drawer."

"My mother?"

"She was quite the little tomboy. Just like you."

"And what did you do when you found a snake in your desk?"

Ms. Guiley shrugged. "Picked it up and tossed it out the window. That sure stole her thunder. I was not then and never have been a lily-livered princess of a female."

"No, ma'am."

A sharp nod acknowledged Gwen's words of respect. "Then there was the time she freed the frogs in biology class. Liberated, she called it. We had no dissection unit that year. Betsy had guts but a heart as soft as spring rain and big as Lake Superior."

All the other stories Gwen had heard of her mother had dealt with her marriage, her years as Mrs. Dr. Bartelt or her short time as the mother of Guinevere. Those stories had always been tinged with the sadness of impending doom, as stories were when told in retrospect about the dead. But Ms. Guiley's stories gave Gwen a view of her mother as a person in her own right.

Gwen thought she would have liked Betsy. She might even have been her friend if she'd been born a generation earlier. Surprisingly, the thought did not make her sad but lifted her heart as not much else ever had.

"There was never anyone for Betsy but Steven, and the same for him."

Gwen's heart fell right back near her toes—the place it always fell whenever she heard these stories. Her parents' perfect love and everlasting devotion was something she'd had to live with. And she wasn't impressed with the results.

"You know they were best friends since child-hood? Just like you and the Colonel's boy, Dr. Dog."

"Drycinski." Gwen's defense was automatic. Her mind spun with the thought of Doc and her mother being best friends, before everlasting love ruined it all.

"I can never remember that foreign name. He an-swers to Dr. Dog."

"I'll just bet he does." If Ms. Guiley called Gwen Mud, she would answer.

"Anyway, they were like peas and carrots, those two. And then when they were teenagers, bam!" She slapped her hand down on the table so hard her empty shot glass jittered. Gwen jumped. "Love like I've never seen before or since. It was somethin' to watch."

Gwen murmured noncommittally.

"I always figured you and Dr. Dog would be the same. But nothin'."

Gwen wouldn't call how she felt about Eli, then or now, nothin', but it sure wasn't love and it never would be. Lust maybe. Lust, she could handle; lust, she could control.

"I'd best be going, girlie. Tell Dr. Dog I'll bring Fifi by on Monday as usual."

"Does Eli give you a shot and a beer, too?"

"Of course not." She moved toward the door with a fresh spring in her step. "He gives Fifi one." She paused in the doorway and sent a wink Gwen's way. "But oh, how that dog loves to share."

CHAPTER EIGHT

AFTER HIS ASSISTANT QUIT because of unrequited love, Eli's day went downhill.

Not that he couldn't perform surgery on three dogs, two cats and a guinea pig named Orville by himself. He could; it just took twice as long to knock them out, stitch them up and ship them out to the room off the clinic where postops processed their snooze juice.

He was supposed to do house calls—more often than not barn calls—on Thursday afternoons while his patients slept peacefully under the care of Candi, who also did the weekly billing. Not only couldn't he leave his patients alone, but he didn't finish surgery until after three-thirty. Then he spent the next half hour rescheduling his cows and pigs and horses.

A muffled *woof* from the front hall drew Eli out of his office. Jake and Elwood sat next to the door, mouths full of tennis balls. How they could get those things that far in and not choke, even he couldn't figure out. Just as he couldn't figure out how they could swallow a sock but leave enough hanging out of their mouths for him to retrieve it, inch by inch, yet never choke on it, either. *Amazing Animals* should do a story on the Blues Brothers.

He glanced outside. "Sorry, guys. Ms. Guiley is walking home."

At the sound of the retired teacher's name, both dogs dropped their balls and lay down with a long-suffering groan. They had tried to make her love them, but Ms. Guiley just didn't feel the magic. She referred to Jake and Elwood as "ye hounds from hell" and recommended exorcism whenever they came within three feet of her and Fifi—a hound from hell if Eli had ever met one. Unfortunately, Fifi was little and fluffy and yowled like a cat, which to the Blues Brothers meant open season.

Ms. Guiley strolled off and Eli was just about to let the dogs out, when Nancy pulled up with Doc in the back seat of her car. "Sorry again. Now I have to help Doc."

It didn't hurt that Gwen was on her way out the door to do the very same thing. Eli had had a bad day. But if he could end such a day with the sight and sound and scent of Gwen, Eli would no doubt remember every bad day as a good one.

"Need a hand?" he asked as he approached the group.

"My hands are fine," Doc growled. "It's a leg I need."

"Looks like a leg to me." Eli observed the cast that covered Doc from ankle to knee. "Maybe."

"Ha-ha. Get the chair out of the trunk, big boy."

"I can get it." Gwen shouldered in front of Eli, tugging at the heavy chair and glaring when he would have helped.

Eli glanced from Gwen to Nancy, who shrugged, then to Doc, who just rolled his eyes. Eli hadn't even seen Gwen today, so what had he done? Or not done?

He had no idea. Eli had little experience with women, and Gwen had never snarled at him before. He helped Doc into the chair and would have wheeled him up the walk if Gwen hadn't booted him out of the way again.

"I'm sure you have plenty to do at the clinic. We won't keep you."

"Actually, I'm done for the day."

"Then I'm sure you have places to go, people to see." She muttered something else he couldn't quite catch, then grunted as she pushed Doc up the slight incline.

Doc glanced over his shoulder at Eli, his frown obviously saying, *What did you do?*

It was Eli's turn to shrug. Nancy moved up to his side. "Did you hear what she mumbled?"

"No. You did?"

"I've got good ears."

"You and every other army nurse."

"Watch it, or I'll try out my Nurse Ratched imitation on you next time you have the flu."

Since she no doubt would, Eli decided to keep a civil tongue in his head. "What did she say?"

"She said, 'Cuties to kiss.' Does that mean anything to you?"

Eli had a sudden image of himself and Candi on the porch. "Oh-oh."

"That's what I thought. You want Gwen? You'd better think with your brain, stud boy."

"Stud boy? Me? You know better than that. And who said I wanted Gwen?"

Nancy snorted. "Please don't insult my intelligence."

"Is it that obvious?"

"Relax. She hasn't got a clue. You're her very best friend, Eli. She'd never dream you were plotting seduction. That is what you're plotting, isn't it?"

"Plotting sounds so devious."

"Thinking? Dreaming? Hoping? How are those?"

"You know what will happen if she even suspects how I feel?"

"You'll see the back end of her so fast you won't know what hit you."

"Right. Seduction is the only way. I believe we were meant for each other. I believe she loves me. I just have to get her to see that Pine River isn't hell and love isn't a lifelong penance."

"Good luck."

"Any ideas?"

"If I knew how to make someone love me, I'd be way ahead of you."

"Huh?"

"Never mind. I think you might be right about Gwen. She saw you kiss who?"

"Must be Candi. She's the only cutie I've kissed lately."

Nancy gave him a disgusted look, as only Nancy could. Eli resisted the urge to cringe like Jake and

Elwood. "I'm not even going to ask how you could be so stupid, because it might have been the smartest thing you've ever done."

"How do you figure?"

"She's jealous, stud boy. And that can't be bad."

"WHO PUT THE BUG up your butt?" Doc asked as Gwen settled him in the single downstairs bedroom that had been used previously for patients awaiting transport to Mercy.

"Me? And this from a man who's had a bug up his butt since 1974."

Doc stiffened at the reference to the year his wife had died. "You do not want to go there, Gwen."

"I'm sure *you* don't. What I want has always been irrelevant."

"You want to fight with an old, injured man?"

"You aren't old."

He sighed. "I feel old."

"Yeah, join the club."

Gwen collapsed the wheelchair and stored it in the closet. Then she propped Doc's shiny new crutches next to the bed.

"Anything you'd like to discuss?"

Gwen cut a glance at her father. What was he after? She didn't believe that after all these years he wanted to discuss her mother. Everyone else in town always did. But Doc? Never.

She doubted he'd give two hoots about her burning annoyance with Eli. If she could even put to words why she wanted to kick her best friend in the shins.

"What patients have you seen?" Doc prodded.

The light dawned. She should have known he didn't want to discuss anything personal. Patients first, always, except for yesterday in the hospital. Under the circumstances his odd preoccupation had been understandable.

Today it was back to business, which was to Doc all there was in life. She'd wanted him to love her; she'd settled for need, instead. He needed her now, for the patients, so she'd discuss the patients. And nothing else. Just like old times.

"Ms. Guiley."

"Is it Thursday?"

"All day."

"She all right?"

"Strong as a horse. Drinks like fish."

Doc's lips twitched. "She does not. She likes a whiskey and a beer. She's older than dirt. Cut her a break."

"How old is she?"

"She's not saying. And everyone who 'knew her when' is six feet under."

"You know she's getting double meds."

"Where?"

"Eli's. For Fifi."

Doc's twitch turned into a full-blown grin. "I wish Fifi would down a few stiff ones and take a life-long nap. That poodle is scary."

"A scary poodle. I've never heard of that."

"You've never met Fifi."

"Seriously, Doc, what are you thinking giving a woman of unknown age alcohol on a weekly basis?"

"I'm thinking she comes for a check-up every week and goes to a hospital every month for tests. I'm thinking she gets out of her house, takes a walk, chats with another human being for a while. Sometimes, Gwen, medicine isn't about medicine. It's about discovering what a person needs to feel strong enough to fight for one more day. You've lost touch with the idea that there's a person beneath the label of patient."

Because she'd been thinking something along those lines herself, and not liking it at all, Gwen struck back. "You don't know anything about me."

"And why is that? You ran off just when you were getting interesting."

"What's that supposed to mean?"

"Everyone always told me, 'Blink and you'll miss them grow.' I shut my eyes for a moment and you were a woman." Doc sighed and picked at the quilt instead of looking at her. "Aw, Gwen, I'm no good at talking about how I feel."

"Really? I'd never have guessed."

He scowled at her sarcasm. "I did my best."

"You mean Mrs. Drycinski did."

"You were a toddler, and I knew nothing about them."

"You're a doctor. You see toddlers all the time."

"Seeing them and raising them are two different things. I could tell if you had a fever, or peek at my handy-dandy chart and see if it was time for a vac-

cination, but when you threw your food on the floor
or woke up screaming at midnight I..." He spread
his hands in a helpless gesture she'd never seen him
use before.

"You paid someone to raise me."

"I found someone who knew what in hell she was
doing. Parents don't have all the answers. Doctors,
either. We do our best, and sometimes it's not
enough."

Gwen stared at Doc for a long moment. He had put
words to one of the secret questions in her heart—her
fear that no matter what she did as a doctor, it could
never be enough. And if her best wasn't good enough,
then what else was there?

THOUGH NOT IMMOBILE—he *had* crutches—Doc
wasn't supposed to partake of any unnecessary activ-
ity during his first week out of the hospital. Not only
was he still in pain, but he was exhausted from the
shock of the trauma and the surgery. That didn't make
it any easier to hear the world moving on all over the
place while he was not a part of it. He hated change—
but everything seemed to be changing, whether he
liked it or not.

His daughter was home and that should make him
happy. Except he didn't know how to reach her, what
to say. He never had. He should most likely bare his
soul, tell her everything in his heart, profess his love,
apologize for his sins—that was what all those television fathers did. It was pathetic to watch.

Doc just wasn't that kind of man. His generation

kept their mouths shut, their troubles hidden, their joys secret. He'd loved Betsy with all his heart, and she'd known that. Hadn't she? Just because he'd never told her didn't mean she didn't know. Look at how he'd mourned her. He'd never touched another woman with love. He didn't think that he could. Somehow that would be a worse betrayal of Betsy than letting her die in the first place.

"Here's dinner." Nancy walked in with a tray almost as wide as her smile.

That was another thing that had changed. Nancy was too damned cheery for Nancy. Doc figured her yippy-skippy attitude must have something to do with Brett, the PT with everything. Why that made him mad, Doc had no idea. Nancy deserved a life. But that tall, dark and handsome boy wasn't going to make her happy. He just knew it.

She was humming when she leaned over to place the tray across his lap. The toneless tune annoyed him almost as much as the way her shirt slipped sideways and gave him a peek of peach skin, right in front of his nose. "I'm not hungry," he snapped.

"So what else is new? If you didn't have to eat to live, you never would. Now you need to eat to heal. Put that fork in your hand and some food in your mouth, or I'll have Gwen put a tube down your throat."

"I'd like to see her try."

"So would I." She grinned.

"What's with that infernal smiling? Did you get

more than a good-night kiss from Brett the incredible pretty boy?''

Nancy's smile froze. Her eyes widened. Shock spread over her face. *"That* is none of your business.''

Doc sighed. She was right. But he couldn't seem to stop himself from wondering. He hadn't been able to stop thinking about Nancy and that kid since they'd left his room last night. He'd seen the guy hovering around this afternoon, obviously waiting for Nancy to arrive. So Doc had gone outside. Then lo and behold as soon as Nancy drove up, there was Brett. It was enough to make a grown man puke.

"He's too young for you, Nance.''

"Also none of your business.''

"What is my business?''

"Medicine.''

He scowled at his leg. "Not at the moment.''

"If you gave Gwen the same third degree over every one of her dates it's no wonder she never told you she was getting married.''

He'd never said a word to Gwen about her dates, mainly because none of them had been serious. She'd gone through boys like lemonade on a hot summer afternoon. The same one rarely knocked on the door twice. Except for Eli.

He hadn't brought up the question of Gwen's sudden marriage for a very good reason. She wasn't serious about that, either, though she might not know it yet. So Doc wouldn't back her into a corner she would fight to get out of.

Eli could handle the problem of Lance Heinrich. The kid thought he was fooling everyone with that best-friend nonsense. But Doc hadn't been born yesterday. He'd seen love like that shining in another young man's eyes only once—from a mirror, one lifetime ago.

"Hey." Nancy laid her hand on Doc's shoulder. "Why the sad face?"

The warmth of her palm seeped through the thin cotton of his well-washed T-shirt and called to a forgotten part of his soul—or maybe a part he had not forgotten but merely chosen to ignore. Doc tilted his head and caught a glimpse of something in Nancy's face that made him reach up and put a hand over hers.

Her hand was large; so was his. But hers was soft. Maybe that was why it seemed to fit against his rough skin like two halves of one whole.

Confusion flickered in her eyes. "Doc?" she whispered.

How long had it been since someone had called him Steve? Another lifetime ago. Oh, Ms. Guiley addressed him as Steven, but no one had ever called him Steve after...

He yanked his hand from Nancy's and started shoveling food into his mouth so he would not be tempted to use it for talking—or more foolish things.

Nancy stepped away from his bed, and Doc kept eating, afraid to look into her eyes and find pity. Pity for a man who had spent a lifetime loving a dead woman and had no idea how to stop? Or for a man who had the guts to tell her that boy was too young, when he himself was far too old?

"Well, I guess I'll see you in the morning," she ventured.

He nodded, still staring at his plate. When the door closed, Doc tossed the fork onto the tray with a clatter that emphasized the chaos in his mind.

For a moment there he'd had the insane urge to press his mouth to the pulse that beat against the blue-veined skin of her wrist. To taste life against his lips.

He'd been taking too many drugs, or perhaps too few. Something had caused him to ache for the forbidden.

Ms. GUILEY TURNED OUT to be Gwen's last patient of the day. She'd fielded a few phone calls, then a single page, a prescription called in, a question or two, and here she was, unable to sleep at midnight. She sipped chamomile tea and stared out at the night. In the distance, thunder rumbled, a lonely sound. She'd never cared much for storms.

Perhaps this odd, restless feeling came from boredom and nothing more. Tonight, even Doc hadn't provided any amusement. She'd gone in to take his dinner tray, and he'd been doing his blob imitation—grunting at her and jabbing the television remote in perfect syncopation. She was going to hurt him if he didn't knock that off.

Gwen frowned at the rain-scented breeze that billowed the curtains above the kitchen sink. Doc wasn't being his usual pain-in-the-neck self—uncannily zeroing in on what annoyed her most. Perhaps postop depression was setting in early.

Since she only had medical journals to go on, she couldn't be sure. But she'd read that depression, combined with a lack of concentration to task, followed many surgeries. If Doc didn't shape up, maybe she'd give him a happy pill instead of a slap up alongside his head. Not that the old goat would take the pill, but at least she'd be doing her job—looking at the person behind the patient.

Gwen grimaced over a gulp of lukewarm tea. Maybe Ms. Guiley had the idea. This tea could use a shot if not a beer. But she'd never drink when she was on call, and she appeared to be on call for the duration.

Perhaps she needed some fresh air. Opening the back door, Gwen peered at the sky. Clouds danced with the moon but no rain fell. She didn't hear the thunder anymore, either. Maybe the storm had blown east on a speedy wind.

After making sure the pager rode her hip, Gwen shut the back door. It would do her good to get out before spring disappeared. Thus far, all she'd seen of the season had been this afternoon when she'd gone outside to wheel Doc inside.

Not that being inside for extended periods was so unusual in her life. In Milwaukee, if it was a particularly bad few days, she might only get a single, lung-cleansing gulp of air from the receiving dock before the loudspeaker blared, "Dr. Bartelt to the ER stat!"

She certainly didn't miss that. What did she miss?

Lance? Her condo? Her friends? Make that friendly acquaintances. The only true friends she'd ever had were Eli and Nancy, and they were here.

Gwen made a sound of impatience and picked her way through the dew-covered grass. Why did she keep thinking subversive thoughts? People instead of patients. Life instead of death. Friends instead of acquaintances. Home instead of hell.

The clearing opened all around her. Without conscious thought, she'd come to Eli's gazebo.

Maybe she'd known all along this was where she wanted to be. Maybe that was why she'd been unable to sleep, unable to read, unable to sit still and drink her blasted tea. Because as soon as she stepped into the clearing and saw the moon glint off the roof, peace flooded her soul. Because of Eli. He had always known what she needed, even when she didn't know herself.

She had stopped missing him with an ache that was a physical pain long ago. Oh, the emptiness had remained, but she'd gotten used to it. Like a clock that ticked through the night, the echo of Eli was always there, just quiet enough to forget for hours, even days, at a time; but he never disappeared completely.

Being with him for this month, as they had been together for so many years, would bring that pain back again when she left. She would go into her marriage missing another man.

Eli? The other man? Now, that was funny.

So why didn't she feel like laughing?

Gwen stepped into the gazebo just as the spring

shower broke and pattered against the glass roof. The gentle ping of the drops soothed her burning confusion. She lay down on the bench and watched the rain run down the glass in rivulets.

The door opened. She didn't need to look to know who had come. Staring at the clouds chasing each other past the moon, Gwen held out her hand—and met Eli's coming in the other direction.

CHAPTER NINE

THEIR FINGERS ENTWINED, palm met palm, and the silence filled with the beat of rain on the leaves. For eternity Gwen could lie there, watching the storm-shrouded sky and holding Eli's hand. Could this be what heaven was like?

"Was your day so bad, then?"

Eli's voice broke the stillness; his words shattered her peace. Gwen turned her head and met his gaze. The benches they lay upon met at the head, putting their faces only inches apart. This close, she could see the boy she remembered in the eyes of the man. She had trusted that boy with all her secrets, so she trusted the man now with her deepest fear.

"No one I loved died on me today. I guess that would make this a good day."

"People you love are going to die, Gwen. There's nothing you can do about that."

"But I don't want to be holding them in my arms when it happens."

"That's your father's fear. Don't make it yours."

"My father's curse, you mean. It happened."

"And it's over. He can't let the past go, but you should."

"I should forget her?"

"Never. But don't let what happened to them ruin your life, too."

"What if it happens to me?"

"How could the same thing happen to the same family twice in one lifetime?"

"Shit happens?"

"Every day. Get used to it."

"I've never gotten used to people dying. I stopped crying over every one, and I don't know if that's good or bad. Seems you should cry when you commit the ultimate failure."

"Failure?" He shifted onto his side and stared directly into her face. "Is that how you see it when you lose a patient?"

"If I can't save them, then I've failed."

"Don't you ever think that maybe it was just their time?"

"No. Medicine is supposed to change that."

Eli snorted. "I don't think so."

"So in other words, you think it was my mother's time on that country road. Lack of emergency services had nothing to do with what happened?"

"If your father couldn't save her, then it was her time. That's what I believe."

"He doesn't."

"Which doesn't make him right, only guilty—at least in his own mind."

She faced the stars again. In the way of spring showers, the rain had stopped as suddenly as it had begun, and the clouds sped off to places unknown.

The moon shone bright, sparking shards of light off the droplets trembling atop the Plexiglas roof.

"You saw me kiss Candi this morning, didn't you?"

Gwen's fingers jerked, and Eli tightened his hold as if to keep her from retreating. She hadn't planned to. Nothing had felt so good in a long, long time as Eli's hand in hers.

"So?"

"She quit. I was just saying goodbye."

"Quit?" Her voice sounded too happy by half. Gwen cleared her throat and tried again. "That's too bad. Why?"

"I didn't love her."

Gwen glanced at him, but Eli stared up at the stars and not at her. "That's a requirement for veterinary assistants? The vet has to love them?"

"She thought she loved me."

"But she didn't?"

"Candi has no idea what love is."

"And you do?"

"I know it isn't lust for someone's body or attraction to a pretty face. Not admiration for their mind, respect for their profession or adoration of their talent."

Gwen stifled a wince. She knew she didn't love Lance. She didn't want to. Then why did she suddenly feel so guilty?

"You know what love *isn't*, then. What is it?"

"I'll know love when I feel it. Because love can be nothing else."

"You've been reading romance novels again."

He grinned. "Someone has to."

Gwen sat up, and the movement broke the connection of their hands. Well, she couldn't very well hold his hand for the rest of the night, now could she? Still, without the warmth of his, her fingers felt bereft.

"I should get some sleep." Gwen stood. "Tomorrow is another day."

"So I hear." He stood, too, and she was struck again by his height, his breadth, all the changes that made him a new man and the similarities that kept him her Eli.

And because he was her Eli, she had to try to tell him what she felt, even though she didn't know why. "I've only been in town a few days, and I find myself forgetting why I hated it so much. I love this gazebo. I could spend eternity here. It's like an enchanted castle, a place out of time."

"The gazebo wasn't here before."

"But you were."

"And I always will be."

His eyes heated and his gaze dropped to her lips as if he meant to kiss her again. When he did things like that he both frightened and thrilled her. She didn't know what to expect from Eli anymore, or from herself.

Forbidden urges came to her every time he was near, and when they were combined with the feeling of safety only Eli could bring, those strange cravings were nearly irresistible.

He touched her face and her whole body leaped in

response. She swayed toward him, wanting to feel again the thrill of his mouth on hers. But he merely pressed his lips to her forehead in the same manner as he'd kissed Candi that morning. When he'd been saying goodbye to someone he didn't love.

"Good night, Gwen."

Good night wasn't goodbye, and what did it matter if Eli didn't love her? In fact, if he loved her that would be bad, because she wanted nothing to do with love. Remember?

Eli moved toward the door. "Eli, why is everything so different here?"

He turned, brows raised. "Everything here is just like it always was, Gwen. What's different is you."

He disappeared into the night, leaving her with more questions now than she'd had when he arrived.

Gwen sat back down and looked at the stars a while longer.

ELI STOOD on the other side of the tree line and watched Gwen. He felt like a Peeping Tom, but this was *his* yard and *his* gazebo—even though he'd built it for her.

He couldn't make himself leave. His mind was full of questions; his body hummed for hers. Things were changing, and he could only hope they were sliding his way this time.

Her mind was almost seduced. She was questioning her bad memories and longing for more good ones. Now Eli had to fulfill his promise of showing her Pine River through his eyes. Without the tint of sadness she always put between her and this place, Pine River could seduce a saint.

When she'd swayed toward him, lips parted, eyes slumberous, he'd barely been able to stop himself from taking everything she offered. If he had, the game would have been over before it had even begun.

So he'd kissed her brow, as a good friend would, and tried not to smile at the disappointment that flooded her eyes. Each step had to come from her, even though they already lived in him. Need would lead to want, would lead to love and then forever. If he could only keep himself from touching her too soon the way he wanted to.

Gwen's sigh drifted to him on the wind, and this time Eli let his smile break free. He could sense his dream hovering at the edge of night. He could smell her on his skin; he would walk with her in his sleep. Because as he'd told her, nothing had changed here, and Eli had always been able to sense Gwen, because she lived in his heart.

As if she could hear him, or feel him, too, she turned and stared directly at the place where he lurked. "Eli?"

Her voice was a whisper, yet he heard it clearly through the night. He stepped back, one step and then another, until he could no longer see her shadow, smell her hair, feel her heat despite the distance. But the siren call of her voice still tempted him.

Tempted him so badly he had to go into the house and lock the door, then lean his hot forehead against the cool panel of wood and tell himself again why he could not touch her now unless he wished to lose her forever.

Eli wandered to the front of his house. A beam of light flashed across his front window—there and gone in an instant.

He stepped onto the front porch. In the distance a light searched the sky, drawing attention to an open field on the other side of town.

"Holiday Carnival," he murmured, hearing the wonder of his childhood reflected in his words, in his voice.

He'd been wondering where he could take Gwen to show her that what she remembered was wrong and what she felt was true. What could he show her that was old yet new, somewhere they had been before and could go again, a place that held their youth in its palm?

He'd been wondering—and here it was.

The door to her house closed, a far-off sound but a comfort nevertheless. She had gone to her bed and he would go to his. If they were thinking of each other when they slept and they dreamed, all the better for them both.

ELI AWOKE with the dawn to the sound of someone pounding on his door. He'd been right. He hadn't slept much, but boy had he dreamed—amazing things.

Because the pounding did not abate, only became more frantic, he hustled downstairs and answered, clothed just in his red-and-white UW shorts. Emergencies never cared if he was completely dressed or not.

The sun split the sky, sparked off the back of the baby elephant in his yard and slapped him in the face. Eli closed his eyes, squeezed them tight, then opened them again.

That was an elephant, all right.

He'd been dreaming amazing things—but not quite this amazing. Eli turned his gaze from the elephant to the bald little old man who had pounded with the force of…an elephant?

"Can I help you?"

"If yer the doctor."

"Depends what kind of doctor you need."

"Eh?" The man cupped his ear and leaned closer.

"For you or your friend?"

"Ah." He dropped his hand. "For Jimmy here. He's feelin' poorly."

"Then I'm your man." Eli stepped onto the porch. "What's the matter with him, Mr.—?"

"No mister about it. Just call me Jazz. Used to play sax down on the bayou. Before my hands went bad." He waved gnarled fingers in front of Eli's face.

"All right, Jazz. I do have a large-animal practice, but Jimmy might be a little larger than I'm used to."

"You're Dr. D., right?" Eli nodded. "Heard downtown that you know animals. Since I ain't found many elephant doctors in these parts, I'd be obliged if you'd give it a go."

Eli was always gratified when people in Pine River said good things. Small towns rarely accepted outsiders as one of their own. But Pine River had accepted him. People had been knocking on his door with their animal problems since he was young. He'd just never had anyone bring him an elephant. Life sure was fun.

"So what's Jimmy been doing?"

"He's not himself. A more gentle animal you'd never want to meet—until lately."

"He's become violent?" Eli frowned and descended the steps to the yard. The elephant wasn't leashed. He glanced at Jazz, who might stand five-foot-four and hit a hundred pounds if he fell in a lake. A leash wouldn't do much good if his elephant got an attitude. Jimmy might be little, but he was a little *elephant.*

"Not violent, exactly."

"Well, what, exactly?" Eli glanced at Gwen's house. All he needed was for her to come outside for the paper and get charged by a mad baby elephant. But her windows remained dark, the door closed tight.

The thunder of eight tiny feet approached and Eli's heart lurched. As if in slow motion, he turned toward the house, just in time to see Jake and Elwood barrel through the open front door and leap off the porch. He could almost see grins stretch their mouths when they caught sight of Jimmy.

Before he could order a halt, they skidded to a stop in front of their guest. One sniff and they started barking. The elephant lifted its trunk and Eli tensed in expectation of a dual slap for the loudmouths. Instead, Jimmy gave a ferocious snort and sprayed both dogs with a little dust—and a whole lot of something else.

"That, exactly," the old man said.

Jake and Elwood tilted their heads, looked at each other and sneezed. Then they glanced at the elephant, which no longer seemed interested in them, and with as much dignity as Eli had ever seen from them, they walked away, stopping only to sneeze on his bare feet as they went by.

"So what do you think, Doc?"

"I guess I'd better take a closer look."

"Sure. He's all snorted out now. Should be safe."

Eli approached Jimmy. He stared at the elephant, stumped. A nose test—for heat and dryness—like he'd do on a dog, wouldn't work very well with that nose. How did you check for fever in an elephant? He didn't know, but he did know the best way to get close to a strange animal.

"Hey, big guy," Eli said quietly. "You're not feelin' too good, huh?" Eli reached out and rubbed his knuckles between Jimmy's eyes. The elephant's gray-brown skin was covered with coarse hair and scratched Eli's fingers.

Jimmy contemplated Eli. He appeared sad. But then, so had all the elephants Eli had ever seen. They reminded him of bloodhounds. He'd never met a chipper bloodhound.

Jimmy lifted his trunk and Eli tensed, waiting for the shower. Instead, Jimmy wrapped his trunk around Eli's back and yanked him close, as in a hug.

"Well, if that don't beat all. He likes you. I guess what I heard was right, Doc. Animals just take to you.

Eli patted Jimmy on the head. "It's my gift," he said dryly.

Jimmy released him but continued to stand as close as he could. Eli stepped back, worried about his toes and Jimmy's occupying too close of a space. The elephant followed, so Eli kept still. Sooner or later, if he kept backing up and Jimmy kept following, Eli would be sorry.

"So the problem with Jimmy is that he snorts on people, is that it?"

"Yes, sir. Lately, whenever any kids line up to have a ride, he sprays them with whatever he can grab. Sometimes it's a lot worse than dust."

"I can imagine."

"If he doesn't cut it out, I don't know what I'm going to do. You think Jimmy's got an allergy?"

"Not unless he's allergic to kids. What have you been feeding him?"

"The usual. Hamburgers, chicken nuggets, tacos."

Eli rubbed his forehead. "Elephants are herbivores."

"I don't hold with none of that and neither does Jimmy. He's a good little elephant."

"I mean they eat plants. Peanuts, maybe."

"Right. That's why he's Jimmy. Carter, you know."

"Uh-huh. Well, he shouldn't be eating meat. He's probably got a bellyache as big as his butt. He's cranky and doesn't want sharp heels kicking him in the side."

"You think that's it?"

"Try cutting out the fast-food and see what happens. Meanwhile, I'll call a friend of mine at the Milwaukee County Zoo. Then I'll come by tonight and see Jimmy. Let you know what my friend said."

"Thanks, Doc. See you tonight."

"You bet you will."

Jazz trotted off in the direction of the open field past Denali Street, where sun sparked off the red-and-white stripes of the beer tent. Tonight polka music would fill the air and hundreds of people would try to dance beneath the canvas. Beer would fly. Popcorn would flow. Everyone would laugh. Traditions were hard to break.

"Were you talking to that elephant?"

Surprised, Eli glanced up and discovered Gwen, tousled and warm, leaning on the porch rail and laughing at him.

"Maybe I was and maybe I wasn't."

How long had he been standing in his yard, barefoot and bare chested, staring at the swaying rump of Jimmy as he walked away?

Long enough for the sun to rise completely.

"Why *is* there an elephant?" Gwen asked.

Eli walked to the edge of his yard and caught Gwen staring at his chest. She appeared very interested. Not pausing to grab a shirt hadn't been a bad idea if she looked at him like that. He pointed downtown. "What do you see?"

"Oh!" Her soft gasp of joy made him hide a secret smile. "It's a carnival."

"Yep. Are you game?"

"Don't we always go together?"

"Always did."

"Let's do it again."

"Seven o' clock?"

"It's a date. I, uh, I mean, not a date, exactly. But, um, yeah, seven is fine."

"Great."

"Look, Eli! They're testing the Ferris wheel."

Gwen sounded as excited as any child on Christmas morning. The carnival represented everything that was good about their past and this town. Gwen had always loved it.

Especially the Ferris wheel. Together they watched the wheel go round and round; Eli could almost hear the *clickety-clack*, nearly smell the cotton candy on the wind.

His stomach flopped and his heart went *pitter-pat* with both excitement and dread. If he couldn't make her see the beauty of this town and feel the magic between them at the top of the Ferris wheel in the dark of the night, he didn't deserve Gwen at all.

Would he kiss her when they reached the top? Maybe he would and maybe he wouldn't. He'd wait and see if she kissed him. He had a hunch that tonight she just might.

CHAPTER TEN

"ANOTHER DAY without disaster." Gwen finished jotting notes on the chart of her last scheduled patient.

"Speak for yourself, sister. Doc's a train wreck."

Gwen glanced up to find Nancy collapsed behind the reception desk. Her usual pin-neat braid had loosened and strands of curly hair sprouted about her face. A huge red blotch marred the center of her pristine white uniform. At least it looked like ketchup, not blood.

"Does he need pain medication?"

"He needs to be sedated, or maybe I do."

Gwen hadn't been in to see her father since breakfast. They'd been busy and she'd been preoccupied. Every moment her mind wasn't absorbed with sunstroke, poison oak, foot fungus or diaper rash, she'd been dreaming about Eli's chest.

If she didn't know better she'd think she was going through puberty again. She couldn't remember feeling such strong urges since her hormones kicked in when she was fourteen. Back then everything had felt stronger, loomed larger, seemed worse than it really was. Kisses were life altering, touches were mind-bending and dreams always seemed just about to come true.

She'd been dreaming of Eli with no shirt, then she'd looked outside, seen him fooling around with that elephant, and she'd been so entranced by all that smooth, supple, burnished flesh she'd had to get a closer look.

Thank God no one had seen her drooling but her. What was happening? She was not a flighty, foolish child. She was a trauma physician. She saw bodies every damn day.

But she couldn't remember seeing one like Eli's. Not ever.

And she couldn't remember wanting to see one again quite as badly as she wanted to see his.

"Hey, Gwen? You want to stay on this planet for a few more minutes?"

"Hmm? Oh, sorry, Nancy." Gwen's cheeks heated, and when Nancy's sharp gaze zeroed in on her face, she returned her attention to the chart she'd already finished with. "What's Doc doing?"

"Besides being a pain?"

"Isn't he always?"

"Yes, but at least when he's working, he growls as he walks by. Now he growls whenever I step foot in his room. He wants to know what's going on out here."

"What does he think? A wild orgy?"

"Interesting example. Ever been to one?"

"No!" Since she'd been dreaming of something close, Gwen put a little too much spirit into her negation. The expansion of Nancy's grin made her blurt, "How about you?"

"There's an orgy at the VFW every Monday at two. I try not to miss it." Gwen just stared at her until Nancy rolled her eyes. "Geez, Gwen, you lived here. The raciest thing in Pine River is Eli watering the lawn in his UW shorts."

"When did you see that?" Gwen narrowed her eyes. "And why were you looking?"

"I'm his friend. I'm not dead. Why? Are you jealous?"

"Jealous? Me? I'm engaged."

"But not dead. I bet Dr. Heinrich doesn't have thighs like Eli."

"Nancy!" Gwen couldn't stop herself from blushing, and Nancy grinned.

"You *have* seen Eli in his red-and-white specials."

Gwen couldn't help but return Nancy's smile. "I'm not blind or stupid."

Gwen had missed such simple girl talk. She certainly had no one she would discuss such things with in Milwaukee. Not that she had that many opportunities to stare at guys in shorts anyway. Eli had always been her best friend, but Nancy had been her girlfriend, and there were certain things you discussed only with a girlfriend—like your best friend's thighs, for instance.

"So what are you doing tonight?" Nancy asked.

"Eli and I—"

"Eli and you?" She wiggled her eyebrows, which Gwen ignored.

"We're going to the carnival together. The way we always used to."

"I'll bet you your father that tonight isn't the way it always used to be."

Gwen frowned. "Why not?"

"You've changed."

"That's what Eli said. I don't know if that's good or bad."

"He's changed, too."

"I noticed."

"And I bet he's very good."

Gwen opened her mouth and Doc's voice came out. "Nancy! I need some water."

Nancy rolled her eyes. "He sure does. Over his head."

"I'll get it."

"No, you get dressed. My date's picking me up here at eight. By then I'll have Doc fed—and medicated into oblivion if I have anything to say about it."

"You're going to the carnival, too?"

"No. Brett isn't the carnival type."

"Too bad."

"Yeah." Nancy's sigh was wistful. "I always did enjoy the carnival. But it's Friday and it's a date. I won't complain." She hurried off, her white shoes squeaking against the wood floor.

Gwen sent up a wish and prayer that her friend would find someone to love who would love her back. Nancy deserved happiness.

Just because Gwen wanted nothing to do with love

didn't mean her way was the way for everyone. Nancy was the kind of woman who loved with all her huge heart, and she wouldn't be happy until she gave that big heart to the one who needed it the most. She wouldn't care if her heart ended up cracked or even shattered for her trouble. Too bad Gwen couldn't take that kind of risk.

The day had turned hot in the way spring days often did. The approaching night would be warm. Gwen had brought one summer dress; she had no idea why.

White daisies printed against a background of sky blue, the pattern had charmed her. Though the dress was too casual for the places Lance took her in Milwaukee, she'd been compelled to buy it, but she'd never had occasion to wear the thing—until tonight.

Gwen slipped the dress on and did a pirouette in front of the full-length mirror hung on her bedroom door. All those ballet lessons had to be used for something, even if it was private dancing.

The long, full skirt twirled about her calves. She whirled the other way, catching the dress in midcircle and watching as the material fought against centrifugal force. Without realizing it, she started humming "I Feel Pretty" and that made her laugh.

When was the last time she'd felt pretty? Certainly not when she had coffee with Lance, wearing bloody scrubs, her hair sweaty and tangled. The funny thing was, she didn't feel pretty at the best restaurant in town, wearing a gold crepe dress with her hair in a French twist, either. She just felt dignified and stuffy and more lonely in the middle of a hundred people than she felt while all alone.

Gwen stuck out her tongue at the woman in the mirror. Then she removed the rubber band she'd used to keep her hair from her face while she worked and shook her head. Freed from captivity, the locks tumbled about her face, brushing her cheeks, her neck, making her shiver. For a change those tresses carried the scent of coconut shampoo instead of the acrid odor of antiseptic.

Gwen brushed stray strands from her eyes. Her hair no longer held the streams of sunshine, as it had when she was a child, but had darkened to the shade of sand. Lance often told her to get highlights, but she never had the time. Eyeing herself now, she decided her hair looked just fine as it was.

The doorbell rang. Gwen grabbed her sweater and the purse where she'd stuffed her pager. She got halfway out the door, then came back and did another twirl in front of the mirror. The sound of her own laughter was so surprising and sudden that Gwen laughed some more. If Lance could hear her, he'd think she'd gone mad. A fact she'd have to consider. Later, when she wasn't in such a good mood.

Gwen still smiled as she opened the door. Eli stared at her as if he'd never seen her before. Her smile faded, and she glanced down at herself. Everything seemed in place.

"What?" she asked.

"You're beautiful."

Her smile returned. "I do feel pretty."

"Not pretty. Exquisite. Sunshine on shadow. Water in the desert. Drowning man, life jacket—gorgeous."

"Thank you. I think. Hold on a minute, I need to tell Doc I'm leaving."

She trotted through the clinic and stuck her head in the back bedroom, where Doc and Nancy played gin, neither appearing happy about it.

"Eli and I are hitting the carnival. I won't be late."

"Must be nice to be able to run off like that," Doc growled.

"It is," she snapped, immediately feeling bad about it. What had happened to her good mood?

Doc, that was what.

"You can page me if you need me," she ventured.

"I'll be fine. Get lost."

"I'll miss you, too," she muttered.

Nancy shook her head and made shooing motions with her hands. "He'll be sleeping by nine."

"I will not."

"Wanna bet?"

The two were almost nose to nose. They seemed a lot happier that way. Gwen shut the door quietly and left them to their fun.

"Doc okay?" Eli asked as they walked toward town.

"Depends what you mean by okay."

"Rude? Cranky? Sarcastic?"

"All of the above."

"He's fine, then."

"Yep."

"It must be driving him crazy not to be able to see

his patients. Have you discussed any cases with him?''

''No. Except for Ms. Guiley, which reminds me… Why are you giving her a shot and a beer every Monday?''

''Not her. Fifi.''

''Fifi shares.''

''Really? I'd never have known that if you hadn't told me. And here I thought that psycho poodle was downing her medicine like a champ.''

''There's no need to be sarcastic. I just wonder if it's good for Ms. Guiley to drink.''

''It's not the drink she needs. It's the attention.''

''That's what Doc said.''

''He's right. She's alone. Never married, no children, her entire family is—''

''Six feet under, I heard.''

''It's sad when you think about it. An entire life, and she's visiting the vet on Monday and the doctor on Thursday. Seems like a person should have a houseful of family to sit around and tell stories about them at the wake.''

''You're being morbid.''

''Just truthful. When you go, don't you want to have them read off a long list of 'survived by' at your funeral? Survived by eight children, twenty grandchildren, various nieces and nephews.''

''I'm an only child. I won't have any nieces or nephews.''

''Whatever. I'm trying to make a point here.''

''So make it.'' Gwen's ''I feel pretty'' mood was

pretty much gone. The really frightening thing was—
she saw Ms. Guiley's life, and it was hers. She'd
thought that was the best thing. No one to mourn. No
one left behind devastated. But no one to remember
her with love, either. Why did that bother her all of
a sudden?

"I want to live a good life," Eli said. "When I go
I want it said that I loved well and was loved in return. I can't think of a better epitaph."

Carnival music drifted on the summer breeze. The
sun hung heavy in the sky, making the lights of the
Ferris wheel shine in cheery mockery. "Could we
stop talking about epitaphs and funerals?"

"No problem."

Eli grabbed her hand; Gwen clung to his. She was
very sick of all the thoughts he was making her think.
Tonight would be a night for fun—just like old
times—no more questions, no more surprise intro-
spection. At least until tomorrow.

"What do you want to do first? Eat? Ride? Polka?
No, the band doesn't start until eight, so I guess it'll
have to be one of the other two. And I need to check
on Jimmy while we're here."

"Jimmy? I don't remember a Jimmy from school.
Is that a friend of yours?"

"New friend. Big guy, hairy, long nose. A little bit
gray."

Gwen laughed. "The elephant."

"None other. Let's ride the Ferris wheel. We can
get a look at the layout and decide what we want to
eat."

"What we want to eat *first*," she said, clarifying. "I plan to eat my way through this fair."

"Which would be just like old times."

"That's what I'm counting on."

DOC HAD BULLIED Nancy into bringing the day's charts for him to read. It wasn't that he didn't trust Gwen. She knew what she was doing. He just couldn't rest easy not knowing what was happening to his patients. Call him overly responsible—everyone else did.

He couldn't find one thing out of place or incorrect. Except for her disapproval in his handling of Ms. Guiley, he and his daughter were on the same wavelength about most everything else. That was a first.

The doorbell rang. Nancy's footsteps moved toward the front of the house. From the sound of the *clippety-clop,* she wore high heels again. He'd like to get another look at those legs.

The thought made Doc scowl even more than the fact that she was all dressed up for pretty boy. He had no business hankering after the legs of his nurse, no matter how great those legs might be. No matter how long and strong, with muscles that flexed and released enticingly along her calves. Doc was a tall man and he liked a long, strong woman.

The thought made him curse. Since when had he liked any woman? And he specifically *could not* like Nancy. She was young enough to be his daughter.

She appeared at the door in another figure-hugging dress, this one bright red. She might be young, but she was definitely not a child. She hadn't been for a very long time.

"Still awake?" she asked.

He'd palmed his pill, but he wasn't going to tell *her* that. He didn't want to sleep now or he'd never sleep through the night. So he grunted noncommittally and tried to keep his treacherous gaze off parts of her he had no business looking at. It was a lot harder than he'd ever imagined.

"See you tomorrow, then."

"I'll be here."

She laughed and he glanced up, catching her smile. He couldn't help but smile back, which made hers falter. "You feel okay?"

"Nancy, we have reservations." Brett's voice came from the hall.

"I'm coming," she called over her shoulder. The face she turned back to Doc appeared torn. "You need me to stay?"

He considered lying, saying he felt funny and yes, he needed her here. But the notion was so preposterous he couldn't make himself do it. So he shook his head and waved his hand in a shooing motion. "Have fun. I'm getting sleepy already."

She didn't appear convinced. But since he never lied to her, she believed him and left. Or at least he thought she'd left. A few moments later he heard her voice, muffled and disturbing. Then a short cry of "Brett!" and a thump.

Doc grabbed his crutches, battled himself out of the bed and across the floor, then he struggled through the clinic. Sweat popped out on his forehead, but he kept hitching on his way.

"You're driving me crazy in that dress."

"Move those hands, buster, or lose them."

"Make me."

Doc did not like the sound of that. He liked what he saw when he reached the entryway of the clinic even less. Brett had those hands all over Nancy's curves and his mouth all over her neck. A rage went through Doc. He leaned against a wall, lifted a crutch and poked Brett in the back.

"The lady said, 'Move those hands.' I think she meant *off* her and not around, like you're doing."

"Doc!" Nancy gasped, her face as red as her dress.

Brett removed his hands and turned. His face flushed scarlet with anger, making him far less pretty. "Do you mind? This is private."

"I do mind. This is my house and that's my nurse."

"If you want her old man, get in line."

Nancy made a soft sound of distress and Doc lost his temper. "Get out of my house, or I'm going to hit you with my crutch."

"I'd like to see you try. You can barely stand."

"Maybe so, but I bet I can hit you if Nancy holds you down. I think she might enjoy that. Wouldn't you, Nance?"

"I think I might." She sounded stronger, not so upset or helpless. Thank God. Doc had never seen Nancy look helpless and he found he did not care for it.

"Fine. I'm leaving."

"And you won't come near her again."

The kid's chin went up. "Or what?"

"You won't have a job, for starters. I delivered the head of the PT department."

"You probably delivered his mother, too."

"Not quite. But she is a personal friend."

"Does everyone in this hick town know everyone else?"

"Pretty much. That's what makes it such a great hick town."

Brett slammed the door when he left. Doc leaned heavily on his crutches. Since when had it gotten so hard to stand up straight for five minutes? God, he was old.

"Good riddance." Doc snorted. "You sure can pick 'em, Nance."

Nancy burst into tears.

ELI AND GWEN rode the Ferris wheel, ate a foot-long hot dog, chased it with a cherry slush, then went back on the Ferris wheel to tamp everything down and make room for course number two.

The sun hovered on the western horizon, painting the sky orange, pink and blue. The breeze smelled like popcorn. The band began to play "Roll Out the Barrel."

Everything was the way it had always been, until Eli laid his arm along the back of their seat. His bare skin brushed her neck. His hip bumped hers; the warmth of his thigh in summer cotton pants seeped through her thin, spring-flowered dress and heated more than her leg. What Gwen felt was nothing like she'd ever felt before.

The wheel sped upward, and her belly lurched in the other direction. At the very top, they stopped and their carriage swayed lightly.

Gwen turned her face toward Eli, and he kissed her, right there at the top of the world.

His lips were familiar, old friends, new sensations. Or maybe old sensations. She'd kissed him before, and she'd wanted to kiss him again ever since.

Her mind became a jumble of new thoughts and old memories, her heart a tangle of new feelings and old emotions. But ever present, ever constant, was Eli. The alluring scent of his skin, the silky slide of his hair beneath her fingers, the taste of his mouth, cherries on ice, and the sound of her name on the wind.

"Gwen," he whispered, touching her face, kissing her chin.

She tugged his mouth back to hers. No more talking, no more thinking. She wanted to kiss Eli and more. Amazing.

Desperately seeking the heat of his lips, the touch of his tongue—teasing, tangling, mating. Hard, rough hands on her arms, at her waist. Why had she denied herself? When had she started to want this more than anything she'd wanted before? And how was she going to stop?

The wheel jerked back into motion and they tore apart as the world came at them from below. For a second Gwen wanted to shout, *Take me back up to*

*that place where he kissed me. That place where I
felt for the first time something I wonder if I've felt
for a lifetime.*

Eli stared at her calmly, as if what had happened
up there had never taken place. But his mouth was
wet and his lips were swollen. She could feel the
scrapes his beard had put on her chin and she liked
them. Licking her lips, she tasted him, and his eyes
went dark with secrets she longed to explore further.

But they hit bottom and the ride was over. Eli
tucked Gwen's hand into his elbow as they hurried
off the landing so the next couple could take their
place.

Once on the ground, Eli stopped and looked up at
the wheel, then down at Gwen, holding her gaze.
"See? Everything here is just the way it always was."

"Maybe it is," she agreed. "I just never noticed
before."

He smiled at her as if she'd said the most clever
thing he'd ever heard, then pulled her into his arms
for a quick hug that made her blood slow and pulse.
Before she could hug him back he released her.

"I have to see a man about an elephant." Eli held
out his hand. "Wanna come?"

Gwen slapped her palm against his. "I can't think
of anything I'd rather do."

DOC BALANCED helplessly on his crutches, unable to
reach Nancy, even had he known what to do if he
could get near her. Shake her, hug her, kiss her, love
her?

"Nancy!"

She glanced at him, her face streaked with tears, her eyes full of a misery he could not bear to see. Doc let a crutch drop. The clatter made her jump and catch her breath, but as soon as he began to totter and slip, she gave a cry of alarm and rushed forward to catch him before he fell.

She put her shoulder beneath his arm to keep him upright. Doc tried not to be distracted by the brush of her hair along his jaw and the strength of her arm around his back. He was unsuccessful. Despite the feebleness in his legs, other parts of him worked with amazing good cheer.

"I think I overdid it."

Nancy stumbled, swore, kicked her high heels, one after the other, against the wall, then hauled him toward the bedroom. Doc frowned at her bent head.

He'd given her the perfect opening, served practically on a silver platter. Why wasn't she, in her motherly way, calling him a moron and telling him all the things that were going to happen if he kept behaving badly? Then he'd tell her to mind her own business, and they could snarl at each other awhile. He'd guarantee she'd feel better once they went a round or two.

Instead, she dumped him on the bed with none of her usual gentleness cloaked by a gruff manner. Then she stood his crutches against the wall and headed for the door.

"Nancy?"

"Leave me alone, Doc." Her breath hitched. "Just leave me the hell alone."

Suddenly he didn't want her to be alone. *He* didn't want to be alone. "I-I think I've got a fever. Can you check?"

"You're the doctor. Stick a thermometer in your ear, or better yet, stick it somewhere else."

His lips twitched. That was more like the Nancy he knew. Now, if he could only get her to look at him. "Why are you mad at me? He was the jerk. Wasn't I your hero?"

She glared at him. It was a look, anyway. Unfortunately, her eyes still shimmered with tears, and his heart flopped about like a fish at the bottom of a boat.

"Come here, Nancy." He patted the bed.

Her face had a funny expression—as if she wanted to come over and sit by him, and then again, maybe she didn't. Either way, she came, grabbed the thermometer off the nightstand and sat on the bed. The mattress dipped, rolling his good leg into her better ones, then she grabbed his ear and squinted, trying to stick the thermometer into the cavity.

Doc turned his head and her fingers slipped off. Their faces were so close he could see flecks of black in the blue of her eyes. He saw something else in those eyes—something that made his stomach fishtail again, and before the thought even took solid root in his mind, he kissed her.

And she kissed him back.

CHAPTER ELEVEN

IN CHILDHOOD she'd adored him; teen years had brought respect; with womanhood came love. But Nancy had never dreamed that Doc might kiss her.

The love she'd felt for him had been like a fairy tale, something she'd known would never go further than her secret heart.

Perhaps in the darkest of night she'd wondered, but she'd never gone beyond that. Because to wonder would be to hope and there was no hope.

Then suddenly there was.

He was not kissing her brow or her cheek or her hand. He was kissing her mouth, and he was kissing her for real. A man-woman kiss that lit her body afire and made her mind swirl with forbidden things.

She had never kissed a man she loved, because she had only loved this man. So she had never known how extraordinary kissing could be. She did not want the miracle to end too soon.

Nancy touched his face, as she'd done once before while he slept. His beard scratched her fingertips, the skin beneath hot but not feverish, the curve of his jaw as familiar as her own. She'd known him most of her life, but she'd never known him like this.

He kissed like a man who had not kissed in a lifetime. Stilted, clumsy, but with a lot of enthusiasm. Nancy had been kissed by pros, but no kiss had ever touched her as deeply as this kiss she'd never expected to have.

The sweetness, the novelty, the soul-crushing beauty, made tears burn her eyes and seep over her cheeks. When his mouth left hers and planted frantic kisses on her face, the drops dissolved against his lips and he slowly pulled away.

She opened her eyes, joy in her heart, passion sizzling in her blood. The horror in his gaze turned everything to ash.

"Doc?" she whispered, uncertain what she was asking.

He flinched at the word and pushed her away. She grabbed his hands and refused to go. But he turned his head on the pillow and stared out the door toward the empty clinic.

"I don't know what got into me. A mistake. Pain and drugs and not enough sleep. Forgive me."

Forgive?

Mortification took the place of newborn hope. Nancy let Doc go and stood. She'd always been terrified he would discover how she felt and then she'd have nothing—not even his respect. But she had not kissed him and ruined everything. *He* had kissed *her!*

Doc had been kissing Nancy Davidson as if he couldn't get enough of the taste of her mouth or the flavor of her skin. Or had he been thinking of someone else all along? The thought probed her mind like a pricker stuck in the thumb. She should not ask, but she had to know.

"Were you thinking of her?"

He turned back, confusion on his face. "Who?"

"Betsy."

He winced and closed his eyes as if in pain. "No," he whispered. "I wasn't. God forgive me."

She was glad to hear it but not so glad that he seemed horrified even more at the thought that he'd been kissing Nancy and *thinking* of Nancy.

"Why is that so terrible?"

His sigh was long, full of sadness, and he kept his eyes closed as if he could not bear to look at her. Nancy's heart cracked just a little. "Sometimes I can't even see her face anymore. I try and I try, but it's just not there."

"I would think that's normal. What isn't normal is throwing your life away because someone died."

His eyes snapped open, the confusion and sadness gone, replaced by a burning anger that made Nancy step back.

"What do you know about it?" he shouted. "Have you ever loved anyone so deeply you would do anything for them? Die for them, cry for them, mourn them forever?"

"I love someone so much I'd live for him. Is that enough?"

"Maybe for you." He stared at her, considering. "Let's just forget this ever happened. Go back to the way things have always been. Please?"

He had no idea she loved him. She should be

thankful. Things could go back to the way they'd been if she only pretended nothing had changed— even though everything had.

Nancy shrugged. "No problem. I can forget it if you can."

Later that night in her large, empty bed, Nancy discovered another thing she'd do for the one she loved. Lie for him.

Because she'd never forget his kiss.

Never.

THE MOMENT Jimmy saw Eli, he trumpeted a hello and stuck his nose through the bars of his traveling trailer. Eli held still while the end of Jimmy's snout wiggled and searched, before coming to rest on Eli's shoulder with a snuffling sigh of contentment. It was good to be loved.

"Another conquest?" Gwen asked. "Is he going to end up in the menagerie shed, too?" Eli glanced at her and shrugged. "You can't be serious, Eli. That's an elephant, not a hawk or a cat or even a skunk. It's an el-e-phant. He'll get bigger."

"I'm aware of that. But if he gets dumped by the carnival, I'll have to take him."

"That's what I love about you." She took his hand. "You are every dog's best friend."

"Jimmy's an elephant."

Jimmy's nose twitched in Gwen's direction, then sniffed along her neck, dipped into her dress, played with her hair. "I'm aware of that."

The elephant's nose traveled down their arms,

curled around Eli's and yanked his hand away from Gwen's. "I think he's jealous," Eli said.

"Of me?"

She sounded so surprised Eli frowned. Hadn't he just kissed her senseless at the top of the world? Wasn't *she* the one hanging on to *his* hand? He'd thought those were good signs, and obviously Jimmy had, too. Trust Gwen to burst his bubble without even trying.

"Hey, Doc, thanks for comin' by." Jazz leaned against the trailer.

"How's he been?"

"The same. I didn't put up the sign to give rides. The kids were mighty disappointed, but I didn't want to take any chances. I let him rest, and you know what? He blew a big pile of—" Jazz glanced at Gwen and shrugged "—unmentionables at some of the kids hanging around. My boss is fit to be tied."

Eli nodded. "I talked to my friend at the zoo. He agreed with me about the diet. He also thought it best to give Jimmy a little time off. Maybe his stomach will settle and he'll be himself again. In the meantime, keep Jimmy away from unmentionables."

"I don't think I can, Doc. He makes his own."

Gwen choked, but when Eli glanced her way, her face was innocent, though her eyes danced. Then her pager went off like the shrill of a telephone just past midnight. Everyone jumped, even Jimmy.

She glanced at the message, then at Eli. Her skin paled. "It's Ms. Guiley."

THE AMBULANCE pulled way, the siren conspicuously silent. The red twirling light did not twirl. Ms. Guiley did not need to hurry anywhere. She was already there.

Gwen had arrived too late. She and Eli had done CPR until the ambulance came. The paramedics had looked at her as though she was crazy when she'd insisted on continuing for another ten minutes. Ms. Guiley had been down for over half an hour, and who knows how long she'd been lying in her front yard before that.

Finally Eli had put his hands over Gwen's, stilling them from their near-frantic thrusts against Ms. Guiley's frail chest. "Let her sleep now. She's earned some peace."

Gwen had nodded and pronounced Ms. Guiley dead—at 10:32 p.m. on a beautiful Wisconsin night.

The crowd she hadn't noticed drifted back to their homes. A few people murmured apologies or praise. Gwen didn't acknowledge either one.

She sat down on Ms. Guiley's steps and put her head in her hands. Eli plopped down beside her and placed his arm around her back, tugging her close to his side. "You didn't fail, Gwen."

"Then why is she dead?"

"You know why."

"Her heart gave out. I just saw her yesterday."

"And she was fine, wasn't she? What does that tell you?"

"I screwed up?"

"No. It was her time. You were here within

minutes of her being found. If you and I couldn't stop it, it wasn't meant to be stopped.''

''You really believe that.''

''Yes, I do.''

''Then what good is medicine at all if what's supposed to happen happens? I went into medicine because of my mother. She wanted me to save the world.''

''You can't save the world, Gwen. You can only bandage your little corner.''

''This from a man who's saving elephants.''

''He walked into my corner.''

Gwen rubbed her forehead. She was so confused. Ever since she'd come home nothing was the way she'd believed it to be—most disturbingly, medicine and Eli.

''I thought if I was the best damned doctor around maybe some other little girl's mother wouldn't die on her. But you're saying none of that matters.''

''I didn't say medicine doesn't matter. I said that once you've done all you can, and the inevitable happens, then that's what was meant to be.''

''I don't know if I can accept that.''

''It doesn't matter if you accept it or not. It is.''

Gwen pushed her hair, damp with sweat from performing CPR for forty minutes, from her eyes. Her dress was grass stained where her knees had ground the cheery material into the lawn while she tried to save Ms. Guiley. She'd never wear this dress again, anyway. What did it matter?

''We'd better go in and see if we can find the name

of her lawyer. Get things rolling.'' Eli stood and held out a hand to Gwen.

Gwen took it. She'd been doing that a lot lately, and she had to wonder why his hand in hers now seemed as natural as breathing, or kissing him. "I guess someone has to."

"That's my girl." He squeezed her fingers and for a minute she wondered what it might feel like to truly be Eli's girl.

The thought dissolved when they entered Ms. Guiley's house and sadness overwhelmed Gwen. She might be able to bear losing Ms. Guiley. She'd barely known the woman, though she'd liked her well enough. But losing Eli?

That would destroy her—a chance she wasn't willing to take.

Doc was still mentally berating himself when the front door opened. He figured Gwen would go directly upstairs, thinking him asleep, and that was fine. He certainly had no desire to chat right now—unless it was to call himself a fool.

He was surprised when Gwen appeared in his doorway. "Doc?"

She didn't whisper, as if to see if he was awake yet. She spoke loudly, as if she planned to wake him up regardless.

"What's the matter?"

"I'm going to turn on the light, okay?"

Doc grunted. He could only hope she didn't want to talk about her mother, her childhood, his life or any of the other myriad topics he was not in the mood for right now. Up to and including his sudden attraction for a woman who was young enough to be his child.

A curse slipped past his lips when the overhead light shot on. "Sorry," Gwen murmured, and crossed the room.

Her hair was tangled and her dress a mess. He didn't like the ice-white shade of her skin or the haunted look about her eyes.

"What in hell happened to you? Did Eli get fresh?"

She gaped at him. "Eli? Fresh?"

"You're right. The boy has more class than that."

Her brow wrinkled, but he waved away her inevitable questions. Let Eli handle his own problems. "What's so important it couldn't wait until morning?"

"This." She held up an envelope with Steven Bartelt written across the front in bold, swirling letters. The handwriting and the name revealed what was inside without him even having to open it.

He leaned back against the pillow. "She's gone."

"About an hour ago. I'm sorry."

"What do you have to be sorry about? I was the one who wasn't there."

"I was. I did everything I could."

"It was her time."

"Not you, too."

He lifted his head. "What?"

"Eli said that."

Doc shrugged. "Sometimes it's just their time."

"So it was Mom's time? If that's true, then why have you been moping around for thirty years?"

"Twenty-seven," he corrected.

"Don't be a smart-ass."

"Why not, when I do it so well?"

Gwen narrowed her eyes. "I can understand why you worked so hard, why you ignored me, why you couldn't be there emotionally for anyone if you thought you'd failed to save Mom. But if it was just her time, then all this—" she threw her hands up in a gesture of exasperation "—was for nothing."

"I do not want to discuss your mother right now, Gwen."

"And that would make today different from any other day of my life *because…?*" She threw the envelope onto his lap. "For some reason that is beyond my understanding, Ms. Guiley wanted you to plan her funeral."

"I know. She told me." Doc opened the envelope and scanned the contents, which didn't surprise him but made him think some more.

When he looked up, Gwen was gone, and that was probably for the best. He thought of calling her back, but what would he say? He could only handle one crisis at a time, and sometimes not even that many.

Doc grabbed a pen and started to make notes.

THE MORNING OF Ms. Guiley's funeral the sun rose bright and hot—spring turned to summer despite the calendar that insisted spring lingered still.

Doc had planned the entire thing from his room, and he hadn't wanted any help. Not from Gwen or from Nancy. He'd kicked them both out every time they'd walked in, which was just fine with Gwen.

And it seemed to be fine with Nancy, too. She'd dropped by Saturday morning, gotten thrown out and Gwen hadn't seen or heard from her since, which was very un-Nancy.

Gwen had only seen Eli from a distance. Watering his lawn, which had proved an interesting distraction on a Saturday afternoon—a distraction that had lasted all the way through Saturday night in her dreams.

Then Sunday morning he'd loaded up his dogs and a few of the menagerie and he hadn't come back until Sunday night—with only the dogs. She'd watched from her window and wished he'd asked her to go along.

But if he had, she'd have missed the ecstasy of Mr. Bray's paronychial infection—translated, infected toenail bed. Or the agony of Mrs. Angeli's five stitches—she'd broken a glass while washing dishes. She might even have missed Mikey Barrabas and his first snotty nose, which would have been a true tragedy. Gwen was becoming quite attached to Mikey.

She was becoming attached to a lot of people and a lot of things. She needed to remember that she was only in Pine River for a few more weeks. But as the days passed, and she was drawn more deeply into a life she'd always despised, Gwen found herself wondering far too often what it was about Pine River that she'd hated so much.

When she went to the grocery store, she liked it when the cashier told her that Doc preferred tangerines to oranges. She enjoyed leaving her car in the driveway and walking everyplace. She loved having people chirp, "Hey, Dr. Gwen," as she window-shopped on Main. And when folks brought up her mother and said how much she resembled Betsy, the words didn't hurt so much anymore. In fact, they made Gwen feel as if a little bit of her mother lived on in her.

The only thing that bothered Gwen was that she hadn't had enough time to pry more memories of her mother out of Ms. Guiley. But there had to be other people in Pine River she could pester. Maybe she'd even yank a few out of Doc.

The doorbell rang at 9:30 a.m. Gwen sent a silent prayer that no serious emergency was going to keep her from the funeral.

Eli stood on the porch. His khaki slacks had a military crease, and his navy-blue shirt looked crisp enough to click. The knot on his tie was so perfect Gwen wanted to loosen it, then muss the rest of him with her mouth. She was definitely losing her mind.

"I thought maybe you'd need help getting Doc to the church," he said.

"Sure. Thanks."

"I don't need any help."

Doc stood, or rather leaned, on his crutches in the archway to the clinic. He'd managed to dress himself in the tan suit she'd brought down from his room. No black at Ms. Guiley's funeral, by special request.

Gwen had gone into Pine River's only clothing store and bought a pink dress with a full skirt. Ms. Guiley would have loved it. Gwen certainly did.

Doc was getting better at an amazing rate. Gwen might be able to leave early if he kept improving like this. The thought did not cheer her as it should.

"Maybe you don't need any help," she said, "but Eli's here, so let's use his truck instead of my car. You can stretch out your leg in the back."

Doc grunted and swung off toward the driveway, nearly knocking Eli over as he went out the door.

Eli drove to the field where the carnival had been. The rides were packed onto their flatbed trucks, but the caravan wouldn't leave until Wednesday or Thursday, depending upon where they were scheduled to bring joy and polka music next. The only structure standing was the beer tent.

"Here?" Gwen asked.

"No moss on you." Doc struggled out of the vehicle, snarling at her when she would have helped.

Gwen raised her hands in surrender and backed off. She raised a brow at Eli. "Obviously, you knew about this."

"Doc asked me to help."

For some reason that hurt Gwen's feelings. She'd been shut out, Eli let in. She shouldn't be hurt. Doc had shut her out all her life. But he hadn't let anyone else help him, either. Silly to be jealous of her best friend, but jealousy was, most often, silly.

The tent was packed. No surprise. Even if Ms. Guiley hadn't taught everyone in Pine River at one time or another, in the way of small towns everyone knew everyone, and a funeral was an occasion for a get-together—kind of like an end-of-life block party. This one looked to be bigger and better than any in recent history.

Eli and Gwen sat in the front row with Doc, who would be giving the eulogy. Onstage a portable movie screen had been set up in the center, a few feet in front of what appeared to be a VCR on steroids. At one corner stood Jazz, complete with saxophone; at the other sat an Oriental urn.

Ms. Guiley.

"What's he doing here?" Gwen whispered, even as she smiled and waved at Jazz.

"Ms. Guiley wanted jazz music," Eli answered. "No bagpipes, no organ. None of that whiny stuff. Jazz said he still had it in him to play a funeral. We lucked out—he's pretty good."

Gwen glanced at Doc, who shrugged. "Sandy wanted a celebration, not a wake."

Sandy? She'd never heard Ms. Guiley called that. But then, *Sandy* had called Doc *Steven.* Gwen had almost forgotten her father's name. No one else ever used it.

"Celebration of what?"

"You'll see."

Doc struggled over to sit on a chair directly in front of the stage. He pressed a button on a cord that led to the machine and still pictures of Ms. Guiley's life sprang onto the screen. Jazz started to play and Gwen became lost in the novelty of the celebration of a woman's life.

A much younger Ms. Guiley appeared in a dress trimmed with fringe, long beads twirling, a flask in her garter. She'd been a flapper! Slides clicked one after the other, and chuckles rose from the crowd, then outright laughter as Ms. Guiley rode a horse, a hot-air balloon, a camel.

Now that Gwen thought about it, Ms. Guiley had often disappeared during vacations. None of the children cared because they were on vacation, too. She'd traveled the world, lived several lifetimes in one. But she was always alone.

Then came the photos of the children. Ms. Guiley had saved pictures from each year she'd taught. Nearly everyone in the crowd saw themselves through Ms. Guiley's eyes. She even had a frame of Gwen and Eli, walking home, heads tilted toward each other as they shared their day. When that one appeared on the screen, she reached for Eli's hand, and his met hers halfway there.

The screen went blank. Jazz stopped playing. A microphone appeared in Doc's hand. "Everyone in this room knew Sandra Guiley. But I bet very few of you knew all that."

Murmurs of assent swept the crowd.

"She was born in Pine River. She died in Pine River. She taught because teaching was her gift. And she saw the world because…well, I'll let her tell you. This is Sandra May Guiley's eulogy, farewell letter and last will and testament all in one."

Doc pulled several sheets of paper from one pocket, retrieved his glasses from another and proceeded to read:

"'If this is being read, I'm dead. I hope I went fast and was no trouble to anyone. That's how I lived my life and that's how I want to die my death. I know I was a character. That's what I always wanted to be. A live wire. Someone who lived, who did, who dared. Chances—first, second and third—are for taking. I grabbed them whenever I could.

"'Now some of you are shaking your heads and saying, "That woman never took a chance on love, on a family or a man." And I'd say, damned right. The life I lived was the life I chose. Not the life chosen for me, by any person, living or dead.

"'I loved kids. But I knew if I had some of my own, they'd consume me as kids are wont to do to their parents. I was born to teach. I was good at it. So I taught kids—I didn't raise them. And I think I did a good job.

"'Now on to the bequests. Every physical thing I own I want sold. Build a library with that money and name it after me.'"

Out of the corner of his mouth Eli whispered, "What about—"

"'And as for Fifi, she goes to Dr. Dog. I know he's always wanted her.'"

"Hell," Eli muttered.

Gwen hid her smile and squeezed his hand. The tent filled with laughter.

"'And as for me, toss what's left off the quarry

cliffs on a summer afternoon in June. I used to watch the kids swim there, and the birds fly, then swoop. At night, when the moon shone on the water, couples would kiss and dream and hope. I traveled for adventure, and now I'm off to the greatest adventure of all, but home is home forever. So toss me off those cliffs and let me fly awhile, then I'll swoop down on the water and wait for the moon, and a part of me will always be in Pine River.'''

Silence pulsed as the last words faded. Someone in the back started to clap, and the rest of the crowd joined in. Then they all got to their feet and gave Ms. Guiley's life a standing ovation. It was the best funeral Gwen had ever been to.

When the furor died down, Doc spoke into the microphone again. ''Ms. Guiley wanted a party and we're going to have one. The tent is ours until tomorrow morning. There'll be music and dancing, food and drinks. Celebrate Ms. Guiley's life, along with her next and greatest adventure.''

Gwen watched Doc. His mouth was moving, the words came out, but his face appeared carved from stone, and she suddenly understood what Ms. Guiley had been up to in having Doc plan this particular funeral.

The life I led is the life I chose.

Had Doc chosen his life, or rather his *un*life? Or had he let circumstances dictate the life he led?

He certainly hadn't been happy, and he appeared mighty unhappy now as he stared at the back of the tent, a ferocious scowl on his face. Gwen followed his gaze all the way to Nancy, who was looking at anyone but Doc. What was with those two?

Until she'd come home, Gwen had been feeling as though life were rushing by and she was standing still. But she was living the life *she'd* chosen, wasn't she? Or was she living the life chosen by circumstances, just like Doc? Was she letting life push her around, when she should be pushing at life?

She'd run off just when she was getting interesting. To spite dear old dad? Or because she'd really wanted to be anywhere but here?

If the big-city ER was where she truly belonged, then why did she feel as if she'd just begun to live a worthwhile life, doing what she'd sworn never to do, in a place she'd believed she would always hate?

CHAPTER TWELVE

"WHAT AM I going to do with Fifi?" Eli grumbled. "She'll drive the Blues Brothers nuts."

Eli and Gwen sat at a table outside where they could still hear the music while they shared a plate of food. They'd danced several times with each other and with acquaintances as the day waned toward night.

"You could give her to some other poor sap."

"No one's that poor."

He gave Gwen a considering glance that made her shudder. "Don't look at me. My number-one rule is no pets."

"Fifi isn't a pet—she's a curse."

"I have a no-curse rule, too."

"You have too many rules."

"So you keep telling me." And so she was starting to believe, but she'd never tell him that.

"But you're not listening."

"Have I ever?"

"No. That's part of your charm."

She snorted. "Tell that to Doc."

"He knows. If you weren't so much like him,

maybe the two of you wouldn't butt heads all the time.''

''I am not like him!''

''Okay. You're not.'' He dabbed broccoli into dip and munched.

''Don't patronize me, Elijah Tecumseh Drycinski.''

Hunching his shoulders, he looked around. ''Hey, watch it. No one knows my middle name.''

''Who are you calling no one?''

''It's not my fault my father thought Sherman was one of the greatest military strategists of all time.''

''Maybe he was.''

''Yeah, tell it to Atlanta. They're still pissed.''

''Can you blame them?''

''No. I'd be mad if someone burned Pine River to the ground.''

''I wouldn't.'' But even as she said the words, she knew they were no longer true. If Pine River burned she would mourn. Once you stopped searching for things to hate, there were a whole lot of things to love.

Like the café that baked fresh cinnamon rolls every morning, rolls people stood in line for before the sun popped over the horizon. Or Tandet's Department Store, which had been family owned for fifty years and where you could still buy a girdle if you needed one. Or maybe the liquor store that also housed the weekly newspaper, or the craft store that doubled as a five-and-dime.

And if you drove out of town, there was the quarry, the bluffs, the river and miles upon miles of fields dotted with cows. The place was a Norman Rockwell painting waiting to happen, and Gwen was starting to like it.

Eli ignored her dreaming and kept on eating. She suspected he needed to fill his face quite a bit to keep up that physique.

She'd always loved being with Eli, talking with Eli, and now she liked looking at him, too. And if, in the darkest part of the night, she dreamed of touching all that smooth, supple, muscled skin, with her hands and her mouth...well, a woman deserved a secret fantasy or two.

Suddenly Eli quit eating, tilted his head and listened as the strains of a song drifted from the tent. He wiped his mouth with a napkin and stood. "One more dance and I'll take you and Doc home."

"I sent Doc home hours ago, and I don't want to dance anymore, Eli." She stuck out her stocking feet and wiggled her toes. "My feet hurt."

"Leave off your shoes. No one cares. Just one more, Gwen. It's Sedaka." He did a fancy Fred Astaire shuffle that impressed her so much she gaped. In the old days he'd have tripped over his huge feet. But the old days seemed to be gone in more ways than one. "How can you resist 'Laughter in the Rain'?"

"I never knew you cared."

"No, you didn't." He tugged her to her feet before she could question that cryptic comment and pulled her through the crowd to the dance floor.

All the songs they'd danced to earlier had been

fast—fifties rock 'n' roll, sixties whatever and seventies disco. This ballad demanded slow dancing.

Gwen and Eli fit together like spoons in a drawer. His new height complemented hers. His new grace made the dance a delight. His familiar scent both comforted and aroused her.

He wasn't doing anything particularly erotic, yet their light summer clothing created a friction that raised the temperature between them several degrees. He held her hand close to his chest. His other hand rested lightly around her back, but his thumb nestled at the curve of her rear, and with every step and dip, he caressed the sensitive skin and made her shiver. Her temple brushed his lips. His breath kissed her cheek.

"Softly she breathes," he murmured.

"And I close my eyes," she answered in time with the music.

But instead of closing her eyes, she looked into his face and caught a glimpse of something she'd never seen there before—a hunger so deep she stumbled, stopping their dance as wonder awakened within her.

"Gwen?" Eli held out his hand.

The heat in his eyes was gone. Had it ever been there in the first place? Or was she projecting onto him all the secret things she felt but was afraid to act upon?

What *did* she feel? Not love. No, that wasn't true. She loved Eli. But not like *that. Never* like that. She wanted him, though, with a strength that was almost as frightening as everlasting love.

If she touched him with passion would she ruin all they had shared up to now? She didn't think she could risk it. But if he kept touching her and kissing her—and why was he kissing her, anyway?—she didn't know if she'd be able to stop herself from touching him and kissing him, too. Which was so unlike her, Gwen didn't know what to do.

One of the old-timers, who spent his retired days drinking coffee at the café, danced by with his wife. "I see you two are together again." He winked at Eli. "'Bout time, too. We were beginning to wonder about you."

"Wonder what?" Eli muttered as the couple danced away.

"If you're gay."

"Me?" His voice cracked with surprise.

"That's what *I* said."

"Well, thanks, I think." He pulled Gwen back into his arms. "Let's finish this, Gwen."

Somehow she no longer thought he was talking about Sedaka and laughter and rain. "What did he mean—together again?"

"How should I know? I'm the one they thought was gay, remember?"

"Seriously. What was he talking about?"

"You know how we always were. Eli and Gwen. Gwen and Eli. Peas and carrots, you and me. We're together again. The old folks like things to be the way they always were."

The twist of Eli's shoulder beneath her palm set off a shout of something hot in Gwen's belly. These inappropriate reactions to her best friend had to stop, but she didn't know how to make her body obey her mind.

Someone bumped her from behind and she stumbled flush against Eli—and discovered that her inappropriate reaction was mirrored in him.

Her eyes went wide; her mouth fell open. Shock made her nerves leap. He wanted her, as a man wanted a woman. Eli, her childhood friend.

But that wasn't what made her run all the way home in her stocking feet.

What made her run was that she wanted him, too. More than she'd ever wanted anyone in her life.

EXCELLENT JOB, Dr. Destruction.

Eli stood on the dance floor and watched Gwen run. Luckily the cut of his pants disguised what she'd run from, because everyone in town was staring at him. He shrugged, grinned and a few folks laughed. He'd never felt less like laughing in his life.

Had he ruined everything before he'd even had a chance to succeed? He couldn't help how his body reacted. He had been waiting to hold her close since he'd realized she was the only woman for him.

He loved her; he wanted her; he needed her. Three out of three—why was that bad?

Eli attempted to leave the party, but it took him a while to make his way from the tent. People stopped him to say hello, to ask his advice, to shoot the breeze. By the time he picked up Gwen's shoes and drove home, stars burst brightly against the black of the night.

He stood on his lawn, watching the Blues Brothers sniff the bushes, and stared up at Gwen's window. It was dark; the entire house still. How could she sleep after what had happened between them? Unless, of course, it had only been happening for him.

No. He didn't believe that. She had trembled in his arms while they danced. Her hands had played along his shoulders, explored the muscles, absorbed his heat. She'd rubbed her cheek against his chin, cuddled against his chest, slid her knuckles along the side of his neck as she swayed with him to the music of their past.

So how was he going to get her to admit the truth? Pine River had seduced her mind—the place, the people, the essence of home. He'd thought that if he seduced her body, her heart would follow. But he loved her too much to manipulate the lust humming between, even if by doing so he could gain the desire of his soul forever.

Eli sighed, and the sound must have been mighty sad, because the heads of both dogs went up, and they trotted over to sit at his feet, staring at him with adoration. Well, at least someone loved him.

"What am I going to do, guys? No guts, no glory, the Colonel would say. No pain, no gain." The dogs cocked their heads, one to the left, one to the right, listening as dogs do. "Only cowards don't take chances. But I think this is a chance I'm too much of a coward to take. I'd rather lose her than hurt her. So call me a fool."

Elwood snotted on his knee. Jake snuffed on his shoes. Their idea of calling him a fool, Eli guessed. What would he do without them? Less laundry.

Eli went inside, the dogs at his heels. As soon as they crossed the threshold, they bolted up the stairs. Eli shrugged and followed more slowly.

Stepping into his room, he reached for the light, then froze with his finger on the switch. The shadow of a woman spread across his floor. He followed the specter to the window, where Gwen stood in silhouette, flanked by his dogs.

"Out," he snapped, and the Blues Brothers whined a plaintive chorus, but they went.

Gwen continued to stare out his window toward hers. She'd changed out of her dress and now wore loose cotton trousers and what looked to be one of Doc's old work shirts.

"Something wrong?" he asked. He could not recall her ever being in his room at night, though he'd dreamed of it often enough.

"I'm not sure." She leaned her head against the glass. "You say everything's the same, that I'm different. But everything feels different—the town, the people…"

"And?"

"You." She lifted her head, but she didn't turn around. "You're different, Eli. And I don't know what to do."

"Why do you have to do anything? Why can't we be the way we always were?"

"Because we aren't and you know it. You can pretend everything is the same, but then, why do you keep kissing me?"

"You don't like it?"

"I didn't say that. But best friends don't kiss the way we've been kissing."

"You want me to stop kissing you?"

"Quit answering my questions with questions!" she cried. "It's not that I want you to stop kissing me. I want *me* to stop wanting more than kisses. But I can't. There's something else between us now. New feelings—or maybe they're old and I just never noticed."

Eli caught his breath. Sometimes a path opened and all you had to do was walk down it.

He crossed the room and stood close enough to feel her heat. But he didn't touch her. Not yet.

"What do you feel?"

"Besides confused?" She shook her head and her hair brushed his mouth. His body hardened in an instant. He clenched his hands to keep them from her. "I want you, Eli. It's insane, but I do. I can't think past wanting you. And though it should feel wrong, somehow it doesn't. It feels more right than anything I've felt in a long, long time."

He closed his eyes. Was this the answer to his prayer? Would making love cause her to see that she loved him? Or was this just another curse, worse than

Fifi, the dog-cat, because all Gwen would ever want was his body and never all that he had to give to her?

"Eli?" Her voice shook, and he heard the little girl he'd known long ago—needing him to be her friend then, needing something more from him now.

Eli unclenched his hands and slipped them beneath the loose hem of the shirt. Her stomach muscles leaped beneath his fingers; his body responded in kind.

She turned in his arms, trepidation in her eyes. "Am I crazy to think you want me, too?"

He shook his head, not trusting himself to speak for fear he'd blurt all his secrets and ruin everything for always.

And Gwen, being Gwen, understood and kissed him for the first time in the room where he'd dreamed of her for what seemed like a lifetime.

GWEN COULD NOT believe she'd sneaked into Eli's house, using the key in the fake rock that Katie always kept on the left side of the porch. As if everyone in Pine River didn't know that everyone else kept those unsecret rocks. But then, who in Pine River would use the spare key for nefarious purposes? And if a stranger was ever seen playing with a person's secret rocks, well, the neighbors would have Sheriff Hardstadt over in a heartbeat.

So she'd used the key and stood in Eli's room and tried to figure out what on earth was happening to her. She'd planned to talk to him, as they'd always talked. But the moment he'd walked into the bedroom her body had turned liquid, and she'd been unable to remember what she'd wanted to say. She certainly hadn't planned to stand there and boldly state she wanted him.

Had she?

Eli had said lust was not love and that was good. Did she dare reach for what she should not touch? If they changed what was between them from friendship to something deeper, would they lose the most important thing they'd ever known?

She had no idea and she couldn't worry about it now. Because she was kissing him as she'd never kissed another man before. Most likely tomorrow would prove this the biggest mistake of her life, but right now she had to have Eli or die.

She'd thought he'd be gentle; she'd thought he'd be tame. She'd been wrong about a lot of things since she'd come home, most of them having to do with Eli. This was one of them.

She'd barely touched her mouth to his, when he lifted his hands from her stomach to her face, tilted her head and kissed her more thoroughly than he ever had before. He kissed her roughly, but he held her gently.

He was Eli on the inside, yet a passionate stranger in her arms. The merging of the boy she'd always known and the man who couldn't seem to kiss her deeply enough made all her doubts disappear. This was meant to be—maybe only once—but meant nevertheless.

The tie on her pants loosened and they fell, tangling

at her feet. Eli tore his mouth from hers and followed them, dropping to his knees and pressing his open mouth to the skin just above her panties.

He rubbed his cheek along the soft skin of her belly. The rasp of his beard made her tremble, then his mouth traced a path to her hip, teeth scraped along bone. Arousal shuddered through her, and her hands clenched on his shoulders, holding him close, never wanting him to go.

He continued to do innovative things with his mouth until her knees went weak. As if he could sense her need, he stood. His face, haunted by her, shadowed with the night, was the face of a man she'd never seen before. Maybe because she'd never seen such passion in Eli's eyes.

He reached for the buttons on her shirt, fumbled a bit, mumbled a curse. She smiled. That was more like the Eli she knew. Reaching up, she touched his hands, shook her head, then released the buttons, one by one, until the shirt hung open. His gaze heated as the material brushed her breasts and her nipples hardened.

"Now you," she whispered.

She'd been dying to touch the body he'd grown into while she'd been away. She'd seen his skin shining in the summer sun; his chest had been the star of her most recent dreams. But having the rippling muscles and bronzed flesh bared right in front of her nose was more than Gwen could stand.

Forget about touching. She had to taste.

Following his lead, she dropped to her knees, putting her mouth to the ridges of his belly, running her tongue between the ripples. When he would have backed away, she grabbed his hips and held him still, trying some of his innovations the other way around as she worked her way up.

She learned the contours of his chest with her lips. Solid muscles; soft smooth skin; his nipples were flat, the tips hard. He tasted like summer sun and salt wind. She'd like to spend a lifetime—or at least a few days—learning all the secrets of his body using only her mouth.

"Gwen," he moaned. "Too fast. Slow down."

His fingers fisted in her hair, holding her closer, proving his words a lie, even if he didn't know it himself. She left his chest behind, tasting his collarbone, nibbling the vein in his neck as she palmed his arousal. The catch of his breath made her lips curve along his chin before she stepped back and tangled her fingers with his.

He looked dazed. A purely female sense of satisfaction rippled through her, and she tugged him toward his bed. Half-afraid he would put a stop to the madness, she swallowed a sigh of relief when he followed.

She would have no idea how to seduce a man. She'd never cared one way or another about sex. Take it or leave it had been another rule of hers. But right now, if Eli decided to leave, she would need to think quickly about how to take.

She lay back on the crisp, military-cornered sheets and her shirt fell open, baring her to his gaze. He looked at her so intently and so long his stare was like a physical touch along her sensitive skin.

He glanced around his room, as if he wasn't sure where he was. "Eli?" His gaze came back to her face and she smiled, then held out a hand for him. "Don't leave me here all alone."

The heated expression she'd seen beneath the carnival tent returned, starker and hungrier than before. He ignored the gentle invitation of her hand, covering her body with his and putting his mouth where his eyes had only touched.

She would never have thought Eli anything but a gentle man, and she was surprised to find she did not want him to be gentle. He chased her up a peak, made her mindless with only his mouth and lips and teeth, then he yanked off the remainder of her clothes with impatient fingers. He learned her shape with callused hands. His clothes disappeared as quickly as hers, and any thoughts of taking things easy and slow faded as she discovered the new body that housed the soul of her dearest friend.

The upstairs room had been hot; now the air turned steamy. Their skin became slick, adding new sensations to the ones they'd already discovered.

They lay body to body, man to woman, hard to soft as he raised himself up on an elbow. The movement pushed him more firmly against her and made it difficult for her to think. All she could do was feel and need and want something that only Eli could give her.

His chest heaved, rubbing against the sensitive

peaks of her breasts. She shifted, empty and aching, lifting to him, inviting him inside without words.

He shoved the damp, tangled hair from her eyes. "Gwen, are you sure?"

She groaned. She'd always loved talking to Eli, but *not now*. "If you stop, I will kill you."

"I don't think it'll come to that." He moved as if to leave her, and a small cry of distress erupted from her mouth as she clung to him.

"Don't. Don't go. Please."

Was that her? Begging? She bit her lip and he kissed her eyebrow. "I just need to get something. To protect you. All right?"

Protect her? From what? She'd never felt more safe or secure in her life.

Then what he had said dawned on her and she blushed. She had been thinking of nothing but him inside her. No future, no past, no consequences, nothing but now, nothing but them. Foolish, irresponsible, idiot.

Which just proved that when you lay naked with the man of your most recent dreams, every rule you'd ever lived by went out the window. And the man who had told her she had too many rules was the one making sure she didn't break one by accident.

She didn't trust herself to speak. Instead, she merely nodded as his lips slid along her cheek. He was gone a second and back just as fast, but while he was away her arms felt bereft and her skin cooled— a reminder of the loneliness that had haunted her, except when he was near.

She hated the crinkle of the foil packet, the clinical *click* that followed, but she would hate being pregnant more. Wouldn't she?

Her conscience didn't answer and she didn't have time to question why not. Because questions were for later, along with the doubts and recriminations. Now was for him, for her, for them, and she turned herself over to the mysterious passion that had been between them since she returned. Perhaps even longer.

"Look at me," he whispered.

He pushed into her, slowly, drawing out the moment, holding her gaze, as if he wanted her to know he was becoming a part of her body, just as he'd always been a part of her mind and her heart.

Staring into his eyes as he touched her more deeply than anyone else ever had made what was happening between them more than sex, and a spark of panic ignited. More than sex? What did that mean?

But the spark was doused by the passion his movements aroused; the questions about what this might mean fled in the wake of questions more urgent.

How could he know just the way to touch her, to kiss her, to stroke her, when she did not even know herself?

He brought her to completion once, and while she was still quivering and shaking with the force of her response, he whispered against her skin, tasted her mouth, her neck, her breasts.

His face in the moonlight was intense, his eyes closed as he listened to his body and hers. She reached up, wanting to touch the expression she saw there, needing to feel the fierceness of that desire against her palm.

His eyes opened and it was as if she stared directly into the most secret part of him—a part not even she had ever seen before.

"Say my name," he ground out, desperation tinged his voice.

"Eli," she said, and he caught his breath. She stroked the cords of tension in his neck, ran her fingers over his shoulders and down the bulging muscles of his arms. "Eli, Eli, Eli."

He pushed inside her, farther and deeper. She pulsed to the beat of a heart. His? Hers? Who cared?

Together this time, they went over the edge. As their breathing evened out and their bodies cooled, he murmured, "Damn, Gwen."

And she smiled into the darkness of their night.

ELI DIDN'T KNOW what to say, so he kept quiet after his first muttered expletive. He had meant to show her his love with his body and not his big mouth. He'd wanted to love her gently, completely, let her know of his heart without saying a word.

So what had he done? Put his ravening mouth all over her in ways he'd only read about. Had hot, sweaty sex on the bed of his youth, where he'd dreamed of her in ways he could never, ever say. Then been unable to find release until he'd begged her to say his name because of an adolescent fear that she didn't realize it was Eli making her come.

Which was silly. She'd said she wanted *him. Eli.*

She had known what she was doing. So had he. But she had not known why he was doing it.

How was he going to tell her he loved her after he'd taken her as if what was between them was anything but love?

Gwen shifted and Eli tensed, waiting for her to shove him away and run for home. Instead, she made a soft sound that reminded him of Cleo when he rubbed under the kitten's chin. Eli frowned. Something touched the hair at the back of his neck and he jumped.

"Sh," Gwen murmured, her breath blowing past his cheek, making him shiver. Then she ran her fingers through his hair, playing with the curls at his nape and the waves over his ear.

He moved so he wasn't crushing her anymore, and her hand flew to his hip, curving around him, holding him near. "Don't go. Not yet."

"Where would I go? This is *my* room."

"Mmm. All the times I looked into your room from mine, talked to you while you lay on your bed and never thought of anything like this. Silly me."

He experienced a moment of discomfort. She was obviously attracted to his new body, just as Candi had been. She probably thought he was an incredible stud, since he'd just performed to heights he'd never even imagined. But that was because he loved her more than life itself, and he'd wanted her forever it seemed—while her desire for him was as new as his extralarge shirt size.

"You're attracted to my body." He heard the disappointment in his voice. Why should she be any different? It wasn't as if he'd wooed her with love. He'd lured her with desire.

Gwen arched back so she could see his face. "Of course. I'm not blind. You're beautiful, Eli. But you're beautiful everywhere—both inside and out. I'm not the kind of woman who has affairs based on appearance."

"Is that what we're doing? Having an affair?"

"Aren't we?"

He sighed. "I think we need to talk, Gwen."

"No," she answered too quickly, as if she wanted to stave off talk of anything serious. "Don't ruin this with talking. Don't take it apart and analyze it. Let me just feel for once in my life. What we have between us is special. Can't you feel it, too?"

Her gaze searched his face and there was such earnest hope in her eyes he could only nod. Was she feeling the magic of them, or the magic of lust? And did it matter so long as she was feeling something for him other than camaraderie?

He could not believe Gwen would be his lover for weeks on end, then coldly leave to marry another man. If he did what she asked and spent the rest of the month in her bed, or rather his, would she see that what they had was love and not lust?

He had believed he would do anything to make her love him. Was that belief a lie?

"Never mind," she whispered. "It's okay. I've never felt anything like this before in my life—"

"Never?" His heart lifted. If she'd never felt like

this before that was because she wanted him *and* she loved him. She just didn't know it yet.

"Never." Gwen trailed her fingers down his cheek and his heart was lost all over again. "Until you, Eli."

"Tell me what you want."

"Can't we just have this for now?"

Because *this* for him was love, he said, "Yes."

Then he showed her how he felt all over again.

CHAPTER THIRTEEN

DOC HEARD GWEN slip in just before dawn for the third day in a row. All these late nights, or early mornings, could only mean one thing. She'd finally seen Eli as something more than a playmate. Or maybe she'd finally figured out that there were better things to play than doctor—if you were playing with the right person.

Doc believed Eli was the right one for Gwen, but he wasn't quite so sure if Gwen was the right one for Eli. Since he *loved* his daughter and *liked* the kid next door, he would keep his mouth shut and hope everything worked out Eli's way.

Because Eli's way would keep Gwen in Pine River, and even though they'd never gotten on as well as they should have, Doc wished he could have a second chance for a relationship with his child. The only way such a thing would happen was if she stayed here longer than a blasted month and didn't marry that prick from the city.

How did he know the guy was a prick? What guy named Lancelot wasn't?

Doc closed his eyes, tried to sleep. It worked as well tonight as it had every night since...

Since he'd kissed Nancy and felt alive for the first time in nearly thirty years.

"What kind of fool am I?" he muttered.

Old fool, worst kind.

His conscience was a pain in the ass.

Ever since they'd agreed that the kiss had never happened, Nancy had acted like a lemon was stuck in her craw. Not that such behavior was any different than usual, but for some reason her sarcasm stung now where before he'd relished the battles.

Doc finally fell asleep after the sun came up, and when he awoke he felt no more rested than when he'd gone to bed. He could hear Gwen, Nancy and one of his patients in the clinic.

Since he could not stand to sit one more day on his sickbed and listen to the world pass by, he got dressed and crutched his way into the exam room.

"Just what do you think you're doing?" Nancy demanded.

Doc took a chair and hoped the sweat on his brow would not drip down his face and prove just how hard it had been for him to drag his sorry butt in here. "What does it look like, genius? Observing. Consulting."

Gwen raised a brow at him over the head of Johnny Kirkendal. "Did I call for a consult?"

He ignored the question. "I see Johnny's here again. Where's his mom?"

"She said she'd return in twenty minutes."

Doc coughed. Mrs. Kirkendal was no dope. "What is it this time?"

"I'm taking out his stitches. Wanna help?"

"Not in this lifetime." Doc sat back with a smirk, waiting for the entertainment to begin.

Nancy shot him a glare. She knew what was going to happen. Johnny practically kept them in business, and the kid had never gotten the concept that sitting still and being cooperative made things go a whole lot faster.

The first touch of the scissors to Johnny's head set off a wail much louder than the boy should have been capable of making. Since Doc had heard it all before, he didn't jump. Gwen did.

Nancy grabbed Johnny's flailing hands. Unfortunately, Johnny's head was thrashing at the speed of light. "Johnny? Johnny! This won't hurt. It'll only take a second if you relax."

But Johnny wasn't going to listen. Johnny was no dope, either.

"Doc." Nancy scowled at him as she kept Johnny pinned down. She'd learned years ago that to let Johnny go was to see the last of Johnny.

He shook his head. He wanted to see what Gwen did about this before he stepped in and prescribed the usual.

His daughter scowled at the howling, thrashing child. Doc could almost see her brain going *tick-tock*. Her gaze flicked to his. "Tell me you don't tranq him every time he needs his stitches removed."

"Okay, I won't tell you."

"Doc!" She looked horrified. *Good girl.*

"He does *not* tranq the kid." Nancy was disgusted.

She had been disgusted a lot lately—whenever she talked to him.

"Restraints?" Hope raised Gwen's voice.

"Nope."

"What then?"

"What is your recommendation, Doctor?"

Nancy grunted as one of Johnny's fists broke loose and hit her in the chest. "Would one of you be a doctor, Doctor?"

Doc ignored her, which was increasingly hard these days now that he knew her mouth tasted like sin in the rain and she smelled like seduction to a very old man. And if he told her those things, she'd kick him where the sun did not shine.

"What would you do if you were in your fancy, schmancy hospital?" he asked his daughter.

"Kids who come in my door need tranquilizers, if they're even conscious."

"You've never had a kid in this situation?"

"Nope."

"Improvise."

"Now," Nancy snapped.

For a minute Gwen looked lost. Then her gaze sharpened and she smirked at Doc. "Nurse, what is the usual course of action for this patient?"

Good call, Doc thought. *When in doubt ask the nurse. She always knows everything.*

"Bribery, Doctor."

"Of what kind."

"A sucker for every stitch removed without complaint or movement."

Gwen's mouth flattened. "Nice, Doc. Sugar the kid up for Mom. Wreck his teeth for the dentist."

"It's my responsibility—make that yours—to get the stitches out. It is Mom's responsibility to ration the candy."

Shaking her head, Gwen leaned over Johnny. "Okay, kid, you win. Sucker for every stitch."

Johnny stopped screaming and thrashing, as if the off switch had been thrown. Doc shrugged when Gwen glared at him. "Treat the person beneath the patient."

"You're beginning to get on my nerves." Gwen snipped quickly and expertly at a now stiff-still Johnny Kirkendal.

Doc glanced at Nancy. "That's what they all say."

GWEN COULDN'T REMEMBER living a happier week in her entire life. If she didn't think about the future but kept her mind focused on the here and now, everything was perfect.

Since Ms. Guiley, no one had died on her, and she'd stopped expecting anyone to. No one had even gone into arrest, something that happened on a daily basis in her ER, and though she'd handled everyone with calm professionalism, her own heart always pumped like a freight train whenever she tried to bring someone back from the great beyond.

She liked her patients. She didn't even mind Doc "consulting," though it seemed to drive Nancy nuts. Go figure. The woman dealt with him all the time and *now* he bothered her.

She and her father were getting along, working together and she was learning things from him that she would never learn from anyone else. Because no one else had been a doctor as long, or as thoroughly, as Doc.

Then there was Eli. He added a new dimension to every facet of her life. They shared their days as they always used to, but now that they shared their nights and their bodies, what they had went deeper than before. She reveled in how special their relationship was and tried not to look any further than the next moment so she wouldn't have to dwell on what in hell she was doing.

Gwen cursed and walked to the window. She was done with scheduled patients for the day. Doc was taking a nap. Nancy had growled something about needing a drink and banged into the kitchen.

Eli and the dogs were outside. He'd picked up Fifi yesterday from the neighbor who had been watching her since Ms. Guiley's death, so now there were three. Plus an elephant.

Elephant? Gwen hurried outside. Had Jazz left Jimmy on the doorstep?

As if he sensed her, Eli looked up the moment she stepped onto the walk. His smile made her face heat. She knew exactly what he was thinking, because she was thinking the same thing. Last night had been better than the night before, which had been better than the night before that. If this kept up they were going to kill each other—or worse.

At her approach Jimmy lifted his trunk, and Gwen

stopped dead between her house and Eli's. Then Jazz came around the corner with a bucket of water.

"It's okay," he called. "Jimmy's reformed."

Gwen shot a glance at Eli, who nodded. "My diagnosis seems to have been correct. Jimmy is a happy little elephant. He and Jazz just stopped to say goodbye."

"I thought the carnival left last week."

"It did. But Jimmy and I hung around to make sure he was cured. Now that he is, we'll join the others. We're scheduled to do the Polish Festival in Wannakazi and we sure wouldn't want to miss it."

"I'd imagine not."

Jimmy sucked water into his nose, then tossed some over his back. Gwen flinched, but the resulting spray on the wind felt nice beneath the blazing sun.

The Blues Brothers came tearing down the grass strip between the houses. Jake had Fifi in his mouth. She didn't seem to mind. She'd stopped yowling whenever they were near, and she'd slept curled up between the two of them last night. It was weird.

But the strangest occurrence had happened that morning. A cat had walked right through the yard, practically beneath the noses of the Blues Brothers, and they had only looked at each other, then turned back to Fifi. Perhaps their cruising days were done— as long as they never figured out that Fifi wasn't really a cat.

The dogs stopped, and Jake placed Fifi gently on the ground. Then all three barked at the elephant. Or rather, two barked and one howled, like a treed cat.

Jimmy turned a morose eye on the trio. Even though Jazz insisted the animal felt better, he still didn't look like the happiest camper. Until he shot a stream of water at the dogs and all three went yipping and yowling back where they'd come from.

Jimmy raised and lowered his head as if acknowledging applause, and there was a glint in his eyes that said he'd been planning that for a long time. In that moment, Jimmy looked very happy.

"Dr. D., I can't thank you enough for helping me with Jimmy. Wherever I go, I'll tell everyone to take any problem animal to you."

"Goody," Eli murmured, loud enough for only Gwen to hear. To Jazz he shouted, "Have a good trip."

The little elephant and the littler man disappeared from Pine River—for at least a year.

Left alone, Gwen and Eli stared at each other. They did that a lot. She'd been looking at Eli nearly all her life, but looking at him was so much better now that she knew what he looked like in nothing at all.

His gaze dipped to her lips, and before he could raise it again to her eyes, she went into his arms and they kissed—long and deep for the entire town to see, if they wanted to. Gwen didn't care. All she seemed to care about these days were her patients and Eli. And she wasn't going to feel bad about that—for at least another two weeks.

A car honked and Eli raised his head slowly, glancing at the street. He frowned and his eyes followed the car as it continued on. Gwen glanced that way too, but she had no idea whose car was whose in Pine River but Eli did.

"Joker?" she asked.

"Candi."

"Hmm." Jealousy reared its ugly head, surprising Gwen. She had no right to feel as though she wanted to throttle Candi until she gasped "Uncle" and promised to leave Eli alone forever. Instead, Gwen cuddled against Eli's shoulder, content in his arms.

"Busy day?" he asked.

"The usual. You?"

He shrugged and his chest slid along her cheek, surrounding her with the scent of summer-warmed man and lemon-lime soap. She resisted the urge to unbutton his properly buttoned shirt and improperly rub her mouth along his smooth skin. Maybe later.

"I need an assistant. I can do surgery without one, but not as many as I used to. If I keep putting people off, I'll lose the business."

"To who? There isn't another vet in the county."

"There is now. In Pecatonica."

"That's twenty miles away."

"Not such a big deal for elective surgery."

"True." Eli absently rubbed her shoulders in a gesture that was becoming habitual. Gwen sighed with contentment. Eli gave the best hugs in the whole world. "Did you ever think of going to the high school?"

"I went there once. I don't want to go again."

"No, I mean talk to the principal, or a counselor, or the work release supervisor. Find a senior who relates to animals, then teach the kid what you want him to do.''

''I don't know, Gwen. I don't want some kid messing with my patients.''

She smiled against his shoulder. His obsession with his patients no longer annoyed her. Even Doc's was becoming less frustrating, because she was starting to feel it, too.

That afternoon Mikey Barrabas was coming in and Gwen could hardly wait to hold him. In a far-off corner of her mind she thought she heard a slight *tick-tock*. Damn Nancy and her mention of biological clocks. Ever since then Gwen had been hearing funny noises.

She tensed in Eli's arms. Ever sensitive to her slightest mood swing, he let her go. She returned to the subject at hand to keep her mind from the subject of *Tick-Tock* Goes My Biological Clock. ''Once upon a time you were a kid who loved animals. I bet there's at least one more like you in this town.''

''I thought I was one of a kind.''

''To me, yes. To the woof-woofs, don't flatter yourself.''

''Hey!'' he protested, but he appeared happy.

In fact, Gwen couldn't recall seeing Eli this happy ever, and for some reason that made her almost as nervous as her sudden fascination with Mikey Barrabas.

She backed away. Eli watched her. He knew she was running, but being Eli he let her.

''Gazebo at eight?'' he called.

She hesitated, wanting to say no, just to see if she could. But they had so little time left she couldn't deny him a moment.

Or maybe it was herself she could no longer deny.

NANCY SAT IN Doc's kitchen and drank Ms. Guiley's whiskey. She didn't think the old lady would mind. Especially not anymore.

She didn't know how much longer she could pretend the kiss had never happened. Doc didn't seem to be having any trouble, though. Damn him.

Nancy finished off the first shot and poured herself another just as Gwen walked in. She stopped dead and frowned. "You still here?"

"I think so."

Gwen looked at the bottle, then the shot glass, then raised her gaze to Nancy's. "Problem?"

"Not for long." Nancy toasted her and sipped.

"That's not going to solve anything."

"How would you know? Have you ever solved anything?"

"Have I done something to upset you?"

"Nope. Go on, Gwen. I know you can hardly wait to go over and jump Eli." Gwen winced. Nancy ignored it. "If I were you I wouldn't waste time talking to me."

"You aren't me and it wouldn't be a waste. I thought we were friends. Let me help."

"No one can help. Especially you." Nancy finished off her drink and reached for the bottle, but it wasn't there anymore. "Hey! Give that back."

''Not until you tell me what's wrong. If it's worthy of this bottle, I'll give it back.''

''Love stinks.''

''Isn't that a song?''

Nancy stared into her empty glass. ''Have you ever noticed that most songs are true? Think about it. 'Imagine,' now there's a song. Lennon was a prophet.''

Gwen sat at the table, but she kept the bottle well out of reach. ''You think everyone should live for today?''

''Don't you?'' Nancy glanced up.

''At the moment, yes.''

Gwen didn't look too happy about it, but Nancy was too infatuated with the idea of songs that were true to worry overly much why Gwen seemed unhappy when she was spending her nights in Eli's bed. Not that Nancy wanted to be in Eli's bed. She *would* like to be in someone else's, however, and she was just plain sick of sleeping alone.

'''Fifty Ways to Leave Your Lover,''' Nancy blurted.

''I don't like that song.''

''I'll just bet you don't. Okay, how about 'Still Crazy After All These Years.'''

Gwen raised an eyebrow. ''Paul Simon a prophet, too?''

''Damn straight.''

''Why not 'Let It Be'?''

''Never works.''

'''Love Me Tender'?''

"No Elvis. Did he write that, anyway?"

"He lived it."

"Well, I don't want to."

"No? Isn't there anyone who would make your life complete, Nancy?"

That was what she'd come in the kitchen to forget. Trust Gwen to make her remember. "Bite me."

Gwen laughed, which wasn't the reaction Nancy had been hoping for. "This is fun. What other songs are true? 'Can't Smile Without You,' 'It's a Miracle,' 'Ready to Take a Chance Again.'"

"If you continue to quote Barry Manilow, one of us is going to get hurt."

"Fine. Tell me what's bothering you, then I'll go away."

There was no way Nancy was going to admit the country-western song that was her life to her dream man's daughter.

"'Eat It.'" Nancy pushed away from the table and went looking through the cupboards. If she couldn't have the whiskey she'd find the next best thing—chocolate.

"Is that a variation of bite me?"

"No, it's Weird Al."

"A prophet if ever there was one."

Nancy returned to the table with her chocolate-dipped Oreo cookies. "I'm glad we agree."

"On something, at least."

"Don't you think love stinks?" Nancy put an entire Oreo into her mouth. Nothing ever tasted so good.

"I wouldn't know, since I've never been in love,

and I don't plan to be.'' Nancy snorted and took another cookie. ''I haven't! I won't!'' Gwen protested.

Nancy offered her the Oreos. '''Crazy.'''

Gwen took two cookies. ''You, me and Patsy Cline.''

CHAPTER FOURTEEN

NANCY STAYED in the kitchen even after Gwen had gone to rendezvous with Eli. What did she have to go home to anyway? No cat, no dog, no kids, no husband. Why had she ever thought that just being near Doc would be enough? Since he'd kissed her, nothing was enough anymore.

The television blared in his room. He'd probably fallen asleep again with it on. She'd just grab his dinner tray, hit the off button and get on home. *Yippee.*

Nancy stepped briskly into his room and froze. Doc wasn't asleep. He glanced up from whatever he'd been watching, and the boredom in his eyes was erased by an expression Nancy didn't want to believe.

There was no way Doc Bartelt had looked at her with desire. She was projecting her feelings onto him. She'd loved him for years, but never gotten past the love in her mind. His kiss had changed everything for her. Might it have changed everything for him, too?

And if it had, dared she let him continue to pretend the kiss had never happened? If she did, what she'd just begun to dream could never come true. Nancy inched toward the bed.

"What?" he snapped. "I'm watching something."

So much for tender feelings. The desire in his eyes must have been merely a flicker of light from the screen.

Nancy sighed, suddenly very tired. "I'll take your tray and say good-night."

Doc grunted and turned his eyes back to the television. But when she leaned over to pick up his tray from the nightstand, she glanced his way and caught him looking at her butt.

The tray clattered back on the table as she straightened. Doc jumped and jerked his gaze back to his show.

He had not forgotten the kiss they'd shared. He did not feel the same about her as he always had. He felt something more; she knew it. So how would she get him to admit those feelings and give them a chance at something wonderful? She had no idea, so she fell back on the tried-and-true.

"How are you feeling?"

"Warm."

Her lips twitched. She sat down on the bed and reached for his forehead.

His entire body tensed and he flinched away from her hand. "I'm fine, damn it. I'm bored and the room is stuffy."

"I'll be the judge of that." Purposefully she reached forward and placed her palm on his forehead.

"Well?" he growled.

"I never could tell this way."

"What way could you tell?"

"This way." Before he knew what she meant to

do, and stop her, Nancy leaned forward and pressed her lips to his brow.

He caught his breath and went very still. Slowly Nancy leaned back, afraid he would say something sarcastic and break her heart forever.

Instead, when her eyes met his she saw that the desire was no longer a shadow.

"Am I hot?" he asked, his voice low and hoarse.

"Uh-huh. Very."

He raised his hand to her neck. "What should we do about that?"

"You're the doctor." She responded to the pressure of his fingers drawing her closer and closer.

"That I am. But I'll need some assistance."

"I'm a nurse."

Their mouths so close, his next words caressed her lips. "Heal me."

"I thought you'd never ask."

She closed the short distance between them.

ELI FELT RESTLESS and he didn't know why. He sat on the floor of the gazebo, throwing a ball of yarn into the corner and watching Cleo chase it around and around.

He should be happy, and he was. Gwen spent every night in his bed. Well, *spent* wasn't exactly the right word. Spent would mean she woke up there. So far, she always left well before the sun came up—as if Doc didn't know what was going on.

Was she embarrassed? Or did she just want to ensure that a certain distance remained between them?

How was he ever going to find the right moment to tell her he loved her? Would it make any difference if he did?

She hadn't mentioned Milwaukee, marriage or Lance in over a week. She hadn't said she was staying, either.

But she did come to him every night, and they made love many, many times. She walked the dogs with him, holding hands. They'd shared a sundae at the ice-cream store and popcorn at the movies. Hell, in Pine River that meant they were practically engaged.

Too bad she was already engaged to someone else—though he hadn't seen a ring on her finger, just the wedding announcement in the mail.

Eli cursed and Cleo skittered underneath a bench. "Scaredy-cat," he murmured. "Come here, girl."

He scratched his fingernail along the wood floor. She couldn't resist the movement or the noise and crept toward him cautiously. Inch by inch she stalked his hand until she pounced with a gurgling purr, and Eli laughed, then lifted the kitten to bury his nose along her soft fur.

"She never stood a chance."

Eli glanced up, to find Gwen standing right outside the screen door. "I do have a way with women."

Gwen came inside. "Furry ones."

Cleo nudged her face along his and purred loud enough to make his ears ring. "Only those?"

"You fishing for compliments?"

He shrugged and put Cleo on the floor. If he had

to ask, he didn't want to know. "Speaking of fish, you're feeding Doc's, aren't you?"

"Nancy is. Where did he get those things, anyway? He's not much of a pet lover."

The kitten wandered over and started playing with Gwen's shoelace. She sat and reached down to stroke Cleo's baby-soft fur. The kitten took that as an invitation to jump into her lap, where she promptly fell asleep.

"I brought them over," Eli answered. "I figured he might grow into something warm-blooded if I hooked him on fish."

"Hooked. Ha-ha. He says fish aren't pets—they're food."

Eli winced. "I guess he wouldn't want Cleo then."

"A cat?" Gwen put a protective hand over the kitten in her lap. Eli hid his smile. She didn't know it yet, but she was hooked, too. "Are you nuts? Does Doc seem like a lover of the cute-and-furry?"

"He could be."

"If you give Doc a cat, it better be one to fit his disposition."

"Like?"

"Got any nasty tomcats, with one eye and a chewed-up ear?"

"Not at the moment. But I'll keep a lookout."

"How come the Queen of the Nile is free tonight?"

"The shed's empty except for her. She's lonely."

"Empty? How did that happen?"

"They all got better and went back where they came from, or on to a new home."

"It'll fill up again."

"It always does."

"And what about her?" She indicated the sleeping cat.

He shrugged. "No one wants her."

"How could no one want her? She's adorable."

"Aren't they all? You want her?"

"Me? Nope. Rules cannot be broken."

Eli let out an exasperated sigh and stood, scooping Cleo from Gwen's lap. He went to the shed and deposited her in her cage, where she curled up on her blanket and fell back asleep like the baby she was. He took a few deep breaths as he returned to the gazebo, but they didn't help. He was still mad. Gwen's rules were ridiculous, and they were starting to get on his nerves. Mostly because he couldn't get her to break even one of them.

Eli remained next to the door; he didn't trust himself to get near her and not touch her, and if he touched her he just might shake her. "I thought you'd given up your stupid rules since you came here."

"They aren't stupid."

"You don't believe in love. What kind of a crock is that?"

"I never said I don't believe. I said I want nothing to do with it. Look at what love did to Doc."

"Love didn't do that. Doc did."

"Nancy was right. Love stinks."

"That's a song."

Gwen groaned. "Not again."

"What?"

"Forget it."

"When were you talking to Nancy about love?" Eli experienced a moment of unease. Nancy hadn't spilled the beans, had she? No. If she had, Gwen wouldn't be this calm.

"Before, in the kitchen. I'm kind of worried about her. She was drinking Ms. Guiley's whiskey and pounding Oreos."

"Sounds serious."

"I think it is. I just wish I knew who she'd gone and fallen in love with. Nancy always seemed so sensible."

"Sense has nothing to do with love."

"That's the truth. What person with sense would fall in love?"

Eli sighed. He wanted very badly to say "Me" and then make love to her for the first time with the truth between them. But he'd just discovered something about himself. He *was* a coward.

Gwen continued to talk, oblivious to Eli's dilemma as always. "Nancy is miserable, and all because of love."

"I've seen dozens of people who were miserable *until* they fell in love."

"It never lasts."

"No? What about my parents?"

"That's love?"

"For them. They have a comfortable relationship, they know each other, they're at peace. What's wrong with that?"

"Nothing. That's exactly what I want in a relationship. Comfort, peace, knowledge. Passion, undying affection, suicidal need? I'll pass. The people who feel those always end up a tragedy. People who can't live without each other usually have to.''

Eli crossed the short distance between them and sat next to Gwen. He couldn't stop himself from tucking a stray lock of hair behind her ear. He doubted she even realized that his touch made her shiver. "And people who *can* live without each other?"

"Don't have to worry about it."

"When did you become a cynic?"

"When I was two."

He had nothing to say to that. "So you don't want passion?" He trailed a finger from the hollow behind her ear to the hollow between her breasts.

Her eyes darkened as her skin flushed and her breathing quickened. "Well, there's passion and then there's passion."

"You want to explain the difference?" He kissed the soft part of her ear and curved his palm around her rib cage. The fullness of her breast pressed against the back of his hand.

"There's what we have." She put her fingers over his and moved them up. "Which I want, very much. And then there's love passion, which I do not want, ever. Love passion drives you crazy."

Hmm, he thought, *the distinction there is pretty slim.*

"And what we have doesn't drive you crazy?" He flicked his thumb over her already hardened nipple and she gasped.

"You make me good crazy, Eli. Make me crazy now."

And coward that he was, he decided to make the distinction a little bit slimmer.

NANCY TASTED LIKE chocolate and whiskey, an intoxicating, tempting blend Doc was unable to resist.

He'd asked her to heal him, only half teasing. He'd been broken for a long, long time, and he had no idea how to fix himself. But from the way he felt as Nancy cuddled up to him beneath the sheets, going to bed with his nurse hadn't been the way.

His nurse! Damn. A woman young enough to be his daughter. Double damn. A friend of his daughter. What had he done?

Something incredibly stupid. He could never replace Betsy. He would never stop loving Betsy. He would never get over his wife.

Still, the constant ache that was loneliness, which he'd lived with most of his life, had abated for a little while. He hadn't been thinking of anything but Nancy and himself for the past hour.

The way she fit perfectly against his lanky frame, her soft form cushioning his hip and his arm, made him remember other things that had fit perfectly. He gave in to the urge to rub his face over the autumn scent of her hair. She had the most beautiful hair.

"Doc?"

He winced and yanked his mouth away from her brow. "Maybe you should call me Steve."

"Sure." She sighed like a lovestruck kid, not the Nancy he knew so well. "Steve."

Doc's chest hurt. How in hell were they going to work together after this? They could agree it wasn't going to happen again, but Doc didn't know if he could stick to that promise. Even now he wanted to touch her, despite the fact that touching her was wrong. If any of his patients had come in here and told him they'd spent the night in bed with their employee, he'd diagnose midlife crisis and tell them to grow up. Doc cursed.

"Shh," she whispered, and her breath brushed his chin. Doc gritted his teeth against a more primitive urge. He hadn't felt alive in nearly thirty years. Why did he have to feel so darned alive right now?

Nancy came up on her elbow and stared at him with a funny expression on her face. She reminded him of a cartoon character who'd been bonked on the head with a sledgehammer. The dopey grin only needed little birds whirling around her head to be complete.

"You okay?" he asked.

"Do you know how long I've loved you?"

Doc's mouth fell open. He must appear dopier than Dopey. "L-loved me?"

Her dazed look fled the instant she narrowed her eyes. "What did you think this was about?"

Doc snapped his mouth shut. He was old enough to know better than to answer that.

"I've loved you so long I can't remember when I didn't."

"Nance..." he began, but he wasn't sure how to finish.

She moved away from his side and the warmth went with her. He could see in her eyes the dawning of the truth.

"This was about sex, wasn't it?"

"No. That's not true."

"Then what? Obviously you don't love me."

"You don't love me either. You just believe that you do."

"Don't tell me what I feel. Why do you think I've hung around all these years? You're no picnic, Doc. Or should I call you Steve? I'm so confused about which is appropriate now that I want to kick your teeth down your throat."

"Relax. This doesn't have to ruin everything."

"Everything?"

Oh-oh, Doc thought. *Wrong word.*

"Everything as in our business relationship? Everything as in my slave relationship? Everything as in how much I've loved you and you never even noticed I was alive until you wanted me?"

"Calm down. Can't you see that this won't work?"

"What's *this,* Doc? An affair. Don't call it a love affair, since I have no idea what love is."

"What do you want from me?"

"All I wanted was to love you. Silly me. I guess I'm never satisfied. Once I thought it would be enough just to be near you. Then you kissed me, and I realized I wanted more. After this, I want it all."

"All?"

"Love, marriage, family."

His heart fell, even though he knew she deserved those things and more. "I hope you find someone to make you happy."

She smacked the heel of her hand against his chest. "Jerk."

"Ouch! What did I do?"

She got out of bed and started yanking on her clothes. "I want *you*, idiot. You to love me, you to marry me, you to give me children."

He couldn't keep the horror from his face. "Nancy, I can't give you what you want. I can't be who you need."

She was tough; still, he saw the hurt flood her eyes even as anger tightened her mouth. "You could if you wanted to. You're a coward. And you've made Gwen one, too. You wonder why she's marrying that jerk from the city? It's your fault."

He opened his mouth to deny that, but Nancy was on a roll. "You taught her that life wasn't for living, it was for enduring. You taught her that love is pain. She'll never even get one chance at what you had with your precious Betsy, never mind throwing away any second chances. You've been waiting for a grave all your life, Doc. Go climb into one. I'm not waiting around to watch."

She picked up her shoes, and for a minute Doc thought she meant to fling them at him. Instead, she left without so much as another glance, but not before he'd seen the tears in her eyes.

And that grave she'd wished on him looked pretty good.

CHAPTER FIFTEEN

GWEN WATCHED Eli sleep. He was so beautiful, and not because of the breadth of his chest, or the height of his cheekbone, or the wavy length of his hair. When Eli stared into her eyes, whether he was deep inside her or merely holding her hand, she felt beautiful, too, both passionate and alive.

They'd made love in the gazebo first—a naughty thrill, considering anyone could happen by, and very unlike her. She'd enjoyed it immensely, almost as much as making love in his bed an hour later.

What she liked the best about Eli's bed was talking the way they always used to back in the days when they would sneak out of their houses and meet in the backyard to stare at the stars and share their secrets. Lying in his arms after they'd just shared their bodies, then talking about everything from her day to his dogs, was the most incredible experience in Gwen's life. When she dozed, then woke up with his body curled around hers and his breath stirring her hair, the loneliness she'd begun to believe would haunt her forever wasn't there anymore.

What *was* there was a feeling that frightened her. They were two halves of a whole; without him she'd never feel right again. She didn't want to leave him—ever.

Because she wanted to stay so badly, she left his bed without kissing him goodbye. She would not ruin the time they had left by thinking too much. Thinking always got her into trouble.

This was the first time she'd lived her life by the force of feelings, the pull of passion. So sue her. She needed this. She needed Eli. For just a little while longer.

Dawn spread across the eastern sky. Gwen let herself in the front door as quietly as she could. Doc knew what she was doing. He wasn't any kind of fool. Still, she didn't want to get caught sneaking in like a teenager, even if she was behaving like one.

A noise near his room made her tense. Damn, looked like they were going to have the conversation she'd been trying to avoid. Too late to run and not seem like an adolescent, so Gwen stood her ground.

Nancy, barefoot and decidedly rumpled, barreled straight into her. Gwen's eyes widened. Her mouth dropped open. Nancy blushed, then scowled.

"Move it or lose it, Gwen. I'm in no mood to be nice."

Gwen couldn't quite get her mind around what her eyes were seeing. "Doc okay?"

"Just dandy."

Nancy reached for the door. Gwen didn't move. "So our conversation earlier about songs? Love stinks?"

"How could I forget?"

"You were talking about Doc."

The deepening of her scowl told the truth. Only Doc could make someone that mad. "None other."

Gwen rubbed her forehead. "Geez, Nancy. I'm sorry."

"Me, too. I have another song for you. 'Take This Job and Sho—'"

"Hey! You can't quit."

"Watch me." She yanked open the door and banged Gwen in the back. Gwen stumbled forward as Nancy escaped.

Gwen hadn't become an ER physician by letting people shove her around. She was right on Nancy's heels when her nurse reached the sidewalk. "Talk to me." Nancy stopped in midflight and turned. "I thought we were friends."

"We were." Gwen winced, but Nancy didn't notice. "But you're only here for a little while, and I'm not going to be able to stay around even that long."

"What happened?"

She raised an eyebrow. "You know what happened."

"Well, why, then?"

"I've loved him forever."

Gwen's mouth fell open. "Doc?"

"Don't sound so surprised. He's a wonderful man. Smart, funny, devoted."

"When you say forever, you mean..." Gwen spread her hands, uncertain.

"When I was a kid it was hero worship, as a teenager a crush. When I was old enough to know better, love.''

''But you *know* how he is.''

''I know better than anyone. I tried to get over him. I dated other guys. Nothing worked. For me, there's only him.'' Nancy sighed and stared up at the old house. ''But for him, there's only her.''

The pain in Nancy's eyes made Gwen reach for her friend's hand, but Nancy waved her off.

''Don't quit on me, please. I need your help.'' Gwen heard the echo of Lance coming out of her mouth, and she didn't like it.

''I can't be around him anymore. Funny, all those years wasted because I couldn't stand to be anywhere but here, with him. And now, one night, a dream I didn't even know I had comes true, and everything changes.''

''In time you'll find someone else.''

Nancy laughed. ''You aren't listening. For me there's only him. Just as for Eli there's only you.''

Gwen blinked. ''What did you say?''

''Open your eyes. Do you think he's sleeping with you for a good time? This is *Eli*. He loves you.''

''Of course he does.'' Her heart thundered far too fast for so early in the morning. ''We've loved each other forever.''

''Bingo. Sound familiar?''

Actually, it did. ''No, not like that,'' she blurted. Nancy just raised her eyebrow. ''We're friends.''

''Friends who sleep together don't stay friends long. Hell, Gwen, I said I'd keep my mouth shut, but what's the point? It didn't do me any good to keep my mouth shut this long, and it's not going to do you or Eli any good to keep kidding yourselves. Eli's always loved you. First as a friend, then as a crush, then for a lifetime. He's spent years waiting for you to see him as something more than the boy next door.''

''He-he's been waiting for me?''

''Who else? The man's crazy for you.''

Her mind spun with the implications, so that when Nancy left, Gwen didn't have the energy to stop her. Instead, she sat down heavily on the porch steps and watched the sun rise. But the beauty of the colors and the peace of the morning did nothing to soothe her roiling stomach.

She thought back over every moment with Eli, every word, every touch. Love had never been mentioned. But that didn't mean it wasn't there. Nancy was right. This was Eli she'd been sleeping with, and Eli wasn't a casual sex kind of guy.

What had he been thinking? That she'd stay? That she'd marry him? Have kids and pets and love everlasting?

She couldn't. Not even for Eli.

Gwen stood, feeling old and tired for the first time since she'd returned to Pine River. The place that had always depressed her in the past had lightened her heart this time around, and the only explanation for that was that she'd seen the place through Eli's eyes. Damn him.

She had to remember the proper course of her life.

The plans she'd had, the rules she lived by, the man she'd agreed to marry and why. But all those things seemed hazy now with the scent of Eli in her hair, the far-off bark of everyone's dogs as they sang to the dawn that spread over Pine River and made it beautiful.

Temptation had never beckoned Gwen before. Who'd have ever thought it would beckon in the guise of Eli and Pine River? The only way to thwart temptation was to bring her future alive before her very eyes. A single phone call would do the trick. Then she would remember everything she knew as the truth, everything she seemed to have forgotten in the shelter of Eli's arms.

ELI AWOKE ALONE, but he was smiling. Because these days, even though his bed was empty every morning, his heart was full the whole day long. The scent of Gwen mixed with the sheets; the indentation of her head still marked the pillow. He ran his fingertip along the dent. *Cold.* She'd been gone a long time already.

What was he going to do? He couldn't force her to make a choice between him and Lance, between her life in Milwaukee and a life here with him. Forcing Gwen was one way to end up without Gwen. But they couldn't continue like this indefinitely.

Eli went through his day in the usual way— appointments in the office, appointments in the field. A cow, a pig, a chicken, then a schnauzer named Bowzer, a Siamese named Lady—that was not—and a hamster named Sam that was more like a Susie. Just another day at Dr. Dog's.

While washing his hands for the final time that day, Eli reflected on Ms. Guiley. He missed her. The woman had been a bright spot to every Monday.

Eli glanced at the Blues Brothers, sleeping in a pile with Fifi between them. At least they'd stopped carting her around in their mouths. It was as if the poodle had filled a space in their lives, completed an unknown something that they were missing. He understood how they felt. He no longer had an ache just below his rib cage.

Jake and Elwood had been nigh on to angels since Fifi arrived. He would have thought the addition of the dog-cat would really start a ruckus. You just never knew how things would turn out—bad turned to good, good gone bad and everything in between.

Next week he could begin doing surgery again on a weekly basis. He'd taken Gwen's advice and hired a local kid to help in the clinic. When school began Eli would do surgery two afternoons instead of one full day, thereby giving Billy a chance for work release. Billy was the perfect assistant—he worked hard, loved animals, wasn't in love with the doctor.

Things were shaping up just fine. He had only one loose end. Eli stepped outside and glanced toward the Bartelts' in time to see a stranger start up the walk.

Frowning, he glanced at the man's car—a foreign sport utility vehicle. The guy was definitely from out of town.

Eli wandered toward the house next door, curious

what a stranger wanted with the doctor. Nancy would no doubt ask the man right there on the porch, loud enough for half the block to hear. But Nancy didn't answer the door—an oddity that slipped his mind when the stranger kissed Gwen full on the lips.

Stifling the urge to thunder over, grab the guy and slam him against the wall, Eli nevertheless strode to the bottom of the steps and pointedly cleared his throat.

The man raised his perfectly groomed blond head. Gwen's gaze shot to Eli, and he didn't like what he saw in her eyes.

Not guilt, as if she'd been caught by her lover kissing a stranger. Not the usual happiness at seeing Eli for the first time that day. Not even passion, as if she'd enjoyed the kiss.

No, in Gwen's eyes Eli saw determination. She appeared very like the woman who had come home a few short weeks ago. She knew what she wanted and precisely how to get it. What she did not look like was the woman he'd made love to only hours ago, a woman who had wanted him and knew precisely how to get him.

"Eli." Her voice was the other Gwen, too, crisp and refined, not a trace of the laughter or the secrets they'd shared. "I'd like you to meet Dr. Lance Heinrich, my fiancé. Lance, this is Eli. From next door."

Heinrich held out his hand. The smile on his chiseled face did not reach the cool blue of his eyes. "Ah, the vet. I've heard about you."

Eli raised an eyebrow at Gwen. "Only good things, I hope."

She shook her head and very nearly hissed at him behind Heinrich's back. He took the show of emotion as a good sign.

"Of course," Heinrich answered, and they shook hands. "You're her very best friend."

Funny how being a best friend was starting to annoy the hell out of him. Eli dropped Heinrich's hand and stepped back so he could see Gwen's face better.

She still had that odd determination in her eyes. Suddenly Eli understood and his heart began to beat again. She'd asked Lance here to break the engagement. That had to be it. She couldn't mean to marry this guy—not anymore.

Eli grinned, ignoring Gwen's puzzled frown. "So did Gwen ask you to town?"

"As a matter of fact she did. It worked out beautifully with my off day."

"How convenient. Like destiny."

"Destiny." Heinrich laughed. "Sure thing."

"Lance, why don't you come in and meet my father."

Eli snorted. That should be a good time.

Gwen glared at him, but in her eyes he saw a shadow that made him take a step toward her and hold out his hand. She shook her head. "I'll talk to you later. Okay?"

Although Eli didn't like that shadow, wasn't sure what it meant, he liked what she'd said. Later they'd talk and he'd tell her everything, and she'd open up completely for the first time in their lifetime. He could feel it. Tonight was the night.

Destiny, he'd told Heinrich and Heinrich had laughed.

Eli didn't think he'd be laughing for long.

GWEN FOLLOWED Lance into the clinic. She glanced at Doc's room, frowned to find his door still shut. He only did that if he was resting, but today he'd been in there all day, pouting. She'd tried to talk to him about Nancy and he'd thrown a shoe at her, so she'd left him alone. Big baby.

Meeting Daddy would have to wait. She'd rather spend some time with Lance, anyway, get the feel of herself again by looking at him. Lance saved a great, big chunk of the world every day in his big-city ER. He was the epitome of everything she wanted to be— brilliant, successful, respected.

So why did she suddenly feel that the way things had been were the worst way they could be?

Shaking her head at her own foolishness, Gwen joined Lance in front of the pill dispensary—an antique cabinet that had been in the family for generations.

"You've got to be kidding, right?" He pointed at the array of brightly colored bottles and packets. "Those are just for show."

"No. This is where we keep our samples."

"Anyone could break in, smash the glass, take what they want."

Gwen winced at the thought of the glass breaking

on this case, which had been sitting right here for as long as she could remember.

"Why would someone do that?"

"Drugs."

"Samples of antibiotics and birth control pills? Whoopee."

"It happens."

"Not here. The last time there was a break-in two teenagers snuck into the high school to make out. *That's* what happens in Pine River."

"Whoopee, as you say."

Gwen was having a harder time remembering why she'd wanted to marry Lance now than when he'd been over a hundred miles away. Go figure.

"Let's sit in the waiting room." She took his hand and pulled him through the hall to the other side of the house. Holding Lance's hand was like holding a bag of bones, not like holding Eli's, from whose warmth and strength flowed over her like summer rain. Gwen cut that thought off with a muttered curse.

"What was that?" Lance sat on the faded love seat that graced the front window.

Gwen sat beside him. "Nothing. Tell me what you've been doing while I've been gone."

"I figured you'd be dying of boredom here. Poor thing." He patted her hand. "I bet you can't wait to come home."

Home? Where was that anymore?

"I haven't been bored," she said. "Far from it. This place is usually a madhouse."

He glanced around the deserted waiting room. "Looks like it."

"My nurse quit. I had to cancel everything but the necessary."

"Mmm, tough break." But his voice didn't sound sympathetic, and when she glanced into his eyes Gwen saw he was already somewhere else. He did that a lot. "You missed a major accident the day you left. Twelve-car pile up on the interstate. Trauma right and left. We really needed you, Gwen."

Lance leaned forward, all earnest passion for his job as he regaled her with the gory details that used to be their prime dinner conversation. Once upon a time she'd loved it. Now her mind drifted to her patients.

Mikey Barrabas was doing great. His initial consult with the orthopedist had gone well. Gwen hadn't seen Johnny Kirkendal since last week. He should show up at any given moment. She couldn't wait to discover what the kid got into next.

The thought made her stiffen in surprise. She really *did* want to be here the next time Johnny showed up. Unless he got here soon, she wouldn't be. When had she started to care so much about the aches and pains of Pine River?

Had it been that first day when she'd held a healthy baby in her hands? Or maybe the second day, as she'd wiped the blood from Johnny's face. Maybe even later, when she'd watched Ms. Guiley slam whiskey and a beer, laughed with her, cried for her, then laid her to rest in just the way Ms. Guiley always wanted.

Lance waved his hand in front of her face and Gwen blinked. "Guinevere, have you heard a word I've been saying?"

He sounded peeved and she couldn't blame him. She'd been staring into space, thinking about her patients. Just as Doc always used to, and it had driven her crazy. But now she could understand why he was the way he was. Because she was starting to be that way, too.

"I heard you, Lance. Keep talking."

Because he was Lance, he did. She tuned him out when he got to the second severed limb.

She needed to get out of this town for more reasons than one. She might have been able to stand Ms. Guiley's funeral, but what happened when some kid she'd delivered, or patched up, or just seen riding his bike down her street, came in seriously hurt? What happened if Doc, or Nancy, or Eli—

Eli! The reason she'd begged Lance to come here in the first place. Eli loved her and she was scared to death. She was already starting to feel Doc's obsession for his patients; would she soon begin to feel heartbreaking, life-ruining, everlasting love?

That was something she could not allow, so she leaned over and pressed her lips against Lance's moving mouth.

He said something, but the words were muffled. Gwen kissed him with everything she had and felt...

Nothing. *Nada.* Zilch. Zip.

Just as it should be. So why did that leave her so empty and sad?

Lance pulled back. "What was that about?"

Gwen shrugged. "Missed you, I guess."

His smile was a mere tilting of lips that did not reach his eyes. "Remember what we agreed on when we decided to marry?"

"Partnership of minds and careers."

"That's right. I think you're a brilliant, fascinating, strong woman. I am attracted to you, but I don't love you."

Gwen heard their conversation in a distant part of her mind, as a little voice screamed she was nuts to marry this guy. He was a cyborg—no emotion, no warmth in him at all. Gwen saw her future self in Lance, and she didn't like it at all.

She reminded herself that *she* had wanted this relationship. Once, Lance had made her happy, and that scared her, too. But not half as much as the thought of loving Eli and losing him.

"And I don't love you, either," she blurted.

His smiled deepened and reached his eyes. "Perfect. Women in love cling. They want their husbands home. They want to have little babies." He shuddered. "I don't have time for that."

Images of babies danced through her head; puppies followed, then tumbling kittens and an elephant or two. She was losing her mind.

Gwen stood abruptly. "I'd better check on Doc."

Lance nodded. "I'll be right here."

She hurried through the clinic. If she was smart she'd leave with Lance tonight. Run away and never come back. Doc would be fine.

If he could rumple Nancy so badly last night she wasn't ever coming back, he was well enough to crutch around and take care of his own practice. Gwen experienced a twinge at the thought of one of her patients not getting adequate care, but she refused to allow the twinge to grow into full-blown guilt. They were not *her* patients, and they never had been.

Gwen tapped on Doc's door. Nothing. She turned the knob and peeked in. No one.

Hurriedly Gwen backtracked to the kitchen. Empty. The bath? Empty. The porch? Empty.

Well, hell, how long had he been gone? *Where* had he gone?

Thunder rumbled in the distance.

Sighing, Gwen grabbed her car keys. Now she'd have to go find him, which shouldn't take long. There weren't very many places to hide in Pine River. Someone would have seen him somewhere, and would be happy to tell her all about it.

Gwen stopped at the waiting room, where Lance read a medical journal. "I have to pick up my father."

"Where?"

"Got me."

He actually looked at her then. "You don't know where he is?" She shrugged. "Then how do you know he needs picking up?"

"Everybody does at one time or another."

Lance appeared confused. For a smart guy, a lot of things went over his head.

"I'll be back soon with my father. You wanted to meet him, right?"

"*You* thought I should meet him."

"Well, shouldn't you?"

"I'm marrying you, not your father. Considering that I haven't met him up until now, I didn't think I'd be seeing much of him after the wedding, either."

"You probably won't be seeing much of him *at* the wedding, knowing Doc."

"I don't understand you sometimes, Guinevere."

"Join the club," she murmured, and ducked into the fading afternoon light.

CHAPTER SIXTEEN

"BROUGHT YOU some flowers."

Doc tossed the spray of roses and baby's breath onto the ground. They landed right below the marker which read: "Elizabeth Marie Mondale Bartelt. Beloved wife and mother. Gone to God..."

"Yeah, yeah, yeah," Doc muttered, glancing around the cemetery.

All alone on a summer night—just how he wanted it. His gaze returned to the wild, overgrown grave. He hadn't been here in a long, long time.

The bright red of the roses, pristine and pure, contrasted starkly with the fluff of lime-green crabgrass and the mint shade of leafy clover, which grew thick at the base of the headstone. The stiff, dried baby's breath mixed with the soft, fresh, purple-white flowers that grew from the thistles.

This tableau would have appealed to Betsy, so instead of collapsing onto the ground and arranging the flowers in the empty bud vase to the side of the marker, Doc just sat on the ground and left his offering where it was.

"I miss you every day."

Thunder rumbled, far-off yet. It might not even

blow this way. Even if it did, he'd come here for a reason and he wasn't leaving yet. Doc cast a suspicious glance at his metal crutches, then shrugged. If it was his time, it was his time. He had no doubt Nancy would consider it divine justice anyway if he got struck by lightning on Betsy's grave.

He'd spent the day so knotted up inside he couldn't think. The last time he'd felt so confused, so lost, so frightened, this was where he'd come. Of course, then he'd just lost his wife. Now what was his excuse?

Absolution? Doc hung his head and spread his palm over the mowed grass that covered her grave.

"Every day I think of you. I can't see your face unless I look at a picture, but I remember things. How you used to laugh when Gwen did. The sound of you two would make me smile. I don't smile much these days, baby. Not much at all."

And she'd hate that.

Doc's head went up. A breeze brushed his hair away from his forehead, just the way she always used to. He sighed as some of the tension left his shoulders and neck. A glance about proved he was still alone, so Doc slid down and put his hot cheek against the cool spring grass.

"I miss silly things—like your hairbrush on my side of the sink, or the way your necklaces always tangled in your hair and you needed me to set you free. I miss the sound of my own name. Only Ms. Guiley ever called me anything other than Doc."

The breeze returned and rustled the new leaves. Their soft whisper sounded like...Steve.

"No one ever called me Steve but you," he murmured, and the grass tickled his lips.

You and Nancy.

Doc shut that thought off right away. Nancy was the problem. He'd betrayed the wife of his heart last night and he'd never forgive himself.

"I've been grouchy since you've been gone. It pissed me off that people who didn't have half what we did got to be together, and then most of them threw away what little they did have. I didn't realize I was setting a bad example for the kid. You said she'd save the world, but she doesn't see that the only world worth saving is a world you love. She's afraid to love—my fault—but I have no idea how to change that."

The wind remained silent. No answers for an unanswerable question. He'd only been imagining the whisper, anyway, because he'd wanted to hear it so much.

Doc took a deep breath and spread his hands across the grass. He liked lying here. He felt close to her again.

"I missed you so bad back then I hurt every minute of every day." Doc paused. Betsy couldn't really hear him. This conversation with her grave was only for his own peace of mind, so why not admit the whole story? Confession cleansed the soul, didn't it? "Except for last night," he blurted. "Last night I forgot everything. Last night I felt alive for the first time since you left. And though I know it's wrong, I want to feel that way again."

Thunder rumbled once more, nearer this time. The breeze should smell of rain, but instead it smelled of...

Doc raised his head. "Betsy?"

The deepest sense of peace he'd ever known swept through him with the force of the wind. Tears flooded his eyes, and for a brief moment he could see Betsy's face as clear as if she'd died only yesterday.

She was saying goodbye.

Then it was gone—the scent, the memory, the wind—but the peace remained.

Doc knew what he had to do, so he put his head back down on the grass and he cried. He never had before.

LIKE A RUNAWAY WAGON, Gwen chased Doc through town. He'd gone down Denali Street and stopped at the florist, where he'd bought roses. Then he'd tottered off to points unknown.

Gwen went to Nancy's but no Doc. No Nancy, either, or maybe she wasn't answering the door. Her car was in the garage, so she couldn't have gone very far.

"Where would he go with flowers?" Gwen asked herself as she pulled out of Nancy's driveway.

The wind blew a piece of paper against the curb, where it stuck straight up like a headstone, and suddenly Gwen knew where Doc had gone. And she was afraid.

How many people committed suicide on the graves

of their departed love ones? Too damned many, that was how many.

He'd been acting weird all day—weirder than usual, at any rate.

She sped to the center of town and wheeled into Pine River Cemetery. She had not visited her mother's grave in quite a while. But a person didn't forget such things.

Gwen drove unerringly to the location. She could see from the road that Doc lay there. For a moment, she couldn't breathe the fear was so great. But having a heart attack would not help her father. Gwen jumped out of the car.

Thunder growled, and Doc's head lifted. Her breath blew out on a long sigh of relief. He was fine. Now she was going to kill him.

She inhaled deeply in an attempt to calm her still-racing heart. The air smelled of...something. Memories tickled—a woman's laughter, then a child's, a young man's smile, a kiss.

She shook her head and the image fled. Pine River made her remember all sorts of things, and sometimes she didn't know if those memories were real.

Gwen took a step toward her father, but he put his head back down on the grass. She froze as the heartbreaking sound of weeping rent the air. He cried as if he'd never cried before. He cried as if his heart were being torn in two right now, all over again, and as she watched him, Gwen's head throbbed and her eyes burned.

She spun away from the sight and put her hot face

against the cool metal roof of her car. She'd come to take him home, but she'd best leave him here alone.

Gwen left as quietly as she could, but she didn't return to the house. Instead, she drove aimlessly out into the countryside as she had a nice long talk with herself.

She still felt shaky at witnessing Doc's grief. Did he visit his wife's grave and weep every month? Every week? Every day? How did he manage to go on? She didn't think she had such strength.

The image of herself, prostrate on Eli's grave, sprang to life in her mind so vividly Gwen's hands twitched on the wheel and the car swerved.

She *knew* she didn't have the strength to love and lose. So she would not love at all—just as she'd planned, just as her rules dictated.

Even though temptation had beckoned and promised beautiful things, she would return to Milwaukee with Lance.

Tonight.

ELI WAITED in the living room, on the front porch, then on the back, in his bedroom, then in the gazebo. The storm that had threatened blew over with only a drizzle, leaving the air clear and warm.

In the office, Billy worked on the accounts. Every time he had a question, he had to search a different place for Eli. The kid gave him a few odd looks, but Eli was the boss so Billy said nothing.

The dogs followed Eli about as he paced. Doc had left and come back. Gwen had left and come back later than Doc. The only person who had not left was Lance. The guy's car still sat at the curb.

How long did it take to dump a fiancé anyway?

Finally he gave up, told Billy where he was headed and went next door. Lance answered the bell.

"Hey, Eli." Big smile. "What's going on?"

That was what Eli wanted to know. But he couldn't very well ask why Lance was still here and why he was so blasted cheery.

Luckily, Doc showed up. "Eli. 'Bout time. Get your butt in here."

Lance shrugged and stepped away from the door. Eli followed Doc through the clinic and into his room.

"Shut the door."

Doc sat on his bed. He seemed a lot better today, even though his face was pale and his eyes a bit red. If Eli didn't know better he'd say Doc had been crying.

"You okay?" Eli asked.

"Forget me. Gwen's packing and I want you to do something about it right now."

"Packing? Why?"

"Why do people usually pack? She's leaving with that pompous ass."

"Leaving?"

"Quit playing parrot and listen to me. What have you been doing for the past three weeks?"

Eli blushed. His mouth opened, then shut. What was he supposed to say to that?

"That's what I thought. Have you *told* Gwen how you feel?"

"I've been showing her."

Doc rolled his eyes. "I never should have left this to you."

"You approve of Gwen and me?"

"I approve of my child coming home. I think you're the best thing for her. I'm not sure if she's the best thing for you, but that's just too damned bad. I'm not *your* father."

"Thanks for your concern."

Doc ignored the sarcasm, perhaps because sarcasm was Doc's forte. Eli was but an amateur. "Get your butt upstairs and spill your heart. Make it fast, but make it pretty."

"She'll run."

"She's running now, genius. Trust me on this, women like words. They may say they don't need 'em, but they lie. So get up there and talk." Doc pointed a finger upward. "Now."

"What about…?" Eli jerked his head toward the front of the house.

"Wonder Doc? I'll take care of him. I'm suddenly in immediate need of a pizza burger at the Crystal."

"Thanks."

Doc paused at the door. "Do whatever you have to do. And I do mean whatever. This is your last chance."

Eli nodded, then waited until Doc and Lance left. Muttering a quick prayer that he wouldn't foul everything up forever, Eli sprinted up the stairs.

She didn't hear him. Probably because she was too

busy trying to figure out how she was going to sneak out of the house and then out of town.

The thought made him angry. He might have agreed to an affair while hoping for love. But he was worth more than this. He deserved better than a phone call or a letter.

"Were you planning on saying goodbye?"

She jumped and dropped the shirt she'd been holding into the suitcase. "Eli! You scared me."

"Sorry." But he wasn't. Eli sauntered into her room. He had not been in here since they were kids. The place appeared the same. Gwen looked nervous. She should.

"So, I hear you're leaving."

"Doc's fine. It's time."

"And you were going to tell me when?"

She turned her back on him and continued packing. "Where's Doc?"

Eli moved closer. From the way her shoulders stiffened, she felt him there. Just as he could feel her near without looking at all. "Doc and Lance went to have a pizza burger."

Gwen glanced over her shoulder. "Lance?"

"I think Doc wanted some bonding time. I hear you're still marrying the man."

"Of course I am. I never said I wasn't."

Eli couldn't take it. He had to touch her. He wanted to shake her. Instead, he put his hands on her shoulders and pulled her against his chest. "Silly me. I figured sleeping together meant something."

"It did. Just not what you think."

She didn't relax in his arms, or melt into his embrace, but she didn't pull away either. Eli slid his hands down her arms, then around her waist, under her shirt, against the trembling muscles of her stomach. He laid his cheek against her hair. Then he didn't know what else to do. He had no idea what to say.

He'd played out his hand, and still she wouldn't admit she loved him. She planned to leave him here, forget what they'd shared and marry someone else. Would telling her he loved her change that? The words were all that he had left.

Suddenly Gwen turned in his arms and kissed him. He tasted desperation on her lips, against his tongue. She kissed him with all the passion that had been between them since the first night they'd changed their friendship into something else forever.

"Make love to me, Eli," she murmured against his mouth. "Love me."

He pulled away and stared into her face. "I do, Gwen." She closed her eyes, shutting him out, but a tear fell on his hand. "I always have."

He kissed her cheek, brushed her hair back from her face. She shook her head, flipped off the lights and kicked the door shut. "Please, Eli. I need you now."

Something else was wrong here, something more than just the two of them. What wasn't she telling him?

Gwen shoved the suitcase off the bed, slid her dress from her shoulders, kicked off her underwear and stood naked before him.

Eli was having a hard time remembering what he was supposed to say and do. His body screamed one thing; his mind mumbled another. When she reached for him, he went.

He'd been fantasizing about how good it would be once he made love to her with the truth of love between them. He couldn't deny himself that, even though he probably should.

Gwen undressed him, quickly, even a bit frantically. Her mouth was everywhere, as if she wanted to memorize every inch of him, as if she needed to take something with her.

He tasted goodbye on her lips, felt farewell in her touch, but his mind refused to accept such a thing. How could she ask him to love her and then stomp on his heart when he did? Gwen wouldn't do that to him. She couldn't.

They'd made love in many moods—from languorous to furious, adventurous to serene, amid laughter but never tears. The single teardrop that had fallen on Eli's hand had dissolved and he never saw another. But tears were between them nevertheless.

When he entered her, she opened her eyes and murmured, "Eli," as she had the first time. When they reached the top and tumbled over, they did so together, falling a long, long way back to the earth.

He'd thought making love with the word *love* between them would be different. Somehow better, deeper, longer, stronger. But nothing had changed, because for Eli, there had been love all along.

Her face pale, her skin cool, Eli flipped the cover over them both, then gathered Gwen into his arms. "Tell me you aren't going to leave. Say you aren't going to marry him."

Her sigh told him the truth before her words smashed his heart. She tried to struggle free of his arms, but he wouldn't let her go. "Lust changes nothing, Eli."

"This isn't lust, Gwen, and you know it."

"I don't know any such thing."

"What's my favorite kind of gum?"

She gave him a look of complete bafflement. "What?"

"Humor me"

"Cinnamon."

"What kind of shoes do I wear?"

"Tennis shoes. Always."

"My favorite food?"

"Mashed potatoes."

"Ice cream?"

"Raspberry."

"And my favorite movie?"

"*The Blues Brothers,* obviously. What is your point, Eli?"

"You like to walk around barefoot whenever you can. You'll wear sandals until it snows just to avoid socks and shoes. You put honey in your coffee when you're sick and lemon in your water when you're hot. You like carrot cake on St. Patrick's Day and turkey for Easter."

"What difference does any of that make, Eli?"

"I know you inside out and I love you anyway."

"I heard you the first time. I can't love you back."

"Can't or won't? Just because you refuse to say it doesn't mean you don't feel it."

"I refuse to feel it, now and for always."

This time when she pushed him away, Eli let her go. He was getting mad. "Why? Explain to me *why* you want to throw away the perfectly beautiful life we could make together?"

Gwen tugged a short, blueberry silk robe from her suitcase and shoved her arms through the three-quarter-length sleeves. "Do you know where Doc was this afternoon?"

Eli's mind blanked at the shift in conversation. "No." He sat up and leaned his back against the headboard. "What does Doc or where he was today have to do with us?"

"Everything. I found him on my mother's grave, sobbing his heart out."

Which explained Doc's red eyes, but little else to Eli.

"That was probably good for him."

She punctuated her sigh with a yank on her belt. "She's been gone nearly thirty years and he's still crying on her grave. I don't want a life like that."

"So don't have a life like that."

"And if I love you and marry you and need you and want you, what happens when you die?"

"I can't promise not to die, Gwen."

"Exactly. And I can't love you."

"You *do* love me. I know you do. You wouldn't have let me touch you in every way I'd ever dreamed—and I dreamed a lot. You wouldn't have let me inside, your body and your mind. You wouldn't have let me hold you all those nights, all night long. I know you, and you would never have shared yourself with me if you didn't love me, too."

"You *don't* know me!" she shouted. "I don't even know me."

"That's the problem here. Not me and you, just you. You've tried so hard to be unlike your father you've ended up *exactly* like him. With one exception. At least he took a chance. You don't even have the guts to try."

She hugged herself and looked away. "Maybe you're right, I don't have the guts. And I never will. I can't bear to love and lose and die inside."

"Why can't you love and keep and live the way you've never lived before? With me?"

She just shook her head. "I can't be the person you want me to be."

"I just want you to be happy."

Gwen moved to the window, where she leaned her head against the casing. "Then leave me alone."

Eli got out of bed and yanked on his pants. He stalked across the room and pulled her about to face him. "You think the life you led before will make you happy now? You think *he'll* make you happy?"

"I won't be sad or crazy or catatonic with grief."

Eli searched her face and saw the stubborn determination that made Gwen Gwen. "You aren't going to change your mind, are you?"

She lifted her hand and touched his face. "I can't," she whispered.

He'd taken a chance; he'd rolled the dice. But he'd never realized just how much there was to lose until he saw goodbye forever in her eyes.

CHAPTER SEVENTEEN

THE PAIN ON Eli's face nearly did Gwen in. But she was doing the right thing, the only thing she could do.

"Love destroys, Eli. It makes you weak."

"You're wrong. Love heals and it gives you strength. I could face anything if you were by my side."

"That's just what I mean. I don't want to be responsible for someone else's happiness. I can barely manage my own."

He stepped away from her touch, the pain replaced by anger. "You *can't* manage your own. When you came home you were miserable and lonely, pale, tired and sad. I wanted to shake you. I still want to. You're going back to a place that haunted your eyes for days after you came here. You're leaving a place that actually brought you joy. Were you lonely in my arms, Gwen? Were you lonely in my bed?"

He was killing her. She wanted to throw herself back in his arms, take him back to her bed. But she couldn't. "You know I wasn't."

"If pain in the future is the price I have to pay for happiness now, I'd gladly pay it."

"I wouldn't."

"Do you think Doc would have chosen never to have your mother at all, never to have you, rather than have her and lose her?"

"I think so."

"I think you're wrong. I think you should talk to him."

"That would be a first."

"Exactly. You live in a 'what-if' world, Gwen, and that's not living. The world is a great big 'why not?'"

"Maybe *your* world is."

His hands clenched. "Damn it, Gwen, I love you and I always will. If you ever grow up, get over a past that's passed and discover that life is what you make it, I'll be right here."

Panic lit her heart. She'd known this would happen, yet still she'd hoped it would not. All her life, Eli had been there—a faithful, constant presence she could count on. "We can't still be friends?"

He looked at her in amazement. "I can't be just your friend anymore. I want it all. And I deserve it."

He walked out without a goodbye or even another glance in her direction. He clattered down the stairs, then slammed the front door. The silence of the house settled over her; the sound of loneliness returned, made her shiver.

"You do deserve it all," she whispered to an empty room. "You deserve so much more than I could ever give you."

Gwen picked up her suitcase and continued to pack.

ELI HAD NEVER had much of a temper. He was a calm, dependable guy. Right now he wanted to smash his fist through a door. But if he did, he'd break his hand and then where would all the poor animals be?

Gwen wasn't going to stay. He had done all that he could, and still she refused to take a chance. He couldn't believe he'd misjudged everything so badly. He hurt so much inside he felt he'd been stomped on by a goat—or something heavier—like Jimmy. Would the pain last all his life? Is this what Doc lived with every day?

No wonder the guy was cranky.

But Eli had meant what he'd said. He'd endure any pain for the chance to have the love of a lifetime—even if he only had her for a little while. Too bad he was the only one with any guts around here.

"Dr. D.!" Billy ran toward him. "Pete Jones just called. Said the hawk you let go out there is up a tree in one of his fields and looks to be in trouble." Billy handed Eli his bag.

"Thanks." Eli welcomed the distraction. If he sat at home he'd just watch Gwen drive away. He needed that like another hole in his heart. "You done with the billing?"

"Not yet. Maybe another hour."

Eli nodded, and headed for his truck. Jake, Elwood and Fifi shot out of the house. All three skidded to a stop in front of him and sat, eager faces and drooling tongues very plainly saying, "Car ride? Car ride?"

"Fine." He opened the door. One, two, three, they jumped in. The boys in the back, the girl riding shotgun. "I'm taking the dogs," he shouted to Billy. Billy waved and went inside.

At the Jones's farm, Eli found Pete in the milk parlor doing the evening run. Dairy farming had changed a lot in the past twenty years. No more lugging full milk pails to the cooler. Now the cows went to the parlor and the milk was pumped directly from the udder to the cooler. A lot less work, to be sure, but someone still had to clean off every cow and hook up a machine. Eli stood by while Pete attended to another Bessie.

"Biggest tree on the back eighty," Pete said. "I'd take you out there, but I've gotta finish this and drive the family to a movie over in Pecatonica. You can't miss the thing, though. Looks like something out of one of those horror movies." He bent his fingers into an imitation of gnarled limbs. "You know what I mean?"

"Uh-huh. When did you see her there?"

"'Bout an hour ago. I moved some cows to that field and saw her swoop in. She was wobbly, so I went over there. Knew it was your hawk 'cause she didn't take off, and I remembered her from when you let her go. She's all hunched over like this."

Pete slouched to the side and scrunched up one shoulder. Eli frowned. He didn't like the looks of that.

Five minutes later, Eli stood at the base of a very big, very interesting tree. He didn't think it resembled a horror movie set. Not with all those cows dotting the fields, placidly chewing and mooing and in the distance Pete's farmhouse small and white, peaceful and pristine against the deepening blue sky and spring-green grass.

No, the tree seemed more like an escapee from *The Wizard of Oz*—the part when Dorothy had tried to take an apple and the tree slapped her hand. That part had always scared the heck out of him as a kid. Never Gwen though. She was tough.

About everything.

Eli pushed thoughts of Gwen out of his mind as best he could. She'd be gone when he got back, and he'd deal with the ramifications then.

Peering through the skyward-reaching limbs, he spared a moment to be glad the tree was old and the leaves sparse, even though the gnarled branches appeared wickedly sharp in places; he could see his hawk clearly about halfway up. He hadn't nursed her back to life to let her die and tumble to the foot of this misshapen tree.

One of the dogs barked, but the hawk didn't even flinch. Eli glanced at the truck. Three heads hung out of the windows. Three pairs of hopeful eyes gazed at him in adoration. "Stay, I said. You can run behind the truck all the way home."

The labs grumbled, always needing the last word, and lay down. Fifi kept panting and drooling. She hadn't a clue what he'd said, but she wouldn't leave the other two. Eli returned his attention to the hawk and whistled. She lifted her head, then as if the action were too much for her, her beak dropped toward her chest again.

"Come here, girl." The hawk remained motionless. Fifi whined. "Not you," he snapped.

Eli sighed. There was nothing else for it. He could call and whistle till one of the dogs came, but the hawk wasn't going to budge. He'd have to climb the tree.

Eli took antibiotic salve and a penlight from his bag and shoved them into a pocket. Then he put on the thick leather gloves he used when working with large birds and started up.

He hadn't climbed a tree since childhood. Gwen had always done it better. When was he going to stop thinking about her? *Never.* He'd best get used to the pain of every memory.

Eli's foot slipped and the hawk jumped, then fluttered up higher. She could fly at least, but something *was* wrong. She should have flown off, even if she did know him.

Eli kept climbing. A glance at the ground proved a big mistake. He'd come up a lot farther than he'd planned. But now that he was here, and so close, he'd get this over with, then get back down.

The hawk perched upon a thick and heavy branch. Eli leaned his chest against a curve and held out his hand. "Here!" he called. Fifi answered.

"Let me see, girl. Let me see," he murmured, over and over. First she ignored him. Then she lifted her head. Eventually, she stepped onto his hand.

Eli drew her close and peered at the side she'd favored. Blood had dried on her wing. The tiny hole was the size of a pellet. Some kid had been shooting hawks for target practice.

Eli stifled his irritation. What was done was done. But he hated it when he had to patch up a bird because Junior didn't have proper supervision. He'd have a talk with the Department of Natural Resources again and remind them to address such things in their hunter safety courses.

Slowly Eli began to climb down. It was harder than climbing up since he had a hawk on his hand. His tennis shoe slipped again. Eli clutched a branch with his right hand, tried to keep his left hand steady, but the hawk screeched and lifted off. She flew straight at Eli's face, and his defensive retreat lost him a slippery foothold.

Tumbling toward the ground, he hit limb after limb, trying to grab something. He slammed into a thick branch, which snapped. He continued to fall. Something tore at his thigh. Pain erupted—first in his leg, then in his back when he slammed into the ground.

Eli gasped for breath, the wind knocked out of him. He tried to calm his racing heart with assurances that when you got the wind knocked out of you it always felt as though you were dying, but you weren't.

Yet even when he could breathe again, the dizziness didn't abate. Eli lifted his head and looked at the fire in his leg.

Nausea washed over him in a sickening wave. Blood streamed from a tear in his pants. A lot of blood, which must be coming from an equal tear in his leg, along with one in an artery or a vein. Neither would be good, but an artery would be very bad.

Black spots swam. He broke out in a cold sweat. His head fell back to the ground with a thump, and he watched the hawk circling like a vulture. She appeared just fine to him. He'd probably scared the pellet right out of her.

Eli laughed and the wildness of the sound frightened him more than the fall had. He needed to do something or he'd bleed to death. He'd never been much good when his own blood was involved. Anyone else, that was just peachy, but not his own.

Closing his eyes, he tried to think what he needed to do. Tourniquet. Piece of wood. His shirt. He could do it. But he had to do it now.

Something bathed the left side of his face, then the right, then his forehead. He opened his blurry eyes to find three dogs blotting out the darkening sky. How could he have forgotten them?

He patted the dogs. They whined and paced. The smell of blood made them nervous.

"Hey, I don't like it, either," he muttered, and slowly pulled his shirt over his head. He felt as if he were trying to run through deep water and not getting very far.

Eli attempted to tear off a strip, but the weakness in his arms wouldn't allow him to—a bad sign. He avoided looking at his leg. He just might pass out if he saw it again.

"Here." He put one end in Jake's mouth and

tugged. The game was an old one and the dog yanked back with all his strength.

Screech! The cloth rent.

Nearby lay a scattering of branches from his free fall. "Go get it!" He pointed to the nearest largest one. Elwood, who retrieved anything, not just cats, brought him the stick.

Eli swallowed the thickness at the back of his throat, took a deep breath and forced himself to tie the tourniquet around his leg. By the time he finished, he was drenched with sweat. But blood no longer flowed—for the moment.

"Go home, guys." He pointed in that general direction.

All three sat and stared at him.

"Lassie you ain't," he muttered.

What did he expect? He'd taught them to stay with him. They got in trouble if they ran off. And what in heck was home to them? It wasn't a command like sit, stay, knock it off.

"I'll just rest a minute and then I'll get to the truck. If I press on the horn, someone will come."

Of course, Pete was gone and the farm was five hundred acres of grassland. Nausea came in a hard, thick wave and Eli gagged, then started to shiver.

"Come here, girl," he murmured. "Guys, too. Sit by me."

But when he looked for the dogs, they were gone.

Eli passed out wondering why they'd left him all alone.

GWEN CALLED Nancy to say goodbye. Her last good friend sounded as if she'd been crying all day, then she hung up the moment Gwen identified herself.

"Nice," Gwen muttered. "I'm glad I don't have to live in the same town with you anymore."

But that wasn't true. Gwen was going to miss Nancy and their girl talk almost as much as she missed Eli and their talks in the gazebo. She loved that place. She'd miss even more the times she and Eli hadn't talked.

Gwen was sitting on the porch, waiting for Doc and Lance to return, when Eli's dogs showed up. They raced in from the backyard and she tensed, expecting him to follow close behind. She didn't want to see him again. The last time had been hard enough.

Gwen stood, with the intention of going inside and hiding. She was a chicken, a coward, a yellow belly. She admitted it.

Then the door to Eli's house opened and she heard his new helper, Billy. "What are you guys doing here? Where's Eli?"

Gwen stepped to the edge of the porch. "Did they run away from him?"

At the sound of Gwen's voice the Blues Brothers' heads went up and the dogs raced toward her. Fifi stared after them for a moment, then followed. All three jumped in foot-high leaps beneath where she stood on the porch.

"What are they doing?" she asked Billy, who had followed.

"Got me. They went on a call with Eli to the Jones

place. Pete saw Eli's hawk and it didn't look good. I wonder why they came back alone. They've never run away since the dog-cat showed up, or so Eli says." Billy shook his head, confused. "If they took off after something they wouldn't come back here."

Jake barked, and when Gwen glanced at him, he ran a few feet, then stopped and barked at her again. Then the other two did the same thing.

Billy laughed. "Is Timmy down the well, Lassie?"

"Oh, shit," Gwen said. "I just bet he is."

"Timmy?"

"No, Eli." She descended the steps, then went onto her knees. The dogs gathered around her. Gwen checked them over, though she wasn't sure for what, except that she'd know it if she saw it.

She did. Fifi had blood on her paws, but there wasn't a scratch on a one of them.

Gwen had been trained to think clearly under frightening conditions, and though panic threatened, only a moment passed before sanity returned. She *had* to find Eli.

She ran for the house. Inside, she grabbed Doc's bag from behind the desk in the waiting room. If she found Eli just fine and playing with that damned bird, she'd smack him and go home. She only hoped that was what she would find.

Gwen stepped onto the porch, where Billy hovered. "Call the Crystal. Tell Doc where I went. Get an ambulance to that farm."

"You think Eli's hurt?"

"I hope not."

"If he isn't, you'll have to pay for a nonemergency ambulance run."

"I'll happily buy the ambulance if I'm wrong."

Gwen headed for her car. She no sooner opened the door than the dogs shoved her aside to jump in. They started butting their wet noses against the windows until she opened them all, then they hung their heads out, their attention on the western horizon, where the sun faded fast. She didn't have much time.

Not even five minutes passed before Gwen wheeled into the gravel drive at the Jones place. The house was dark, hers the only car in the drive. "How am I supposed to find him now?" she muttered.

The dogs leaped out through the windows and streaked for a cow-dotted field to the west.

"Ask a stupid question..." Gwen pulled Doc's black bag out of the car and hurried after them.

She did not feel like Dr. Woman. She felt like a frightened little girl. If Eli was hurt, would she be able to save him? What if she panicked, as she'd always feared she would when faced with the injury of someone close to her? What if she did more harm than good? What if she kept her head, used all her training and he died anyway—just like her mom.

The realization hit her so hard she stumbled; then she forced herself upright and onward. She *did* live in a "what-if" world, and suddenly she wished with all her heart that she'd agreed to live in the "why not" world with Eli. If she ever had another chance...

Regrets would wait for later. Now she had to find him. Gwen scanned the field. But all she saw were countless cows, three dogs and one very ugly tree with a log at its base.

The screech of a hawk drew her attention upward. The bird circled the tree, vulturelike, a dark shadow in the descending night.

Gwen shivered and lowered her gaze. That wasn't a log underneath the tree; it was a person. "Eli!" she shouted, but he did not move.

The dogs beat her to Eli. They nudged his face with their wet noses, but he did not respond.

Too much blood. She could smell it on the night wind; see the dark blotch against his pants, on the grass. Panic made her hands shake as she reached for the tourniquet and released the pressure.

Blood welled. A lot of blood.

"Oh, Eli," she whispered, and heard the sobs in her voice. If she couldn't get control of this, or herself, he might not make it to Mercy.

She would *not* let him go. She'd been waiting to save the world most of her life. Without Eli there wasn't any world.

Still, her mind raced; her heart thundered. She wasn't sure what to do first, because there was so much to do. She was used to thwarting trauma in a fully equipped ER, not plugging a dike with her finger in the middle of a field full of cows.

The sound of a car, the flash of headlights across both her and Eli, announced the arrival of Doc and Lance. The sight of her father slowly getting out of the passenger seat made Gwen's panic recede a bit.

Doc knew how to save lives in desperate situations. He did it every day.

"Dad, help me!" Her voice cracked in the middle. Doc's face, harsh in the glare of the headlights, revealed his surprise.

"Shouldn't Wonder Doc give you a hand?"

"No." She dismissed Lance easily. He was used to supervising in an ER with all the amenities. "I need *you*, Dad. Please."

Doc nodded and lowered himself carefully to the ground. Watching him check Eli, his gnarled fingers sure, his face certain, comforted her. She no longer felt so all alone.

"Gwen, I think I'd better lend a hand," Lance interrupted.

"No. Don't touch him." Her voice, now a bit shrill, surprised not only her, but Lance and Doc, too. The latter cast her a shrewd expression as he checked the tourniquet.

"Doc knows what to do. Right?" The last word sounded like that of a child asking a parent if the monster in the closet was truly not real. Unfortunately, Gwen's monster had just jumped out and said "Boo!"

Doc ignored her question and got down to business. "We need a better tourniquet."

"Like what?"

"Blood pressure cuff." Gwen yanked the item out of the bag.

"Here." Doc pointed. "Tamp it tight."

Doc put his hand against Eli's throat. "He's shocky."

Gwen glanced at Eli's face, so still and pale the sight made her chest hurt. Shock could kill as easily as the injury itself. "I don't suppose you have an IV in your magic bag?"

"Of course. You'll have to start it, though. Haven't had to do one in years."

"I have." The repetition of her usual routine had a calming effect on Gwen. As long as she didn't look at Eli's face, her hands didn't shake.

She inserted a thick needle into his vein. IVs always felt as though you had a knitting needle sticking out of you but Eli never moved.

Gwen took a deep breath, which wasn't steady. Doc reached over and touched her shoulder. "You're doing all you can."

"But what if—"

"Forget what-if. You can only do what you can do."

"What do we do now?"

"We wait."

"I'm no good at waiting."

"Neither am I, so we'll wait together. Every step of the way."

Nancy had been right. There wasn't a calmer or saner voice amid chaos than Doc's. Gwen was living her nightmare—the nightmare that had once been Doc's reality—though you'd never know it by looking at him.

He might not have been there for her in the past,

but he was here now when she needed him the most, and while they tended Eli together—checking the tourniquet, his vitals, the IV—the hard knot of resentment Gwen had never been able to shake dissolved and disappeared.

"Once you got past the beginning, I've never seen a steadier hand or a better eye. I'm proud of you, Gwen."

Holding on to Eli, she raised her gaze to Doc's. In his eyes she saw the love she'd always longed for. She was starting to wonder if a lot of things had been there all along; she'd just never known how to look for them.

"I made a lot of mistakes," he murmured. "But I think I've also done a lot of good. You were the most good I ever did."

Gwen opened her mouth to ask him a hundred questions, then stopped at the sound of thunder from the sky. Glaring light swept over them both, and they looked up as a helicopter swooped low over the field.

"What the—?"

"I called my office." Lance's voice made Gwen start. She'd forgotten all about him. "Had them send the nearest trauma flight."

"Thank you." Gwen wanted to say more, but she didn't know what. Now that she'd done all that she could do, shock was setting in and her mind kept stuttering. She wanted to sit down in the middle of the field and cry. But superwomen weren't allowed.

She didn't let go of Eli's hand until the trauma team loaded him onto the helicopter and nudged her away. Eli remained unconscious, his skin clammy and gray. He needed blood soon and surgery. With the helicopter, he'd get to the hospital in time.

There was no room for Gwen inside. As Eli lifted into the sky, tears she could no longer stop spilled down her cheeks. She didn't want to let him out of her sight ever again. The thought shocked her almost as much as the realization that she didn't want to leave Pine River. And she wasn't going to.

"I'll take you to the hospital," Lance offered.

"Thanks. I'll tell Doc." Gwen searched for her father, and found him talking to some of the neighbors, who had come on the double after seeing a helicopter bank over the Jones place.

At her wave, Doc excused himself and hobbled over. They stared at each other, a lifetime of unexplored feelings and unsaid endearments heavy upon the air.

"Uh." Lance shuffled his feet, no doubt as uncomfortable with the hovering emotions as Gwen and Doc were. "I'll wait in the car."

Neither of them answered or looked Lance's way when he left. Something had changed between her and her father, Gwen just wasn't sure if things were better or worse.

She wanted to have the relationship with him she'd always needed, but she didn't know how to ask or what to do. So she stood there feeling awkward until Doc did the one thing that made everything all right. He held out his arms. Gwen tumbled into them, and as he held her close to his heart their relationship was almost the way she'd always dreamed it could be if her father loved her.

The only thing missing were the words. Yet none came.

Gwen opened her mouth to try, but her fear tumbled out. "I was so scared, Dad. Really scared."

"You'd never know it to look at you. I told you, your hands were the steadiest I've ever seen. You did great. Much better than I ever could have. And he'll be fine now, because of you."

"Was that how it was with Mom?"

Doc stiffened, but Gwen held on, afraid he'd put her from him as he'd done a hundred times before. Instead, he sighed, the sound coming from the depths of his pain, and his hand glided over her hair.

"I was all alone in the middle of a great big nowhere. With no one left alive but her and me. No helicopters back then. No cell phones. I did everything I could and it wasn't enough. I'm sorry I couldn't save her for you. I know you've never forgiven me."

Gwen gazed into his haunted face. "You think I blamed you?"

He shrugged. "I blamed me."

"Really? I'd never have guessed." He scowled at her sarcastic tone. "Maybe we both need to get over a past that we can't change."

"Maybe." Doc stared over her head, back toward town.

"Can I ask you something, Dad?"

He stared down into her face. "I like it when you call me Dad."

"I'll have to do it more often."

"Yeah, do that." He hugged her, a bit stiff and clumsy yet, but he'd get better with practice. She hoped. "What did you want to ask me?"

"If you'd have known that Mom was going to die and it was going to hurt so bad, would you rather you'd never met her at all?"

"Hell, no! Where did you get that idea?" She tilted her head and just stared at him. "Never mind. I'm sorry. I was wrong to grieve as long as I did. I was a fool and you paid for my foolishness."

"I'm all right."

"Are you? I saw your face when you looked at Eli. I heard your voice when you told Lance not to touch him." His lips twitched on the memory. "You love him. When did that start?"

"I don't know. If love is what I'm feeling, then I guess I've loved him all along."

"And you were going to leave him so you wouldn't ever know the pain I did." He sighed as he shook his head, then brushed his knuckle across her still-damp cheek. "But then you'll never know the joy, either."

"Is a little bit of joy worth a lot of pain?"

"Joy is never little. Grab any chance for love that you can. Hold on to it tight. And if the worst happens, at least you took a chance. At least you had some time. And you never know, you might have a lifetime."

"I love you, Dad."

He blinked at her. "You do?"

"Of course. Did you think I didn't?"

"I don't deserve it."

"Maybe you should start to believe that you deserve some happiness. Chances are for taking you said?"

"Yeah."

"Does that mean second chances, too?"

He scowled at her. "What are you getting at?"

"Nancy. She loves you, fool that she is. I say you grab her and take a chance."

He sighed. "She wants it all—love, marriage, family."

Gwen laughed. "This should be good. I can't wait to watch."

His mouth twitched. "Me, either." He kissed her forehead and released her. "You okay to go with Wonder Doc to the hospital?"

She nodded. "I think he and I need to talk."

"I've got some talking of my own to do. I'm sure someone can give me a lift back to town."

"Go get her, Dad."

"Let's hope I'm not too late." He began to limp off, but stopped a few steps away and turned back. "Did I tell you how much I love you?" She shook her head. "Always have. I just didn't know how to say it."

"You open up your mouth and let the words fall out."

"Like this? I love you."

Gwen blinked back a fresh spate of tears. Hearing her father say those words was every bit as wonderful as she'd always dreamed it would be. "Yeah, just like that."

"Hmm. I think I need to do better for the army nurse." He walked off murmuring, "I *love* you. I love *you*. *I* love you."

As Doc left, wonder spread through her at the amazing twists and turns of life. If a hardheaded old coot like that could admit he'd been wrong for nearly thirty years and start talking about second chances and second families, she should admit that love had to be better than lonely.

Maybe she ought to start reexamining some of her rules, consider breaking a few.

Gwen started toward the car and her fiancé. Looked like she'd be breaking a few promises, too.

CHAPTER EIGHTEEN

DOC STOOD ON Nancy's porch. Inside, lights blazed; music blasted loud enough to wake the world—some song that had a chorus of "love stinks." *Very nice.* Doc figured that was a hint from above not to bother ringing the doorbell.

If Nancy was like most people in Pine River she didn't lock the door unless she went to bed for the night or left town for a weekend. Doc turned the door-knob, then let out a sigh of relief that Nancy *was* like most people.

He stepped into the front hall, where the music was so loud he couldn't hear himself think. Maybe that was what Nancy was aiming for. Doc found the CD player and turned the annoying song off. Then he waited. But not for long.

Nancy walked into the room in a thick white robe, hair loose, feet bare. Doc caught his breath as the love washed over him in a warm, sweet wave. It had been so long since he'd felt much of anything his emotions seemed stronger, deeper—almost as if it were the first time he'd felt such things.

Now that he'd said goodbye to Betsy and unhar-dened his heart, he realized he'd felt this way about

Nancy for a long, long time. The sarcasm and the constant sparring had been his only defense against feelings he hadn't deemed appropriate or deserved.

Nancy took one look at him and pointed at the door. "Get out!" Then she spun on her heel and left the room.

Doc crutched into her kitchen. A bottle of wine, half full, and a single glass, half empty, sat on the table. Nancy took a sip and stared at him over the rim. "Have you gone deaf as well as dumb, Doc?"

"Steve."

"Bite me."

"All right." He started toward her, became annoyed with his hitching gate and tossed the crutches to the floor so he could continue on unencumbered.

Nancy's eyes widened and she stumbled back. "No! You stay over there." He kept coming. She kept retreating until her rear end hit the kitchen counter. "I mean it, Doc. I'm—"

"Steve." He put a hand on either side of her hips, trapping her against the counter, then he kissed her.

She resisted only a moment before a tiny moan that was half surrender, half denial rumbled against his lips. He gave all that he had, used all that he knew, allowed all that he felt to flow into his embrace. She wrapped her arms around his neck and gave back. He thought he'd reached her, until he tasted her tears.

Doc pulled away. Tears ran like a storm down her face and his heart bled. "Don't cry, Nance. I can't stand to see you cry."

"I can't stand to kiss you and know that's all there

is. Don't do this to me." She opened her eyes and the pain he saw there made him wince. "Please, don't."

"What am I doing?"

"I never realized I was so weak. I always thought I was strong and capable."

"You are. You're the strongest woman I know. Give or take one."

"I'm not. I told Gwen she was a coward for not loving Eli, but really she's brave. It takes more guts to turn your back on something you want with all your heart, even though you know it'll destroy you. I certainly can't do it."

"I have no idea what you're talking about."

The tears in her eyes shimmered as they tumbled and fell. "If you ask me, I'll do anything you want. Even be your lover, knowing it'll kill me inside. I want a husband and a family and a life. But if all I can have of you is what we had the other night, I'll take it if you ask. So don't ask me, Doc. Please don't ask."

She thought he'd come for sex. He should be insulted, but he deserved it, he knew. What he did not deserve was her, a second chance, a life. But he'd learned that people rarely got what they deserved— be it good or bad. So he'd take this chance; he'd build a life with her and he'd make her happy for as long as they had.

"I'm only going to ask you one thing." She closed her eyes with a shaky sigh and waited, as if for a

bomb to drop. So he dropped it. "Marry me, Nancy."
Her eyes snapped open. "I love you."

"Did you get hit on the head?"

"If I did, then I didn't get hit soon enough." At
her confused frown, he shook his head, then put his
fingers over her lips to stall any further questions. "I
had a talk with my oldest friend. I needed to say
goodbye."

Understanding dawned in her eyes. "You okay
with that?"

"Must be. I haven't felt so good in years."

"I want it all, Doc."

"Steve. And I'll give you everything I have. Think
it'll be enough?"

"Let's find out." She lifted her mouth to his.
"Steve."

ELI HAD BEEN dreaming of Jimmy the elephant. He
awoke feeling as if a herd of Jimmys had walked all
over every inch of him.

Eli struggled to open his eyes. When he saw the
hospital room, everything came back in a rush. The
hawk, the fall, the blood, cold and pain. Especially
the pain. He moaned, then cursed as the sound caused
a fresh shaft of agony to shoot through his leg.

"Decided to rejoin the living, did you?" Eli turned
his head toward the voice, to find Doc sitting at his
bedside.

The concern in the old man's eyes made Eli wonder how bad off he was. Then the realization that *Doc*
was here made him ache worse. Because by now

Gwen was gone. For a minute he wished he wasn't going to live. What did he have to live for if his dream was dead? If Gwen was gone?

"You need to get better and quick." Doc grinned, an odd expression, considering the situation.

"What for?" The despair in his voice shocked Eli. He sounded like Doc, or how Doc used to sound. Right now, the man appeared far too chipper for Doc Bartelt—and the twinkle in his eye was downright weird.

Had Eli gone to sleep in one world and woken up in a parallel universe? What kind of drugs were they giving him that such things seemed possible and almost right?

"There's someone waiting to see you, boy." Doc nodded toward the other side of his bed. "But don't wake her up. She's been sittin' here for two days, fiddling with you."

Figuring he'd have to endure Candi and her ministrations, Eli turned to look with very little enthusiasm. The world spun, lurched, then finally shifted into focus.

Gwen lay on a cot near the window, sound asleep. The summer sun mixed with her loose and tangled hair. The shadows under her eyes looked too dark against her pale face. Her clothes were wrinkled and she'd lost a sock. She was the most beautiful thing he'd ever seen.

Why was she still here?

The click of the door announced Doc's departure. Gwen's eyes flickered, then opened. She stared at Eli, sleepy and disoriented. Then she shot into a sitting position, stood and stumbled to his side.

She opened her mouth, then shut it, reached for his hand, then pulled back before she touched him. She looked afraid and Eli didn't know why. Unless she planned to break his heart again. He didn't think he could bear it.

"Hey," he said, then paused, as uncertain as she was.

"How are you feeling?"

The impartial question confused him. Was she here as Dr. Bartelt? Or as his Gwen for always?

"How should I be feeling?"

"Dead."

"Then I guess I'm feeling remarkably well. Who found me?"

"I did."

Suddenly everything became clear to him—her reticence, the circles under her eyes, the pale cast of her skin. Because of him, she'd had to face her nightmare.

"I'm sorry, Gwen."

She frowned. "Sorry?"

"Because of me, your nightmare happened."

She didn't answer and an uncomfortable silence fell between them—something that had never happened before. Not with them. Would it be like this forever now that he'd touched her and loved her and begged her to be his? If he took back everything he'd said, would she let things be as they once were? Or were they better off never seeing each other again?

"You remember telling me that everything here

was exactly as it always was, but the difference was in me?''

''Yeah.''

''You were wrong.''

His heart sank. She *was* leaving him. Why had he expected anything less? She'd told him she was. Saving his life didn't change the life she'd decided to live. And the worst part was, he wouldn't have her friendship, either. He'd have nothing because he'd tried for everything.

''There's no difference in me.'' She slipped her hand into his and clung. Eli caught his breath, afraid to hope, afraid to believe. ''What I feel for you now, I felt for you then. It took nearly losing you to make me see the truth.''

''What truth?''

''Your dogs are right. Life *is* beautiful. But only a life with you in it.'' She took a deep breath, then plunged ahead. ''I love you, Eli. I can't remember when I didn't.''

He blinked at her, certain he was still dreaming, but there wasn't an elephant in sight. Gwen had just said she loved him. Had she ever said those words before? No wonder she'd been acting so odd. Knowing Gwen, she'd had to practice those simple, wonderful words for days.

''Eli? Did you hear me?''

''Uh-huh.''

She felt his forehead, then kissed it. He grabbed the end of her hair before she escaped and held her face close enough so their breath mingled.

"What about all those rules of yours?"

"No kids, no pets, no everlasting love?"

"Those would be the ones."

She smiled. "Want to help me break a few?"

"No."

Her smile fell and uncertainty filled her eyes—an uncertainty he planned to erase forever.

Eli tugged Gwen closer and right before he kissed her he murmured, "I'm just the man to help you break every single one."

The GUARDIANS

An action-packed new trilogy by

Kay David

This time the good guys wear black. Join this highly skilled SWAT team as they serve and protect Florida's Emerald Coast.

#960 THE NEGOTIATOR
(January 2001)

#972 THE COMMANDER
(March 2001)

#985 THE LISTENER
(May 2001)

Look for these
Harlequin Superromance titles
coming soon to your favorite
retail outlet.

HARLEQUIN®
Makes any time special ™

Harlequin proudly brings you

STELLA CAMERON
Bobby Hutchinson
Sandra Marton

in

MARRIED
IN SPRING

a brand-new anthology in which three couples find that when spring arrives, romance soon follows…along with an unexpected walk down the aisle!

February 2001

Available wherever Harlequin books are sold.

HARLEQUIN®
Makes any time special ™

From bestselling
Harlequin American Romance author

CATHY GILLEN THACKER

comes

TEXAS VOWS

A McCABE FAMILY SAGA

Sam McCabe had vowed to always
do right by his five boys—but after
the loss of his wife, he needed the small-town security
of his hometown, Laramie, Texas, to live up to that
commitment. Except, coming home would bring him
back to a woman he'd sworn to stay away from.
It will be one vow that Sam can't keep....

On sale March 2001

Available at your favorite retail outlet.

HARLEQUIN®
*M*akes any time special ™

Visit us at www.eHarlequin.com

PHTV

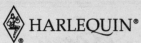 **HARLEQUIN®**

makes any time special—online...

eHARLEQUIN.com

your romantic life

•—Romance 101————

♥ Guides to romance, dating and flirting.

•—Dr. Romance ——————

♥ Get romance advice and tips from
our expert, Dr. Romance.

•—Recipes for Romance —

♥ How to plan romantic meals for you
and your sweetie.

•—Daily Love Dose————

♥ Tips on how to keep the romance
alive every day.

•—Tales from the Heart—

♥ Discuss romantic dilemmas with other
members in our Tales from the Heart
message board.